The flesh beneath her hand gradually dissolved, until that elegant hand rested upon bare white bones, until heart and lungs could be clearly seen.

The man felt the pattern of his breathing change to match hers, felt the dark winds swirling past him and toward her smiling lips. Wide-eyed, the man struggled for air, eyes riveted on the impossible creature who stood before him, on her heaving lungs as she drew in his last breath.

Above the pounding of his heart, he heard music. Then he was gone.

Also by Linda Crockett Gray
published by Tor Books

Tangerine

LINDA CROCKETT GRAY

SIREN

TOR
HORROR

A TOM DOHERTY ASSOCIATES BOOK
NEW YORK

SIREN

Copyright © 1982 by Linda Crockett Gray

A TOR Book
Published by Tom Doherty Associates, Inc.
49 West 24 Street
New York, NY 10010

Cover art by Jim Warren

ISBN: 0-812-51838-1   Can. ISBN: 0-812-51839-X

Library of Congress Catalog Card Number: 81-84144

First Tor edition: February 1989

Printed in the United States of America

0 9 8 7 6 5 4 3 2 1

CHAPTER 1

❖❖❖❖❖❖

I met a lady in the meads
    Full beautiful, a faery's child;
Her hair was long, her foot was light,
    And her eyes were wild.

——KEATS

Lauri Taggert glanced apprehensively at the minute hand on the dresser clock as she wriggled into her swimsuit. Hurriedly sliding the straps over her pale shoulders, she grabbed for the loose blue sweat shirt to tug over it and poked her toes into her tennis shoes. Then she heard the rear door of the house slam shut.

"You home, honey?" Ralph Taggert's low voice evoked a sigh from the young girl who stood motionless at the foot of her bed. "Lauri, honey. You home?" The unmistakable anticipation in his voice brought a grimace to Lauri's lips.

"I'm just leaving for swimming practice," Lauri forced herself to reply as she raced from her room, intent on heading him off before he came upstairs. "I'll be home a little after six, Dad," she said rapidly as she clumped down the steps two at a time.

Taggert was already at the bottom. "Anyone else home?" He reached out with one hand, blocking the lower end of the stairway. His thick gray hair still clung to his forehead in an even row where the hard hat had rested. A day's growth of beard darkened his square jawline.

1

Lauri glanced down at him with deliberate wide-eyed unconcern. "Mom will be home as soon as she gets off work."

"So it's just you and me." Taggert's thick lips spread into a smile.

"You'll have the house to yourself." Lauri shifted feet uneasily. "I'm almost late to swimming practice. I'd better get going. Today is the first day." She waited impatiently two steps above him, keeping her eyes from meeting his.

"I just need a little attention, honey." Ralph Taggert spoke the familiar word softly. "Come on closer, honey. Give the old man a little hug."

"There isn't any time." Lauri's protest was little more than a whisper. "I have to go."

Taggert stepped forward and grasped the front of the loose sweat shirt, tugging Lauri toward him. Standing just one step below her now, he could face her eye to eye.

"You're such a pretty thing," Taggert breathed as he eased one hand under the sweat shirt, sliding it over the silky swimsuit. "You'll be a beautiful woman one day," he asserted low in his throat. "With your big brown eyes . . . soft golden hair . . . and smooth skin . . ." Now both hands moved rhythmically over her hips, then slid upward.

"Daddy, I have to go," Lauri groaned reproachfully. "Please . . . if I'm going to be on the team, I really have to get to swimming practice."

"Just let me touch your boobs." Taggert ignored her protest. His thumbs spread over her chest, caressing the slight mounds of warmth that had begun marking Lauri's transition from child to woman.

"Oh, God, Lauri," he gasped. "You're so pretty. You feel so good." He moved his arms around her, pressing her young body against his. "Feel it? Do

you feel what you've done to me?" he whispered in her ear as he ground his bulging crotch against her. "You feel how much I need you, Lauri?" he whined.

"I have to go to practice," she persisted. "Mom said I could go."

"OK, OK," Taggert growled hoarsely. "But do me first, honey." He grabbed her hand and forced it toward his zipper. "Just do me quick. You know how good it makes me feel." He kept one hand around her wrist while he fumbled with the front of his pants. "Do me, baby," he groaned. "It don't take long, honey." He pressed his mouth against hers. Lauri stood rigid in his embrace.

"You're not going anywhere until you take care of me." His lips curved up in a tight smile. Lauri still stood motionless. "It goes faster if you let me touch you," he mumbled against her neck as he slid his left hand down the back of her swimsuit.

"I can't reach it if you do that." Lauri twisted away from him. "Just do it the regular way," she sighed in resignation.

Taggert sat on the lower step and leaned back, spreading his legs and closing his eyes. "Do me, baby doll," he repeated as Lauri jerked her arm rhythmically up and down. "Oh, baby. Oh, honey," he murmured with increasing rapidity. Finally he stiffened his limbs, his breath coming in short gasps as a stream of semen arched into the air, splattering on the front of his work pants.

Ralph Taggert was still panting, spread-eagled on the stairway, when Lauri bolted out the back door and raced for her bike.

"Ten-year-olds here." The dark-haired coach blew a quick blast on her whistle to call the group together. "Eleven-year-olds, go with Coach Martin." She pointed to the tall blond woman wearing

the bright green warm-up jacket. "Twelve-year-olds, sit on the bleachers. Come on, now!" she yelled good-naturedly. "Let's get organized."

The assemblage of young girls in all shapes and sizes gradually drifted apart as giggling twosomes and threesomes and a few stragglers wandered toward the appointed areas.

"Come on, girls, hustle," the coach yelled once more. "Get in the right group—*now!*"

"Miss Callazo." A petite brunette with elaborate braces on her teeth grinned up at her coach. "I'm ten now but I'll be eleven on May first. . . ." The coach was already nodding and smiling down at her. "Where do I go, Miss Callazo?"

"Go with Coach Martin." Traci Callazo patted the young girl on the shoulder. "You'll swim with the bigger girls."

The metal grin grew wider as the child loped off toward the blond coach.

"Let's get your names and addresses." Chris Martin sat down amid "her girls" and rested the clipboard against her knees. "Please tell me whether you have a birth certificate and your permission slip with you when you give me your name." The gangly-legged eleven-year-olds grouped around her, gazing with awe at the neat french braids fitted close against the woman's head like a golden coronet. Jockeying for position, they nudged against her, touching her soft jacket, breathing in her perfume, and brushing their down-covered legs against her smooth, lightly tanned ones.

"You married, Coach Martin?" The child gazed at the long slim fingers. There was no pale mark indicating the placement of a ring.

"No, Janie." Chris smiled as she checked the columns marked Bir. Cert. and Permission. "I'm not married."

While Chris continued listing the required information on each child, muted whispers and half-suppressed giggles rippled through the cluster of curious girls.

"You got a boyfriend?" an ebony-skinned youngster asked, grinning.

"No boyfriend," Chris replied easily.

"You should," the girl countered. "You look like a princess."

"Well, thank you." Chris smiled at her. "And you look like you'd make a nifty diver." She finished the last of her notations and put aside her clipboard. "OK, girls." She stood. "Let's go on over to the side of the pool and you can all show me what you can do."

"But it's too cold!" several voices protested loudly.

"By next month you'll be saying it's too warm," Chris answered quickly. "How about a deal? If I go in, you girls come in, all in one big splash." The twenty-one youngsters in the eleven-year-old group eyed one another cautiously. "How about it, girls?" Chris cajoled as she unzipped her jacket and pitched it onto the bleachers. "Any of you healthy young things going to let an old lady beat them into the pool?" She turned toward the massive aqua L-shaped pool, then paused on the side to glance back at her reluctant entourage. "Perhaps you'll let the ten-year-olds go first?" She arched her brows dramatically and turned to face the water.

"Nooo!" came the shrieked reply. The slapping of feet against the cement heralded a minor victory as the girls bumped into line on either side of the coach.

"Who can do a cannonball?" Chris shouted. "Jump forward, grab your knees, and hit on your fanny! Let's go!" A moment later, amid squeals and

shrieks, Chris Martin surfaced. "Let's do some warm-up drills," she yelled to the girls, some of whom were sputtering and shivering in the chilly water. "Swirl the water with your arms—like this." She made large backward scooping motions. "Do ten quickly. It builds your shoulder muscles and heats you up. Come on, now. One! Two!" By the second set of exercises the girls had forgotten their discomfort and were enthusiastically jogging in the chest-deep water from one side of the pool to the other. "Step—leap! Step—leap!" Chris yelled out to keep the rhythm.

Suddenly her glance shifted from the bobbing heads to the slight figure emerging from the recreation center bathhouse. The sandy-haired youngster stood staring uncertainly at the groups in the pool.

"Do about ten jumping jacks—legs apart, arms straight—like this." Chris demonstrated. "I'll be right back." She swam the few strokes to the side of the pool and climbed out. "Glad you could make it," she greeted the young stranger. "I'm Chris Martin. I have the eleven-year-olds. Coach Callazo has the tens and twelves." She waited for the girl to speak.

"I'm Lauri Taggert," the child replied. "I'm eleven."

"Great! You're mine! Do you have your permission slip?" Lauri nodded and handed it to her. Chris grinned. "Come along and we'll get started. I'll do your paperwork later."

The girl hesitated.

"We can jump in together," Chris urged her. "Just stick your sweat shirt here, next to my stuff." Obediently the youngster peeled off her shirt and dropped it.

Lauri poked one toe in the water. Her nose promptly wrinkled in displeasure.

"Let's go," Chris prodded her. Lauri shifted her eyes from the cool blue water to the blond woman beside her. Slowly she reached out her hand to the woman, silently seeking a joint effort. "OK." Chris took the offered hand. "Now."

When the sizable splash subsided, Chris slid her arm around the shivering youngster as she introduced her to the multitude of blue-lipped mermaids. "You folks do a few laps across the pool. Get moving!" she ordered with a grin. "Three laps and we'll call it a day." When she released the young Taggert girl to join the others, Chris knew she had found one. She had felt it in her touch. She had breathed in the unmistakable scent that set these girls apart from the others. Her heart thundered with the familiar rage as her green eyes lingered on the sandy hair of Lauri Taggert.

"You are not alone anymore, my child," Chris mused silently. "So it begins again. . . ."

"OK—out of the pool before you turn into icebergs!" Traci Callazo yelled from the far side.

Chris promptly blew her whistle. "Everybody out!" She hurried the girls from the poolside to the steam-filled shower room. "Take it easy," she advised. "Don't let the water get hot—just warm, so it won't be a shock to your system. Thaw out slowly." A chorus of *ahhhs* filled the misty room as the girls sought out the warming spray under a dozen shower heads. "It's only the sixteenth of April. By May the water will be great. Don't get pneumonia between now and then."

By five forty-five the steady stream of youngsters spilling from the front entrance of Savannah's West Broad Street Recreation Center had ceased. Chris Martin clutched an armful of soggy towels and trudged toward the laundry room.

"Got some nice kids?" Traci eyed her as they

stuffed the towels into the massive washer.

"Great ones!" Chris replied cheerfully.

"Then you think you're going to like this?" Traci quizzed her. "Remember, I warned you. It'll take up a lot of your spare time." Two months earlier Traci Callazo had posted a sign in the teachers' lounge begging for volunteers to coach the spring swimming program. Chris Martin had been the only one to sign up.

"I'm sure I'll like it," Chris assured her. Side by side they walked through the abandoned bathhouse, slamming closed the metal locker doors as they passed.

"You want to eat out with us tonight?" Traci asked as she snapped off the last light. "Burt and I are going to be in your neighborhood this evening. We're dining at the Beer Parlor. You could bring your niece," she added hopefully as she locked the rear door.

"Perhaps another time. Sylvie and I have big plans already." She grinned. "We're going rollerskating. If I crawl into school on Monday all black and blue, you'll know I wasn't hit by a truck."

"See you Monday, then." Traci waved as the twosome separated, each heading for her car across the large parking lot.

Chris pitched her clipboard onto the seat and slid behind the wheel of her silver MG. Momentarily her eyes rested on the last entry on the list: "Lauri Taggert, 11, 211 Jones St."

Checking the girl's school records would have to wait until Monday, she resolved grimly. Tonight she had more than one commitment that could not be put off.

Edwin Muir woke a few minutes past midnight to the peculiar aroma of something burning. Easing

his feet onto the floor, he glanced at his wife, open mouthed and asleep on the far side of the bed. Sniffing, Muir padded out of his room, tracking the strange odor. The smoke alarms throughout the house were silent, he noted as he walked along the hallway.

"Damn paper mill," he muttered, then shook his head. "No—that ain't it." He stopped and sniffed repeatedly, opening the door to his daughter's room. Nothing. Mary was sleeping soundly. He closed the door softly and resumed his search.

At the head of the stairs Muir stopped. A peculiar realization swept over him. The entire house was eerily silent. No hum of the air conditioner. No ticking of the hall clock. Apprehensively he waited for a few seconds, then shrugged and continued, sniffing as he proceeded down the stairs toward the source of the odor.

"What in the hell are you doing here?" Muir narrowed his eyes and peered at the young blond girl clad in jeans and a T-shirt who stood in the center of his living room, apparently waiting for him. Behind her on the mantel stood a burnished candelabrum in the form of a hand in a gesture of benediction. Each upraised finger supported a slender green lighted taper. The candle on the extended thumb was unlit.

"What the hell is that?" Muir demanded as the child began to hum a soft, low tune. "You're Mary's friend—aren't you?" He took a step toward the girl as he spoke. "What are you doing in my . . ." His voice faded to silence as the young girl continued to hum, her eyes riveted to his. Suddenly unable to move, Muir stood mesmerized by the vision and the strange melody.

From the shadows a second form emerged— taller than the child but like her, blond and slender,

serene and green eyed. The child retreated into the
darkness as the blond woman took over, swaying
and chanting in a soft whisper that seemed to
reverberate in the stillness of the house. Slowly the
woman brought her hands up from her sides. Muir
watched unblinking as she began unfastening the
buttons down the front of her shirt. He stood
rigidly in place, unable to take his eyes from those
long slender fingers and the widening opening of
her shirt. Finally spreading it apart, the woman slid
it from her shoulders, standing bare breasted before
him as the garment fluttered to the floor.

Then Muir heard a new sound—a slow hissing
that emanated from the woman and seemed to
encircle him. A sudden clamminess crept over him
as he watched her eyes—luminous, intense emeralds shimmering in the candlelight. The curving red
lips and even rows of white teeth gleamed in what
at first appeared to be a smile; then gradually the
grin turned threatening as the ominous hissing
increased. Muir was sweating now; isolated drop-
lets stood out on his forehead, then trickled down
his ashen face. He could neither move nor shift his
eyes from the half-naked creature.

Finally she lifted her left hand and drew it across
her chest, pressing it above the right breast. Her
gold bracelet, coiled like a serpent around her wrist,
supported a spiral-shaped seashell ornament. Muir
stared at the golden shell, transfixed.

Then it began.

As he watched the hissing creature, the flesh
beneath her hand gradually dissolved. Radiating
out from those fingers, the skin, muscle, and blood
vessels of her entire right torso disappeared until
the elegant hand rested upon white bare bones.

Now the hissing became more insistent. Like
dark winds swirling into an abyss, the currents in

the room swept past him and toward her smiling
red lips. Muir panicked as his own breath came in
anguished gasps. Wide-eyed, the man struggled for
air, his gaze still riveted on the woman before him.
Beneath the skeletal torso of the creature he could
see her beating heart, her heaving lungs as she drew
in the air, pulling out his last breath. Muir could
hear the relentless hissing gradually yield to the
louder, rapid thundering of his own heart, desperately pounding out the rhythm of her song.

His mouth hung open.

He could not scream. He could not breathe.

Moments later the pale creature with the blond
hair blew out the candles. She folded a lilac cloth
over the poised golden hand and gently slid it into
her shoulder bag. Already the scent in the room was
diminishing. Already the ticking of the hallway
clock and the hum of the air conditioner had
returned. From the shadows the young blond girl
stepped forward as the older woman stood
buttoning her shirt. Neither of them looked at the
limp, lifeless form of Edwin Muir on the floor.

"Come, Sylvie," the woman said softly. "We can
go home now."

Mike Fuller leaned over his note pad, staring at
the irregular lines of scribbling he'd made on the
way to the hospital. He ran his fingers through his
curly sun-bleached hair as he contemplated a few
undecipherable wriggles that apparently were intended to be words. Shrugging in surrender, he
shoved his pad aside and turned his attention to
the half-filled cup of coffee before him. Across the
room several nurses hastily downed their lunch
while the intercom summoned someone called
Oberman to a coded destination. Steadily Fuller
moved his gaze from table to table, impassively

contemplating the other occupants of the small cafeteria on the basement level of Savannah General Hospital.

The bushy head of George Parsons, Fuller's partner on the homicide squad, bobbed above a cluster of white-clad attendants in the narrow doorway. Fuller looked up quizzically as the large black man silently shrugged. Fuller echoed the gesture, then George headed out again, turning right toward the emergency room.

"Nurse Baker to I.K. One," the voice on the intercom purred.

"That's me," the woman at the next table told her companion. "See you later." She wadded her paper napkin into a ball, tucked it into her coffee cup, and crossed the room hastily on foam-soled shoes. Fuller turned to give a sympathetic smile to the abandoned coffee companion and found himself staring into the greenest eyes he had ever seen.

"Your friend got called away," he said, trying to recover smoothly when he realized he had been staring.

The woman with the green eyes nodded.

"You come here often?" he pressed on with forced casualness, inwardly cringing at his incongruous remark.

The woman suppressed a smile. In anguish Fuller forced his eyes back to his coffee cup. His neck was hot with embarrassment; she must think him a bumbling idiot.

"You look like you're working on something," the calm, low voice said, interrupting his self-conscious silence. Fuller took a deep breath and tried to relax. Again he looked into those green eyes. "Can we talk about your project?" the woman asked with a slight smile. "I'm going to wait awhile in case my friend comes back."

"Yeah, sure." Fuller turned in his chair and half rose. "Well—no . . ." he corrected himself abruptly as he hung midway between sitting and standing.

"Yes, we can talk, and no, not about your project?" she asked, articulating his thoughts as she motioned for him to sit. He did, then shifted around so he could face her table.

"Police business." Fuller found himself staring again as he explained. "I'm waiting to find out if I've got a case or not. I'm with homicide. They call us in when it looks like there's a murder. Right now I'm waiting to see if I have a witness or a corpse. The victim made it here alive. We're waiting to see if she pulls through." Then, as an afterthought, he added, "Oh, I'm Sergeant Fuller. Mike Fuller— Mike." He stressed the less formal designation.

"She's in the intensive unit?" The woman arched her brows with interest. "That's where Katie just went."

"I don't know where she is," Fuller answered flatly. "My partner is standing by till something is settled—one way or the other. Maybe she's been moved to intensive care."

"It may be a good sign," the woman added hopefully as her eyes shifted toward the hallway.

After a short silence Fuller asked, "You want another cup of coffee?" The green eyes settled back on his.

"Sure, Michael." The woman spoke his name with pleasing familiarity. "My name is Chris Martin. I'm a schoolteacher." Fuller extended his hand. She grasped it firmly, still holding his gaze. "It's nice to meet you, even under such grim circumstances."

When she released his hand, Mike rose from his chair, lifted both cups, and strode toward the counter for refills, glancing back a couple of times

to assure himself she hadn't moved. From his vantage point he could see her long tanned legs tucked back under her chair. *Five-nine, maybe five foot ten*, he observed with a professional eye. *She isn't a raving beauty*, he conceded. *No big tits. Kinda long and lean.* "But Jesus," he sighed, "them eyes." He balanced the cups and wove his way through the maze of tables and half-pulled-out chairs. Setting the cups on her table, he slid into the chair directly facing her.

"Well, Michael," she said softly, "if we can't discuss business, we can dwell on pleasure. Tell me where you've been skiing. I assume that's where you got your tan."

"Golf," he corrected her. "I play a lot of golf."

Her eyes dropped to his obvious midriff, then back to his round face.

"Yeah, I know it doesn't show." He grinned sheepishly. "I also drink a lot of beer."

"To cool you off after you've played a lot of golf," Chris completed the thought. Her sudden laughter brought a rosy flush to Fuller's baby face.

"Something like that." He chuckled in spite of his embarrassment.

"I swim," Chris admitted in a conspiratorial whisper. "Someone told me it was great for developing the chest muscles." She watched his color deepen as his eyes lingered on her modest chestline. "I now have shoulders like a stevedore," she said, grinning, "but no *muscles*." She held her hands ten inches in front of her chest in a graphic display of what hadn't developed.

"You don't need, ahhh . . ." Fuller groped for an appropriate end to his sentence.

"Muscles?" Chris bailed him out.

"Yeah, muscles." He smiled at her.

"And you don't need to cut out any more than one or two beers a day," Chris shot back with an amused sparkle in her eyes. "Or are you a junk food addict, Michael?" she asked, pleasing him by saying his name again. "What are your favorite foods?" She listened with keen interest as he began listing his choices. Somewhere between lasagna and seafood gumbo, George Parsons stepped up to their table. The woman in I. K. One was dead.

"The sorry creep didn't even know who she was," Mike muttered angrily. "A bunch of punks hangin' around a shopping center—rippin' off purses from the shoppers. This gal shows up, fights back, and he blasts her through the spine." Fuller stared glumly at the pages of his notes. "So it's our case," he concluded as he pocketed the note pad and stood to leave with Parsons.

At the doorway he paused, then spoke quietly to his partner, then crossed back toward Chris. "Look, I don't want to seem out of line or anything," he said, looking down at her, "but I would really like to see you again." He shifted uncomfortably. "It's just that this isn't exactly the time or place to be making social plans."

"Got a pencil?" Chris reached across the table to receive pen and note pad from Fuller. She flopped to the rear of the book and jotted her name and a series of numbers. "Not this weekend, Michael," she said quietly. "Try me next week—when things aren't so hectic."

"Right, sure." He took the pad and pen. Uncertainly he offered his free hand. "I'll be thinking of you, Chris," he said as he shook her hand slowly. "You and your muscles." He flashed a startlingly boyish grin, then strode off to join his partner.

Chris glanced at her watch, then checked it with

the wall clock in the cafeteria. With a sudden sigh she tucked her purse under her arm and strolled toward the exit. Conversation and Katie Baker would have to wait. Meeting Sylvie at the roller rink couldn't.

On Monday Chris sat in the conference room next to the principal's office methodically dialing the Savannah schools with sixth- and seventh-grade classes. On the third call she located the one Lauri Taggert attended.

"Let me speak to the guidance counselor, please," Chris requested. Within five minutes Chris had all the information. It fit the pattern precisely. Lauri Taggert was the older child—had a brother four years younger. Excellent student. Always volunteering for special projects. Quite popular. Homeroom vice-president. All-American wholesome type. Chris nodded while the guidance counselor at Randall Middle School praised the child. "And she probably does windows," Chris muttered bitterly after she'd replaced the receiver. "Another superkid—never letting anyone down—trying to be everything to everyone—and having nothing left over for herself." Chris glanced over the few notes she had made. Mother—Marion Taggert, store clerk. Father—Ralph Taggert, construction supervisor with the city engineering department.

"Now, how do we get to this one?" Chris pondered the logistics of the Taggert case. Abruptly the sharp jangle of the hall bell signaled the end of her planning period. Tucking her papers into the zippered pocket of her handbag, Chris stepped out into the school corridor, which was awash with a sea of little people, crowding, giggling, poking, and winding their way toward their next classes. Traci

Callazo waved above the swarm, then ducked back into the PE gym, where her students were convening. Chris continued on to the farthest wing of West Broad Street Middle School toward the language lab—her domain. Twenty cubicles complete with earphones and microphones were rapidly being occupied as Spanish I students bounded into the room. When the tardy bell rang, Chris was perched on the tall stool above the electronic console with her own headset in place.

"*Buenas tardes, señoritas y señors.*" She beamed down at the upturned faces.

"*Buenas tardes*, Señorita Marteen," they responded in unison.

"*Buenos días*, Wilma." Chris flipped the console button to cubicle fourteen. "What did you do this past weekend?" Chris asked in Spanish.

The dark-skinned child hesitated, twisting her mouth into a grimace while she formulated the reply. Finally she leaned forward toward the microphone and responded, slowly but correctly saying she'd gone to a restaurant.

"*Bueno*, Wilma, *bueno.*" Chris nodded appreciatively. Then she flipped another button. "Caroline, *buenos días*," she said, and continued the greetings and simple questions until all the students had related details of their weekend activities. On the chalkboard behind her Chris had listed key words from their responses: *restaurante, teatro, dentista, nadar, biblioteca.* Next she led the class in unison as they practiced the assigned dialogue from the textbook, each child intent upon the serene face of the teacher. Fifteen minutes of written work followed. Then at last came the part they liked best. Chris lifted a six-stringed guitar from behind the console and slowly strummed a chord. Then she sang a soft,

rhythmic Spanish melody as the students swayed
and tapped their fingers to the music. She repeated
the chorus, then looked at them expectantly. This
time they joined in—self-consciously at first as
their tongues stumbled over the words, but then
with increasing authority as the music and their
own enthusiasm urged them on. Three minutes
before the period bell they finished their songfest
with a burst of applause. While the students stacked
up their books and passed in their written assign-
ments, Chris plugged a Carlos Montoya tape into
the console audio system to provide a soothing
finale to the session. The light ripple of flamenco
music floated through the room and spilled out the
transom into the hallway.

With perfect timing Chris reached for the door
handle just as the hall bell clanged. When she
pulled open the door she found herself staring into
the wide brown eyes of Mike Fuller. He stood
against the far wall while the flood of students
emptied from the classrooms into the wide hall.
Fuller zigzagged his way through and leaned against
the doorjamb.

"I was in the neighborhood," he began unconvincingly, then shrugged and grinned at her. The
guitar music from the classroom still played on.
"Wanna dance?" he joked. By now a crowd of
curious students hovered around them, giggling
and nudging each other.

"Miss Martin has a boyfriend!"

"He's real cute."

"You think he'll kiss her here?" A flush of color
flooded Fuller's cheeks.

"Perhaps you'd like to step inside." Chris smiled
at him sympathetically. "They'll be discussing the
color of your socks by the time they get through

with you." Mike looked down at the three girls who had stopped to stare at him, blocking the traffic flow. Books clasped against their pubescent chests, a network of orthodontic apparatus on their teeth, they looked like a miniature inquisition.

"Pardon me, ladies." Fuller gave the girls a brief nod. "I have a conference with Miss Martin." He excused himself suavely and ducked inside the language lab. The girls tittered in approval and reluctantly hurried on their way.

"Do you have another class?" Fuller gazed into the green eyes.

"Latin," Chris replied. "Last class of the day."

"You think we could get a quick cup of coffee when you finish it? I mean, if you're not busy," he added hurriedly. "I know I was supposed to wait and call you," he went on rapidly, "but I just kept thinking about you—and I remembered you said you were a teacher. So I checked around . . ."

". . . and here I am." Chris laughed at his obvious discomfort. "So that's how detectives work."

Fuller turned crimson. "So I'm not subtle," he said, chuckling. "How about the coffee after school's out?"

"I'm sorry, Michael, but I can't. I have a date." Before his chin got too firmly set, she added with a smile, "With a group of eleven-year-old swimmers. I have to coach them at the recreation center Mondays, Wednesdays, and Fridays."

"I should have called," Mike mumbled. "I just wanted to see you."

Chris grew suddenly solemn as she detected a distressed quality in Fuller's voice. "You must have had a grim weekend," she guessed.

The tall detective momentarily flashed his boyish smile and stared into her eyes. "Not much worse

than usual," he said in a low voice. "They just figure down at the office that those of us who aren't married shouldn't mind being the first ones called in. I get tired of being taken for granted." He shrugged. "Maybe I'm just getting older and the hide isn't as tough as it used to be." Her sudden glimpse of his vulnerability prompted Chris to reach out and enclose his hand in hers.

"If you're free tonight, how about dinner?" she offered. "My place?"

Again the impish grin spread across Fuller's face.

"Don't get any ideas, big boy," Chris cautioned him. "You'll be sharing potluck with me and my niece. The invitation is for dinner—and conversation."

"I accept!" Mike bobbed his head enthusiastically. By now the hallway was nearly abandoned as the last few stragglers raced to their classrooms.

"Walk, please," Chris reminded one youngster who had hurried back into the classroom to retrieve some forgotten books.

"Where do you live?" Fuller asked hastily. "And when is dinner?"

"Six o'clock, two-oh-nine East River Street. Apartment four." Chris watched Fuller's eyebrows rise in surprise as she gave the address. "A bit plush for a schoolteacher," she acknowledged, "but the apartment belongs to my aunt. Don't panic, Michael—just show up at six or a little after." She grabbed a roll book from the console and stepped out into the hallway once more. "My next class is that way." She tilted her head to the left. "Dress casual," she called over her shoulder. "Very casual." She waved before making a sharp right along the next corridor.

As the period bell shrieked above his head, Fuller stood grinning down the vacant corridor where the

green-eyed woman had been. Humming softly, he turned toward the exit, his long strides echoing against the pale green walls.

"Well?" His dark-skinned partner leaned against the car waiting for him. "Did blondie dump on you?" George Parsons demanded. "She told you she didn't hang out with cops, right?" He grinned.

Fuller opened the passenger door of the unmarked car and folded his long legs under the dash.

"Well, asshole," Parsons hooted as he slid behind the wheel. "What did she say?"

"She invited me to her place—" Fuller barely got the words out before Parsons was crowing.

"Whoooee! Big night tonight!" Parsons clicked his tongue.

"—to have dinner with her and her niece," Mike finally interjected."

"Tough break, fella." Parsons laughed again. "But maybe the kid hits the sack early—and you and blondie can fool around."

"It's not like that." Mike looked ahead as he spoke. "This one is a real nice lady—real classy. She calls me Michael," he added, smiling.

Parsons shot him an uneasy look. "Hey—they all be the same in the dark," he tried to joke.

"This one doesn't make me want to turn the lights out," Mike said quietly. "She's got a way of looking at me that makes me want to look at her."

"Oh, brother," Parsons moaned. "Ain't love somethin'," he cackled as he dropped the car into gear and merged into the light traffic.

"I don't remember," Fuller said grimly. "It's been so long I forgot what it's like."

His dark companion riveted his eyes on the traffic ahead. The white-toothed grin on Parsons's wide face was gone. "Yeah . . ." he finally breathed. "Yeah. . . ."

In a flower-filled meadow atop a rocky island off the coast of Italy dwelled the Sirens. These pale-haired creatures of exquisite beauty filled the salty sea winds with their songs. A ship passing too near Siren Island would find its full sails reverberating with their enchanting melodies—promises of love or fame or riches, whatever one's heart might desire. All men aboard would fall beneath the Sirens' spell, forgetting all else, and would turn their vessel toward the source of the marvelous song or throw themselves into the water in an attempt to join the Sirens. But beneath the jade waters surrounding the island, barely hidden beneath the white-crested waves, sharp-edged rocks awaited the spellbound sailors and their ships.

The keel boards would be ripped apart and the tall ships split asunder, casting crew and cargo upon the ruthless rocks and swirling waters. Across the pale sands of the island were strewn the parched bones and refuse of seamen who had been tempted by the Sirens' song.

When brave Odysseus, on his journey homeward from the Trojan War, learned that he must pass the

island of the Sirens, he asked the sorceress Circe for
aid. He wished to hear their singing but he did not
want the fate that had befallen others whose minds
had been beguiled by Siren promises. Circe directed Odysseus to stop the ears of his men with
wax, so he alone would hear the songs. To prevent
him from casting himself onto the rocks, Circe told
him to have his men tie him to the mast with sturdy
bindings. This was done, and the ship passed near
the rocky island.

The beautiful Sirens sang to him, promising him
great wisdom and the knowledge of events to come
hereafter if only he would join them. "You will
know all these, Odysseus," they sang, ". . . know
what the years ahead hold for you and your
countrymen . . . know now of the end of your
wandering." So they tempted the great warrior.
Odysseus struggled against his restraints, but the
ropes held fast. Though he cried aloud and yearned
to be among the golden-haired Sirens, his men
would not release him and he could not break away.

Finally the rocky island was left behind; the ship
had passed beyond the reach of the Sirens' song.
Odysseus ceased to struggle and a deep melancholy
darkened his countenance. His men unbound him.
Eagerly they seated themselves on the thwarts and
smote the whitened sea with oars, proceeding on
their way.

Three of the Sirens, touched by Odysseus's suf-
fering and vexed by his escape, dived into the sea
and swam toward the distant shore. No longer
content to wait for fate to bring men and ships to
them, the Siren sisters moved landward into the
human realm.

CHAPTER 2

✦✦✦✦✦✦✦

The half-forgotten thought burns bright again,
And memory fills with momentary warmth
  The dark abyss of yesterday.

—GRAY

"Come on, Sylvie," Fuller called to the towheaded girl peering down into the dark water of the Savannah River. "Slip and fall in *after* dinner, kid," he teased her. "I'm ready to get to the food."

Sylvie bobbed her head upright, sending a haughty ripple through her long blond hair. "Some people are so bossy," she asserted with feigned indignation. "You invite them for dinner and they think they own you." She trailed off into a giggle.

"Move it, short stuff," Fuller said, grinning over his shoulder as Sylvie fell into step behind her aunt and the tall, curly-haired detective. Chris tucked her arm under his as they strolled along the red brick walkway of the waterfront with several moored vessels on one side and ancient River Street with its rows of restored warehouses on the other. In between, islands of green grass, rows of benches, and lantern-shaped street lamps invited passersby to look and to linger in old Savannah.

The fading sun sent long thin shadows across the moving water. A hint of a cooling evening breeze touched the faces of the three smiling people.

Mike Fuller walked in silence for a while, taking it all in.

"You know, I've worked in this city for eight years and I've never ridden one of these," he said as he jerked his thumb toward the low-decked tour boat with red-and-white-striped canopy. "You want to go on one with me one day—maybe next weekend?" he asked, trying to sound casual.

"They cruise at night too, Michael," Chris said softly. "All the streetlights are lit, the shops and restaurants are full of people, the music drifts out over the water." She made it sound almost magical.

"That means yes, I assume." Michael squeezed her arm gently as the green eyes shifted slowly from the dark river to meet his gaze.

"Feed me first." Chris smiled impishly. "I'll give you a definite answer *after* dinner. By then we will be even."

Mike grimaced. He had used the excuse of repaying Chris and Sylvie for their hospitality when he'd invited them to dinner. Now he'd have to face the consequences. On the telephone Chris had hesitated when he'd made the offer. "Michael, this isn't a business arrangement," she had said firmly. "We don't keep score of who does what for whom."

Mike had begun apologizing instantly, but Chris had cut him off. "You like me," she noted. "And you like Sylvie. And we like you. We seem to get along individually and as part of the group. So drop the repaying bit, my friend. Say what you mean."

After ten seconds of embarrassed silence, Mike had managed a reply. "I want to be with you—both of you. How about dinner Friday?"

"Very good, Michael," Chris had replied. Mike knew she was smiling. "I want to be with you too." He had felt his heartbeat accelerate at that. "I'll have to check with Sylvie. She'll want to know where she's going and what's on the menu before she commits herself," Chris had added. She had let

Mike ask the obvious questions: what Sylvie usually ate and what restaurant she liked.

"I'd really like her to go," Mike had said, "so you pick the place."

"Sylvie's favorite restaurant is just down the street from our place. The Shrimp Factory. There's music, it overlooks the waterfront, and it has a kids' menu."

"Is that OK with you too?" Mike had asked.

"It will be quite lovely—this time," Chris had agreed. "Next time, when we're alone, we'll go somewhere more intimate. We will have to get off by ourselves sooner or later and find out how we manage. But for right now this will be great."

Mike had had to force himself to speak. The lady put it all out front. There was no game playing with this one, he reminded himself. "Right," he had finally croaked. "See you at six."

"Right," Chris had breathed into the phone. "Good-bye, Michael."

Fuller had stood with his hand on the phone for nearly a minute after he'd replaced the receiver, waiting for his thudding pulse to return to normal. *It isn't so bad when I can look at her,* he had reflected. But on the telephone—when all he had was her voice—it was almost incapacitating. "Next time," he had muttered aloud, grinning. "Already she wants a next time."

The aroma of seafood wafted enticingly across the river-front plaza, mingling with the sea air.

"Hey, Michael." Sylvie suddenly raced up beside Fuller. "Walk a little faster, please. I'm starving." Obediently Mike grabbed her hand and lengthened his stride, with Chris keeping pace beside him.

"Offer someone dinner and they think they own you," he teased.

"Oh, Michael," Sylvie sighed dramatically. "You

can be so silly." She fluttered her long lashes. Abruptly she pulled Mike to a stop at the gangplank of the old three-masted ship moored by the walk-way. Her sails were down and she strained slightly at the tie lines. The current tugged persistently, as if it were urging her toward the high seas. She seemed less a permanent tourist attraction than a seaworthy vessel that had drifted in through a time warp and only paused long enough to load before venturing out again. Mike and Sylvie stood in silence admir-ing the fine old ship.

Gently Chris slid her arms under theirs and led them away. "Come on, you two." She smiled as she steered them across the plaza, over the irregular stones of River Street, and along the sidewalk to the restaurant with the gold shrimp emblazoned on its rough wooden sign above the door.

Banjo music and the heavenly aroma of seafood embraced them as they stepped between the sturdy doors and into the restaurant. Deep red carpets and weathered gray walls muffled the sounds of the river traffic. The tanned, slender hostess led them to a small table where the silent outside world could be glimpsed through windows bordered by frosted etching. From his perch in the lounge the banjo-playing singer filled the rooms with his music.

Fuller hesitated in mid-step, turning to glance toward the source of the song. Chris patted his hand and pointed to his chair.

"Something wrong?" she asked with slight amusement.

"It's just the song—'Leaving on a Jet Plane,'" Fuller explained as he held her chair for her. "Peter, Paul, and Mary were big when I was in high school—a bit before your time." His eyes drifted back across the room toward the lounge.

"Surprisingly little is before my time, Michael,"

Chris said, smiling. "I know the song and I know who Peter, Paul, and Mary are. I'm not that young, my friend."

Fuller's eyes shifted back to the green-eyed woman seated beside him. He'd guessed she was twenty-five. Then his glance settled on blond Sylvie, who, at eleven, looked maybe thirteen. She was staring at the old beached boat and the open treasure chest that occupied the center of the room. Her slender fingers gently tapped the rhythm of the song as she sat entranced.

"I guess I only connected their music with my generation—where I was and what I was doing when I first heard their songs," he apologized. "I used to love to listen to them." His voice took on a boyish quality. He smiled for a moment, then shrugged. "Then I got out of school and joined the navy." He abruptly picked up a menu.

"And did what?" Chris asked.

"And sat off the coast of China listening to them jabber at one another," he replied. "And counseled some dopers . . . and took R and R in Hawaii . . . and saw the Orient."

"And . . . ?"

"And came home and went to college on my G.I. Bill."

By now the red-aproned waitress was placing the water glasses full of regular squares of transparent ice before the threesome. She paused while they made their selections. Sylvie promptly headed for the salad bar, leaving Mike with strict instructions. "Shrimp . . . boiled," she insisted.

"Same for me," Chris informed Mike. "You might try the seafood bisque," she suggested.

Fuller rested his finger beside the two fish-tailed creatures that framed his choice on the menu: half a pound of Thunderbolt shrimp served steaming hot

in the shell with drawn butter and lemon wedges. "We'll take two of these." He turned the menu so the waitress could see.

"Two Mermaids," the young woman said, nodding as she wrote.

"And one of the same, only child sized," Mike added dutifully.

"Mini-Mermaid," the waitress acknowledged.

"And a cup of seafood bisque for me," he concluded. He looked up to find Chris smiling at him. "Is that right?" he asked.

"Perfect." She smiled more widely.

"Please help yourselves to the salad bar," the waitress said.

Across the room came another familiar tune from the sixties—the kind that tall, white-blond Mary Travers would stand and shake her silky mane and sing.

"You seem a bit wistful." Chris looked at Fuller's somber face. "I thought we'd come here for fun and relaxation," she said, trying to coax him out of his glum mood.

"We did. I guess I'm feeling a bit jaded," Mike muttered. "Remembering all my big ideas—somehow flushed down the great john of life." He shrugged, then forced a philosophical smile. "Maybe I'm just getting cynical."

Chris eyed him intently. "I see how that could happen in your line of work," she commented.

"It's the compromises that wear me out," Fuller asserted. "The plea bargaining—early releases—clearing a case on paper instead of really solving it." His glance drifted back toward the lounge. "It erodes one's idealism," he said softly.

Chris simply nodded, her eyes fixed on his face as he spoke.

Fuller abruptly turned and arched his brows. "I

sure know how to get an evening off on a light-hearted note," he apologized. "How about starting over? Let's go get the salad," he suggested.

Sylvie had returned with a frosted plate topped with a mound of greenery. By the time Mike and Chris completed their trip around the salad bar, Sylvie was cheerfully devoting her rapt attention to level three of the elaborate salad she had constructed.

Mike sat across from her and began eating in silence. After a moment he looked up, took a deep breath, and smiled at her. "Tell me how things are with your swimming, now that you've joined Chris's team," he said.

Sylvie glanced up briefly, assuming the question was intended for Chris. Instead Fuller was looking at her.

"Sylvie . . . ?" Chris prodded her niece.

Sylvie nodded cooperatively, then pointed in distress to her mouth while she diligently chewed.

"I was just wondering how you're doing on Chris's swim team," Fuller said, rephrasing his request in an attempt to give the youngster a little more time. "I bet it's a little rough hitting that cold water . . ."

Sylvie shook her head as she finished devouring a large spinach leaf. "I love it," she insisted. "All the kids are getting used to it now. And I've met some really nice girls," she added, "most of them from other schools. I think that makes us more eager to show off in front of each other. No one wants to be called a baby."

"Nothing like a little peer pressure," Chris joked.

"Have you got some pretty good swimmers?" Fuller asked.

"A kid named April Jones is good at freestyle," Sylvie noted. "Lauri Taggert is a good diver." She

smiled across the table at Chris. "I'll get to know the rest of the names in a week or so," she concluded in a matter-of-fact tone. "Right now I just know a couple of them."

"Do you have scheduled swim meets that are open to the public?" Fuller asked deliberately, spooning into the bisque that had just arrived.

Sylvie's pale green eyes shifted from Mike to Chris, then back again. "You mean you'd come?"

"If I'm invited." He directed the comment at Chris. "I don't want to intrude and I don't want to make anyone self-conscious." Chris looked over and nodded to her young niece.

"You're invited," Sylvie declared happily. "In a week, next Friday at five thirty, we have a meet. Parents and guests get in free," she said. "You can be my guest."

Mike smiled slightly. "I'd be proud to be your guest. I doubt if you two eat beforehand, so maybe we could all go out afterward for a late dinner."

"Let's just agree that we will all do *something* after the meet," Chris suggested. "What we do will depend on how the meet goes and how tired some of us are." She rolled her eyes in Sylvie's direction. "We may all end up with a carryout order of something, collapsed on the floor at home."

"Fair enough," Mike agreed with relief.

A dark-haired waitress made her way to their table, carrying a large tray stacked with plates. Eyeing his platter of steaming pink shrimp, Mike breathed in appreciatively. Quietly he inspected their choices and his eyes narrowed.

"Are you two vegetarians or something?" he finally asked. When he'd dined with them earlier that week, dinner had consisted of something called West Indies salad—chilled crabmeat with spices on a bed of lettuce and spinach. Later, sitting on the

floor of the vast, high-ceilinged living room, they
had assembled their dessert from a serving board
full of grapes, nuts, and dried fruit.

"We're the 'something,'" Chris responded. "Seafood, fruit, nuts, vegetables—that's about it."

"No steaks?" Fuller groaned.

"Only for you." Chris laughed softly.

"Well—to each his own," Fuller declared. "Not
that it doesn't look great." He promptly picked up a
curving pink shrimp and peeled off its shell.

The troubadour had shifted to a medley of sea
chanteys—spirited, rhythmic songs about life on
the rolling waves. Amid the cheery sounds of the
music and the muted chatter of the other diners,
the threesome at the window peeled and dunked
and devoured their feast.

By the time they emerged from the restaurant,
the last rays of the sun had completely disappeared
beyond the horizon. A low layer of clouds had
turned from rosy purple to a soft gray. The pale
glow from the long row of plaza lanterns illuminated the waterfront walkway. Shop windows and
doors spilled swatches of light across the old stone
road and sidewalks. Wordlessly the three contented
diners ambled to the riverside. Before them was
spread the network of ropes and rigging of a
tall-masted square-rigger, the *Barba Negra*. The
boat was outlined with rows of white lights that
stood out against the deep gray velvet sky.

From the ocean a cool evening breeze drifted up
the Savannah River, rippling the tree branches and
filling the waterfront with a salty scent. Only a trace
of the pungent odor from the paper mill nearby
disturbed the pleasant atmosphere. Young couples
strolled hand in hand around the plaza. Older folks,
some in pairs, some alone, sat on the benches facing
out over the river. All the sounds of day had been

supplanted by the gentle whispers of evening.

Mike walked with his arm around Chris's shoulders while Sylvie loped ahead, peering off into the night at the distant shore, then stopping to crumble bits of bread smuggled from the restaurant and letting them fall into the swift, dark river.

Finally they turned between the warehouses, climbing up the old stone stairway to the park on the upper bank, where ancient moss-hung oaks spread their boughs. From the park they cut back over to the pale yellow building, taking one of several metal bridges that vaulted back into the upper floors of the warehouses, above shops and galleries.

"One drink," Chris offered as Mike hesitated by the inner door near the elevator.

"One drink," he promptly agreed.

Minutes later Sylvie was tucked in bed and Mike stood on the iron-lace balcony looking down over the wide river. He held a slender glass of Amaretto, occasionally sipping the almond liqueur while he waited for Chris to return. At first he'd been intimidated by the classy address—the fourth floor of a restored warehouse on the historic waterfront. But then he'd stepped inside. Two rooms closed off on the far end of the condominium held a conglomeration of antiques. "My aunt's things," Chris had explained during his first visit. "She's living at the beach now, so we have the place, Sylvie and I. We sort of updated it," she'd said as she led him about.

Chris's rooms were reassuringly like her—shades of gold and ivory on walls and high ceilings, carpets and low chairs with pillows in varying greens from the faintest pastels to startling emeralds, corners filled with ferns spilling over in huge hanging baskets, and standing plants reaching leafy branches toward the light. In the living room great

pastel watercolors lined the walls—seashells, star-fish, sea anemones, sea horses, and lacy water plants.

"I got them in the gallery downstairs," Chris had said, staying beside Mike as he moved from one painting to another.

"They are lovely," Mike had breathed. "You must feel you're living in an aquarium or in the tropics." Chris had merely smiled as she tugged a brownish leaf from one of the plants. On the mantel a carved alabaster pelican perched atop a twisted piece of driftwood peered down, half-amused, at the passersby. From the first moment in her sanctuary, Mike had felt unexpectedly tranquil and comfortable. Now, as he stood on the balcony looking out into the dark sky, he felt at peace.

"How's the search going for the guy who did the shopping center shooting?" Chris's voice came from close behind him.

Mike turned to face her. She had opened the conversation with the very topic that had just entered his mind. "We've got a kid who says he was there. His thing is shoplifting, maybe snatch a purse from time to time, but he's scared about this killing business. He gave us a name. Parsons is prowling the project tonight with another cop."

"Black kid?" Chris asked solemnly. Fuller nodded.

"You'd be a bit conspicuous in that neighborhood," Chris acknowledged. "Of course," she added, smiling at his six-foot-three-inch frame, "you'd be a bit conspicuous anywhere."

"You don't exactly fade into the woodwork yourself." He reached out to encircle her in his free arm as she stepped onto the narrow balcony. "Who could miss those great muscles?" he joked, stroking

her shoulder gently. Chris leaned her head against his chest.

"Are you thinking of making love to me tonight?" she asked quietly. Fuller almost dropped his drink. Chris eased away and looked up at him earnestly.

"That's not exactly a one-sided issue," Fuller said, recovering. "I was thinking about how good you feel next to me. I'd like to hold you and kiss you." He felt compelled to tell her the truth. "But no, I wasn't thinking of jumping into bed with you. Not tonight." He felt almost apologetic. "But if you're interested in negotiating . . ."

"I'll go along with plan A," Chris replied brightly. "Plan B should wait a bit. Put down your drink."

Fuller bent low and placed the glass on the floor just inside the balcony French doors. When he stood, long, tanned, graceful arms encircled his neck.

At first their kiss was light, tentative, cautious. Fuller eased her body closer. He could feel the steady pounding of her heart through his soft shirt. More firmly, languidly, he pressed his mouth to hers, feeling the lips part as she slid her hands upward into his soft, curly hair. Fuller reached toward the silken coil of pale blond hair held neatly in place with a mother-of-pearl comb.

"Not tonight," Chris told him breathlessly. "Once you begin undoing things"—she kissed his nose perfunctorily—"you may want to amend your earlier statement."

From the parking lot below, a couple of teenagers spotted them and began hooting and whistling at the twosome. "Do it! Do it!" one kid yelled as his buddy guffawed.

"A bit crass, but my sentiments exactly," Mike whispered.

"Not yet." Chris rested both hands on his shoulders. "We'll know when it's time." She tilted her head to beckon him inside. "Let's say good night," she insisted softly.

"When can I see you again?" he asked hoarsely as Chris smiled and handed him his jacket.

"When I get back from the beach Sunday night."

"You're going to the beach for the whole weekend?"

"I go every chance I get. I need the surf to calm my nerves," she explained. "My aunt has a house on Hilton Head, right on the coast. Maybe one weekend you'll come with us," she added. "Right now I've got to get off by myself and think about things."

"Things . . . like me?" Mike asked as he reached for her.

"For the time being that's precisely what I intend to do—*think* about you." Chris pressed a firm hand against his chest. "So good night, Michael." She raised her mouth to his in a final, lingering kiss.

As Fuller strode across River Street toward the parking lot, he glanced back up at the iron balcony and the pale light beyond. Sliding behind the wheel, he shoved the key in the ignition, whistling softly between his teeth a snatch of the folk song they'd heard earlier in the evening. *Take it easy*, he cautioned himself. *Whatever you do, Fuller, don't blow this one.* His glance returned briefly to the balcony, but the rooms beyond were now dark. As Fuller eased his car away from the curb, he sang softly to himself, feeling happier than he had in a long, long time.

Amid the shimmering blue waters of the Danube, the golden-haired water divinities—the Rusalki—make their home. Cloaked in robes of mist, they rise with the moon and sing enchanting songs into the night air. With their alabaster beauty and sweet voices, they entice the passerby to linger near their shores. To be embraced in the arms of a Rusalka, to hear her song and taste her lips as she draws one softly beneath the water's surface, is almost a pleasant way to end one's life, for one's last breath mingles with the whisper of the waves and one's body is encompassed by the timeless waters of the Danube.

The fishermen know well these water spirits who rise on waves or perch on rocks to watch them. Sometimes the lovely creatures sing songs of great beauty, sometimes they shriek warnings of treacherous rocks or other perils of the deep. The capricious Rusalki frolic beneath the surface, bringing the fishermen heavy catches of glistening fish or, just as frequently, tearing or tangling the wide nets. With similar playful abandon the Rusalki send water coursing through a mill wheel, causing it to

strain, or stop the wheel altogether and bring all work to a halt. They swirl the water against the dikes till the barriers groan against the pressures, sometimes causing great damage, sometimes only drawing apprehensive stares from the people whose land is threatened.

In the cold seasons of the year the Rusalki remain in the dark and chilly waters. But in Rusalki Week, when the summer sun warms the waters, they emerge from the river and linger in the forests along the riverbanks. There soft winds and green leaves refresh and shelter them. Never far from their aquatic home, the Rusalki choose for their own a graceful willow or a tall pale-barked birch whose slender branches can from time to time dip down and let them slip unnoticed beneath the shimmering surface of the river.

In the night these river spirits call to one another, swaying upon their tree branches, their pale long hair gleaming in the moonlight. Then they climb down from their airy perches and leap through the forest to a clearing, where they clasp one another hand in hand and dance to their exquisite songs. Where the Rusalki tread in their dance, the wheat then grows more abundant and the green carpet of grass more dense.

Some say that once in every century a Rusalka chooses a human lover, then returns to her river home to bear a daughter like herself. Others say that each Rusalka is the soul of a dead maiden who by accident or suicide has drowned in the river. Such a tale is told of a rock in the Rhine River, the Lorelei. In despair over a faithless lover, a maiden cast herself into the river. Now she lingers on that rock and fills the air with her siren song.

CHAPTER 3

❖❖❖❖❖❖

Beneath the lamp the lady bowed
  and slowly rolled her eyes around.
Then drawing in her breath aloud
Like one that shuddered, she unbound
  the cincture from beneath her breast.
                    —COLERIDGE

"You got a kid down there?" asked the thick-necked fellow with mammoth biceps, turning toward Mike Fuller. The massive form became less awesome when a shy smile spread across the big man's face. Gentle gray eyes settled upon Fuller's wary expression.

"Not me," Mike said, shrugging and looking around the nearly empty bleachers. "I don't have any kids," he said almost apologetically. "I'm a friend of one of the coaches. I know one of the kids too," he added earnestly, trying to justify his presence.

"Which coach and which kid?" The gray eyes brightened with interest.

"Miss Martin and the blond kid by the starting block—Sylvie Martin." He pointed to Sylvie's slender form poised by the end of the pool.

The big man slowly grinned. "My name's Rambo —Burt Rambo." His meaty hand jutted out in greeting as he slid down a row to sit beside Fuller. "I'm a friend of the other coach—Traci Callazo." He narrowed his eyes at Mike. "You must be Chris's cop," he asserted.

Mike responded with a bewildered smile. "Mike

Fuller," he managed to reply as he shook the large
hand. The thought of being Chris's anything pleased him—but this fellow's knowing about it was
another matter.

"Traci told me Chris had been seeing a cop.
That's all she told me," Rambo assured him, as if
sensing his discomfort. "But Traci thinks a lot of
Chris—so it stuck with me when she mentioned
you." Again he smiled warmly. "Nice gal, that
Chris." Rambo's square head pivoted back toward
the pool.

"She sure is," Mike agreed and fell silent, atten-
tively watching the team doing a few warm-up laps.

"You and Chris got plans for after the meet?"
Rambo asked without turning his eyes from Traci
Callazo's dark curly hair, barely visible above a
cluster of quivering twelve-year-olds.

Fuller felt his mouth suddenly go dry. It had been
one hell of a week. The shopping center killer had
been tracked to a neighborhood in the East Side
project but hadn't been caught. A stiff with a bullet
in his head had been found floating downriver. And
a knife fight in the project had left one dead and
maybe two—and Parsons was down with the flu.
Mike hadn't been able to keep any of the dates he'd
made with Chris. Tonight he had plans indeed.
Sylvie was spending the night with Lauri Taggert
and he was taking Chris to a quiet place on a pier in
Thunderbolt. And when he brought her home, they
would be by themselves.

"We're going out for dinner," Mike almost
groaned. The large head swung to face him.

"You two want company or you want to be by
yourselves?" His gentle voice made a startling
contrast with his bulk. Then the gray eyes widened
at Mike's hesitation. "Hey, no problem," Rambo

said with an easy smile. "I know how it gets. Maybe some other time we'll get together. Traci really likes Chris and they don't get much time to socialize in school or here. Maybe in a couple of weeks, after a meet one night, we'll go lift a few beers together."

"Sounds good," Mike breathed in relief. The cool April breeze swept over the bleachers and sent shivers through the kids huddled along the bathhouse wall. Mike found himself smiling at the longlegged little creatures, some knobby kneed and awkward, some with rounded fannies and half-formed breasts, some with gleaming metalwork on their teeth, some so slender it was difficult to tell their gender. But they were beautiful in their youth and energy. Mike watched their bright faces, listened to their whispered, excited voices as they waited for their meet to begin.

Chris sat cross-legged by the girls, patting them reassuringly when they reached out to touch her, sliding her arm around the timid ones who huddled close in need of comfort. It was almost hypnotic watching her slender hands slide from child to child, patting a shoulder, smoothing a wisp of hair, smacking a fanny in encouragement as a kid headed for the starting block. In the third heat, Sylvie was to compete. Mike blinked to break his gaze at Chris, then turned his head to watch Sylvie, wondering whether she would appreciate a shouted encouragement. He decided to remain silent lest he make her nervous.

Sylvie had drawn the far lane. At the gun she launched herself through the air with the precision of a gymnast as a cheer went up from her teammates. Fuller watched in wonder as the child emerged, then began slipping through the sparkling water, her lean body barely disturbing the surface

as she reached out with long, even strokes. *She looks like she was born in the water*, Mike thought as he shook his head in amazement. At first Sylvie spurted ahead of her competitors, but then she settled back about half a body length behind the girl in lane three, who was the early leader as they approached the far wall of the pool. Mike stared at the thrashing of the other girls as they made their flip turns and began their second lap. Sylvie barely made a ripple, calmly stretching and plunging her arms into the water without any apparent effort. But still she hovered a half length behind the leader as they neared the finish. She was holding back. Fuller edged forward as he watched her.

"Come on, Sylvie!" Mike yelled, standing abruptly. Then he glanced about in embarrassment at the amused grins of the other spectators, mostly parents, who peppered the bleachers. Chagrined, he settled back down beside Burt Rambo.

"You think the kid's part fish?" Rambo joked as he watched Sylvie. "She's really smooth."

Fuller nodded and forced his teeth to unclench. "She sure is," he breathed.

"You ever see Chris swim?" Rambo arched his brows curiously.

Mike shook his head. "Not yet," he said lamely.

"Like a damn mermaid. Both of them take to the water like dolphins—right at home," Rambo declared. "Whatever it is, it sure runs in the family."

At the end of the race Sylvie touched the wall a fraction of a second behind the winner. Mike stared at her as she climbed from the pool to be congratulated by her shrieking teammates for her second place. All Mike could think was that she could have won. With just a bit of a push at the end, Sylvie could have won.

By the end of the meet the sky was dark and star-studded and the heavy scent of flowering dogwood and Japanese magnolias mingled with the salt air from the river to form an invigorating blend. The West Broad Street Recreation Center had eased out Derenne Center by an ample margin of eighteen points, and Sylvie was the possessor of two second place ribbons. Chris walked her niece and freckle-faced Lauri Taggert toward the green Ford parked beneath a far oak. A husky man in his forties with thick gray hair and deep brown eyes leaned against the front fender.

"How'd it go, honey?" Ralph Taggert asked his daughter.

"Fine, Daddy." Lauri avoided his eyes and reached out for Chris's hand. "Dad, this is my coach, Miss Martin, and this is my friend Sylvia Martin, but we call her Sylvie."

Ralph Taggert fixed a smile on his thick lips, nodding to each in turn. "You're spending the night with Lauri, so I hear," he said to Sylvie. His tone was pleasant but Chris watched his eyes as they shifted from one young girl to the other. There was no threat in those eyes, only a remoteness that could not be deciphered. If he really was one of the enemy, he had their skill at maintaining appearances. She was most interested in what lay beneath that normal surface. Sylvie would find out. Sometime in the night Sylvie would learn what fears haunted her small brown-eyed friend.

"You have a nice time, Sylvie." Chris leaned down and kissed the child. "Don't stay up too late. Remember, you're in training," she cautioned the two youngsters as they clambered into Taggert's car. The door closed behind them with a dull thud. The abrupt roar of the engine cut through the still

night. One pair of green eyes sought and held the other for only an instant; then the sedan pulled away into the darkness. Chris stared after them solemnly. Finally she turned and crossed the parking lot to Fuller's car.

"Are you Sergeant Fuller?" the worried-looking, pink-cheeked hostess asked as she greeted Mike inside the Pier Restaurant. Mike grimaced, then nodded dejectedly.

"You got a call for me?" he guessed.

"Sorry, sir." The young woman looked at him sympathetically. "A gentleman named Kline called and left this number for you."

"He's no gentleman," Mike mumbled. "Chris— duty calls." He shrugged and followed the girl to the telephone, leaving Chris behind.

Chris walked about the foyer, gazing at the heavy nets and scarred floats draped along the walls of the old restaurant. When the young woman in the uniform returned, she was shaking her head. "I guess this ruins your evening."

Chris held up her hands in mock surrender. "It comes with the territory," she said, sighing. "Do you have takeout orders?"

"Not usually." The girl suddenly brightened. "But under the circumstances I think we can come up with something. What would you like? Lobster? Shrimp?"

"Anything that's ready and cold." Chris smiled. Behind the hostess she could see Mike scowl and slam the receiver into place and start back toward her.

"How about a big seafood salad?" the girl asked. Chris nodded enthusiastically. "Two minutes," she promised, and raced toward the kitchen.

"Don't say what you're thinking," Chris told Mike as she slid her arm around his waist and gave him a hug. "Just get out your wallet and we'll be on our way in a minute." She led him to the cashier's desk. "I ordered a salad to take with us. We have to eat, Michael." His dark look softened slightly. "Or isn't missing the dinner what's so upsetting?" Her eyes gleamed with amusement.

"Man cannot live by bread alone," he muttered.

"No, but it does keep your motor running," she said, laughing.

"It was running fine." He kissed her temple, stroked her smooth shoulder.

"Pay the lady." Chris nudged him as the flushed hostess emerged from the kitchen with a small Styrofoam ice chest.

"We couldn't think of anything else to put it in," she said, breathing heavily. "One of the guys uses this for beer—when he's off duty, of course." She smiled.

"Tell him we'll get it back to him tomorrow— with a six-pack inside," Mike replied. "It's real nice of you to fix . . . whatever this is."

The hostess rang up the total. "Ten dollars and forty cents," she announced.

"For a salad?" Mike stared at the red numbers on the register.

"Wait till you see this *salad!*" the girl responded confidently.

Chris gave him another poke in the side. Obediently Mike counted out the bills, grabbed the ice chest, and headed for the car with Chris in step beside him.

"Have a nice evening," the hostess called from the doorway.

"Fat chance," Mike grumbled as he slid behind

the wheel. They were halfway out of the parking lot before he spoke again. "I'll swing by your place and drop you off." His eyes were intent on the traffic.

"Is that official policy or would it be all right if I simply rode along with you?"

"You sure you want to go with me?" he asked cautiously. "Knifing, in a bar. Looks like a prostitute got it in a row with her pimp."

"How long will you be there?" Chris looked at his weary face. In profile the boyishness was absent.

"Maybe a couple of hours. Could be more, could be less. Depends on how many witnesses."

"If you don't mind, I'll stay with you," she said softly.

He shifted his dark eyes from the traffic momentarily and examined her calm expression. "I don't mind," he said. "I just hope you're up to it."

"We'll see," Chris whispered. "In the meantime how about a crab leg?" she asked as she brandished a slender shaft with pale crabmeat protruding from the end.

"For now it'll have to do," Fuller said, grinning. Munching on the chilled delicacy with satisfaction, he eased through the light traffic toward the west end of Savannah.

"His name is Butch. I don't know his last name." The pockmarked face of the tall youth who spoke seemed riddled with holes in the peculiar light. "He said he has a few girls. This one was kinda new. Only around about a month or so." His heavy-lidded eyes lingered on the outstretched limp hand on the floor, the only part of the girl visible around the hulking forms of the two men from the medical team who were working the scene. The

police photographer circled the body, repeatedly adjusting his camera as the flash illuminated detail after detail.

"Will you go down to headquarters and let the staff artist work up a sketch of this Butch character?" Mike drew the man's attention away from the body. "You think you could come up with a face for us?"

"Yeah, sure," the guy said, nodding. "I've seen it done on TV. I could do it." He seemed eager to try. Mike summoned a patrolman to take the fellow away while the memory was still fresh. He watched the two men disappear out the door, then turned again to survey the room. Three more witnesses to go. On the far side of the oblong room Chris sat in a narrow booth talking quietly with the sallow-skinned waitress who had known the dead girl. Mike already had her statement. Angela Jackson was her name, and she hadn't been a lot of help. Visibly shaken, Angela had retreated into the corner booth where Chris was sitting. Chris had promptly gotten the woman a drink. Now on her second or third bourbon, the dull-eyed waitress leaned across the table, resting a hand on Chris's arm as she spoke.

Fuller crossed toward the two women, hesitating for a second to catch their attention before he spoke. "Look, I've got three more witnesses and a few details to straighten out," Mike sighed. "It may be a while," he added as he stood next to Chris. "I'm gonna get a car to take you home, miss." He nodded toward the waitress, then turned back to Chris. "You want the guys to drop you off too?"

"How about letting me borrow your car and I'll take her." Chris cupped her hand gently over the

woman's tense fingers. "Then I'll go on home myself. When you get finished, have someone drop you off."

"It may be awfully late." Mike shook his head dejectedly.

"Just ring the bell a few times," Chris said, smiling. "I'll be there." Her green eyes soothed him.

"OK," he said quietly as he reached for his car keys, then dropped them into her outstretched palm. "You'll get no argument from me. See you—whenever." He straightened his slightly drooping shoulders and escorted the two women to the doorway. "You get a good night's sleep, miss," he said briskly. "We'll get back to you in the morning. Take it easy," he said in a lowered voice to Chris as a sort of good-bye, and turned back toward the bar.

"Good night, Sylvie." The muffled voice on the far side of the bed stifled a yawn.

"'Night, Lauri," Sylvie sighed. She lay very still, staring intently at the shadows in the room until the slow, regular breathing next to her made it clear that Lauri Taggert was asleep. Silently Sylvie eased her legs from under the covers. Crouching in the corner of the room, she unwrapped the lavender cover and placed the golden hand upright on its base. There were four in the Taggert family, so Sylvie set four tapers in place. She struck a match, lighting first one, then the next, then the next candle, then finally touching the small flame to the fourth taper. It would not light. Sylvie waited patiently for several minutes as she sat cross-legged in concentration; then she tried the fourth candle again. This time the flame flickered, then spread along the wick. Now she knew the last one was

sound asleep. None would awake while the tapers flamed.

Sylvie walked around the bed toward her sleeping friend. She touched the fingers of her right hand to the girl's temple and began to hum—softly at first, then gradually louder as she swayed, her left wrist pressed to her chest, a miniature fan of coral on a slender gold chain encircling her long neck. The third candle flamed higher, sending its musky scent into the still air.

"Unburden your heart, my child," Sylvie sang. "Let your sorrow become my sorrow, let my strength become your strength." Her childlike voice repeated the chant as her green eyes slowly closed. Gradually her heartbeat blended into the same rhythm as the slow, regular pulse of her companion. Her fingertips remained pressed against the child's bare temple as she listened to a lament without words.

"Let me help you." Chris opened the passenger door of the car and leaned down so the waitress could drape her arm around her neck. Holding her unsteady companion upright, Chris shoved the car door shut with a foot, then escorted her slightly drunk charge toward the old house. Once a beautiful planter's mansion, the ancient three-story wooden structure sat dilapidated and forlorn, divided by dim hallways and dingy doors into low-rent apartments for Savannah's unfortunates. The city's historic reclamation project had not yet touched this fringe of the inner city.

"Your keys," Chris demanded quietly as she helped the woman up the stairs.

Inside the nearly bare room Chris locked the door securely, then began to hum as she sat the

limp woman on the bed and started to unlace the heavy-soled work shoes the woman wore. Carefully she removed the waitress's clothing, leaving her seated on the edge of the disheveled bed. Then Chris stepped into the bathroom and turned on the shower.

Still humming, she stood in the center of the dim room facing the motionless woman. As she slowly removed her own clothing, dropping the garments onto the floor, she focused her green eyes on the glazed ones of Angela Jackson.

"Unburden your heart, my child," Chris sang. "Let your sorrow become my sorrow, let my strength become your strength." She reached out and took the woman's hands, leading her toward the running water as she repeated her song.

"Wash away the darkness, my child." She eased the woman under the warm steady stream of water. "The shadows of your childhood do not belong with you. Give the shadows to me. Claim the once-dark recesses of your being for your tomorrows." The golden-haired creature stepped under the pounding water and embraced the sallow-skinned young woman whose face was a mask of sadness. She pulled her close against her bosom and sang softly to her. "Let your sorrow become my sorrow," she repeated as the water coursed over their entwined forms. "Let my strength become your strength," she murmured as they clung together. Finally the darker-haired woman heaved a massive sigh. She shuddered as a long low moan seemed to draw the tension from her form. Then her knees slowly buckled as she collapsed against her comforter.

With little effort Chris lifted her companion and carried her to the bed, easing her down on the

crumpled sheets. She retrieved a towel, patted dry the naked form, and lifted the covers over the unconscious woman whose plain face was now calm and peaceful in deep sleep. Chris stood limply, as if her slender form struggled to support an unseen burden. Wearily she dressed herself and silently retreated, pulling closed and locking the door behind her.

A half hour later, in her own green sanctuary, Chris opened wide the balcony doors, letting the breeze from the river fill the darkened room. She lifted a large reed basket from the mantel and began placing its contents—bits of pale coral and gleaming white seashells—in a circle on the carpet. Only the soft moonlight illuminated the circle. Moving to her bedroom, Chris undressed with slow, labored movements. Finally she returned to the circle, bearing in her slender hands a massive conch shell and a small velvet case. She stepped inside the circle, pointing the deep purple core of the conch shell toward the open doors so the wind could glide into the shell's throat. The silence gave way to the low whisper from the conch telling tales of seas and souls and time.

Chris unbraided her long pale hair, still moist from the shower. Lifting an ancient gold comb from the velvet case, she closed her eyes. With long, smooth strokes, she slid the gleaming comb through her hair while the song of the conch shell and the sea wind rippled through the room. At last, with smooth strands of gold caressing her shoulders and the soft sea song in her ears, Chris laid her cheek upon the deep green carpet and slept.

It took five rings before Mike Fuller heard any movement inside the apartment. The entire second

floor had been completely dark when he stood on the street below, looking up at the iron balcony. But behind the lacy railings the French doors were wide open. He could see the sheer ivory curtains fluttering in the light wind. So he had rung—five times—and had poised his finger for a sixth when he heard her voice.

"Just a minute, Michael," Chris called sleepily; then there was silence again. A full minute later the door swung open.

"I figured it was going to work out like this," he said, shaking his head. "It's too late. If you hand me my keys, I'll just go."

"You look tired," Chris said as she took his arm and tugged him gently inside. Mike only shrugged. She had wrapped a deep green robe about her body and her pale hair fell almost to her waist.

"Chris . . ." He formed her name but no sound escaped his lips.

"You want to talk?"

Fuller shook his head wearily.

"Hungry?" she tried again.

Another silent no.

"Would it help if we held each other?" Her green eyes looked up at him intently. She moved nearer so his arms could close around her. Mike held her gently, slowly pressing his face against her hair, breathing in her clean scent. He felt her arms move within his embrace, then the deep green robe slid from her body.

"Come with me, Michael," she breathed against his throat. She stepped back, taking his hand and leading him down the hallway toward the far room. Beside the wide bed she turned. Softly she brushed aside his hands as he tried to unfasten his tie. He stood watching her as she removed each piece of his

clothing. Finally naked, he waited while she pulled back the sheets and slid into bed. He followed her in silence, glancing down uncertainly as the undulating motion beneath his touch distracted him.

"Water bed," he muttered when Chris noticed his reaction.

She smiled and stretched her long arms toward him. "There's a life jacket under your pillow," she whispered with a smile as he inched his way into her embrace. When her cool skin touched his and her pale hair fell across his face, Fuller lost all sense of time and movement beyond the languid rhythm of his warm flesh against hers. Her gentle touch unraveled the twisting muscles in his back. Her soft kisses closed his weary eyelids. Fuller's mouth traced the contours of her body, savoring the slightly salty taste of her skin. Wide-eyed and smiling, Chris whispered his name again and again, arching toward him as he moved above her and willingly drowned in her embrace.

Cradled in each other's arms, they drifted off to sleep as the pastel dawn filtered through the morning mist. Below, long, low barges inched their way along the Savannah River toward the dark waters of the Atlantic and their distant destinations across the seas.

At the stroke of midnight the young daughter of Sir Graillonner withdrew into the woods beyond the castle walls to pray in solitude. There she invoked the spirit of her dead mother to watch over her. This particular night the maid's passage to her secret grotto was not as it had been on other evenings. As she walked beside the river that wound through the forest, a sudden breeze rippled the dark surface of the water, and the rushes by the river's edge whispered low.

Nearby, beneath an ancient oak with branches hung with mistletoe, the maiden chanced upon a green-eyed lady lamenting that she had lost her way in the unfamiliar land.

"Come with me into my father's hall," the maid invited, extending an open hand toward the lady. "You can pass the night with me, and in the morning we will ask my father to help you."

The pale-skinned lady smiled, clasping the proffered hand, pressing it with her own palm as she stared deep into the maiden's clear blue eyes. At the threshold of the nobleman's hall the lady's step faltered, but the young maid held her securely,

supporting her and leading her inward. She summoned servants to bring food and wine for her guest. Later, in the maid's chambers, they disrobed in silence and slid side by side beneath the heavy coverings of the massive bed.

The maiden's sleep was fraught with dreams of strange and terrible things. She saw an emerald serpent encircle a falcon with its coils and contract itself so tightly that the feathered prey perished. The green-eyed lady cradled the young maiden against her bosom and sang softly in her ear. "You no longer need to seek the solace of the night forest," she whispered. "I have come in answer to your summons."

In the morning the maiden recalled nothing of what had passed in the night. She escorted the lady through the winding halls to the large room wherein the nobleman received his visitors. With proper courtesy befitting so elegant a lady, the maiden presented her guest to her father. The nobleman stood and gazed into gleaming green eyes as the lady once again told of her distress. As was customary when a guest of such excellent bearing came into one's halls, the nobleman offered his assistance. The lady asked only for his men to serve as bodyguards to see her safely to her own land.

That very day the lady bade the maiden farewell and praised the nobleman for his excellent hospitality. As a parting gesture she placed a kiss upon his lips. Accompanied by two brave knights as escort, the lady rode off toward the river, which she said would lead back to her home.

Sir Graillonner stared after her, his eyes glazed, his countenance ashen. Throughout that evening he sat by the fire, shunning all companionship as he gazed listlessly into the flames. He accepted neither

food nor drink. Three days he sat without speaking. Three nights he tossed in restless sleep, tormented by some demon dream he could not recall upon waking.

On the last night, as he lay sleeping, some spirit stole away his soul, for with the light of dawn he was dead. The two knights returned to the castle bewildered, unable to remember where their mission had taken them or how they had managed to return. They prayed in the chapel, giving praise for their safe return, for they were convinced that they had been in the thrall of an enchantress who had sealed the fate of their lord with her scarlet kiss.

The fair maid blossomed into womanhood, finally choosing one from among her suitors to rule with her and oversee her father's lands. However, often as she strolled along the riverbank, especially when the gentle evening breeze whispered in the rushes, she would hum a soft and melancholy melody, a half-remembered tune without words.

CHAPTER 4

❖❖❖❖❖❖

"I've got to pick up the girls at eleven." Michael Fuller felt a cool hand on his shoulder as the soft voice drew him from his dreams into the real world. Rolling over, he shifted his gaze upward, focusing on the stream of pale hair, then the oval face and green eyes that had filled his night. The slow, easy motion of the water bed increased beneath him as Chris leaned over to kiss him lightly. "Eleven," she whispered against his cheek. "That's in twenty minutes. I'm leaving to get the girls."

His arms softly enclosed her.

"Michael . . . I don't go in for quickies," she said, resisting his embrace. "I woke you so we could have brunch together"—she smiled—"nothing more complicated than that. You are hungry, aren't you?" She nodded in anticipation of his reply.

"Now that you mention food"—he stretched and grinned at her—"I'm *starving*." He pulled himself to a sitting position, then caught her gently by the shoulders. "Chris . . ." His smile faded as he stared intently into her eyes. His brow furrowed in distress as he tried to articulate his thoughts. "Oh, Chris." He lifted a hand to touch her cheek tender-

ly, slowly trailing his fingers down over her lips, then lower, along her slender neck, returning them to rest on her shoulder.

"I think so too, Michael." She spoke in a whisper, returning his earnest look.

Fuller nodded in relief as his characteristic smile slowly returned. "So long as you understand," he floundered.

"I think I do." Chris chuckled. "So get dressed." she chirped as she leaped away from the bed. "There's cold lobster; shrimp, grapes—a veritable feast of leftovers."

Thirty minutes later Mike Fuller was at his desk, diligently transferring his handwritten notes to specified locations on the police forms.

Homicide
Female, 16 years old, Caucasian
Address unknown
Name: (possible) Marsha
Cause of Death: Medical examiner's preliminary report (attached) lists as cause blood loss from two stab wounds in the abdomen, one stab wound in the chest which severed an artery.

Methodically Fuller compiled the file on the case: a slim folder with the statements of witnesses, the artist's composite drawing, and the list of personal items on the girl's body. Finally his attention settled on one small white envelope clipped to the corner of the file. It was hardly a thing he would have expected to find in the purse of a prostitute lying dead on the floor of Sunny Jim's Bar—a contribution envelope bearing in Old English script the name of the Cathedral of Saint John the Baptist.

Tucking the envelope and a black-and-white photo of the dead girl in his coat pocket, Fuller shoved his chair back from the desk.

"Saint John's—in case anybody needs me," he called to the detective beside the door as he left.

The hundred-year-old Catholic cathedral, flanked by huge moss-hung oaks, faced Lafayette Square where banks of flowering azaleas rimmed the winding walkways. Inside the silent cathedral Fuller stared up at the massive stained-glass windows sending bright beams of red and blue light down upon the smooth, dark wooden pews. A few tourists strolled the aisles, gazing at the delicately carved wood scrollwork and the lofty marble pillars that distinguished the old structure. Rows of candles, each dedicated to a certain saint, flickered beneath pale statues of creamy stone. Fuller's eyes rested on the velvet-curtained confessionals as a white-haired old woman placed a triangle of lace over her tight curls and stepped into the wooden chamber to the far right.

Mike strode up the aisle, then turned toward the unmarked door opening to the offices beyond. A young priest seated behind the desk looked up at him curiously.

"I'm Sergeant Fuller—homicide," Mike said, nodding to the fellow. "We found one of your contribution envelopes on the body of a young girl. I have a picture. Perhaps someone here could help me in identifying her." He lifted the black-and-white photo from his pocket and placed it on the desk before the young man. The priest examined the picture of the pale, dark-haired girl whose long-lashed eyes were closed. Instinctively he crossed himself and murmured a prayer.

He finally spoke.

"I do not know her. However, there are others here who may." He rose from his chair. "Let me take this for a few moments, Sergeant." He lifted the photo from the desk top. "Please wait here."

Mike paced the polished wooden floor of the small room, occasionally glancing up at the blue-eyed, oval-faced Christ in the gilt frame above the desk. Finally he sat on the small armchair facing the door, his long legs awkwardly thrust out. Twenty minutes passed before the young priest returned with a second man, taller and older, gliding smoothly in his wake.

"I am Father Trent," the older priest said as Fuller rose. "Father Williams showed me the picture of the poor child. I have spoken with her on several occasions. Seeing her . . . like this . . . is quite a shock." He returned the photo to Fuller. "Father Williams said you are from the homicide department. Was she—ah, what happened to her, Sergeant?"

"She was killed, sir," Mike responded. "Allegedly by the man she worked for. But we haven't positively identified her and have very little information about him. Any help you could give would be greatly appreciated. Do you know her name?"

"Marsha," the older priest said reflectively. "Marsha is all I know. She gave me no last name." His brow furrowed in thought. "I'm sorry," he sighed. "I'm truly sorry."

Mike expelled a long audible breath. "Marsha . . ." he repeated softly, then lifted his eyes to catch the gaze of Father Trent. "Anything, Father. Anything you can recall that could help us trace her family or friends. Where she lived. A street. A neighborhood?"

"I know she had become a prostitute," the priest

replied bluntly. "And it tormented her," he added grimly. "She was barely sixteen. She'd lived in Savannah most of her life and she had recently left home. She was very troubled and very determined to be independent of her family. This occupation of hers was only a means to an end—so she said. She was putting money aside, putting it in the bank, so she could take care of her sister." He suddenly seemed reluctant to continue. He cast a narrowed gaze in Father Williams's direction and the younger priest silently turned and slipped from the room, closing the door behind him.

Mike watched him go, then turned back to Father Trent.

"Sergeant, most of what I know she told me in confidence. I do not wish to break her trust."

"The girl is dead, sir," Mike persisted. "Someone is responsible for her death. We don't have a full name for the death certificate. We cannot notify her family until we know who she is. Please . . ." Mike lowered his tone earnestly. "Anything you can tell me."

"There is nothing more to tell," the priest said, shrugging. "I know only of her remorse. I know nothing that would aid in identifying the girl or locating her family. Believe me, I tried to help her. She didn't want her family identified. She would not let the church intercede."

"Intercede in what?" Fuller narrowed his eyes.

"In the family problems she left home to avoid," he replied.

"What kind of problems did they have?" Mike pressed him. Problems often meant police and police meant reports. "Money, drinking, fights?"

Father Trent shook his head slightly. He was sharp. He knew Fuller's line of reasoning. "Sorry,

nothing so public as that," he said flatly. "The problem was more intimate. The problem was incest."

Mike closed his eyes slowly. "Her father?" he asked.

"Not genetically, but psychologically, yes. Her stepfather married her mother when Marsha was quite young. She ran away to escape his . . . demands."

"And you couldn't help her?" Mike sounded uncertain.

"She wouldn't tell me very much, no details, only rather general statements. She didn't seem to want to hurt her mother by making this public. Marsha just wanted to get away from the man and to get the younger sister out too." The priest's shoulders drooped with sudden fatigue. "All I could do was comfort her, offer her the protection of the church, hear her confession—and pray with her." He hesitated a moment, then decided to add something more. "She had a special fondness for Saint Maria Goretti." He smiled sadly.

Mike shrugged defensively. "I'm not Catholic, sir."

"Well, son, many Catholics aren't familiar with Saint Maria Goretti. She was but a child when she died resisting the advances of a young man." His dark eyes dropped to the coat pocket in which Fuller had placed the morgue picture of Marsha. "You told me a young man is suspected of the act," Father Trent said.

"Marsha died of stab wounds." Mike guessed what the priest was thinking.

"So did Maria Goretti," Father Trent sighed. "Perhaps now they can comfort each other," he whispered, his face ashen, "and find peace with our

Savior." Again his eyes shifted to Mike's jacket pocket. "Where is the body?"

"Savannah General morgue."

"It is a bit late, but I would like to see her—to provide a final prayer. If no formal arrangements have been made, our diocese will see she has a proper Catholic funeral."

Mike thanked Father Trent for his help, then let himself out of the small office. Father Williams was waiting outside to escort him through the cathedral to the main entrance. On the front steps Mike shook the young priest's hand, then strode away toward his car. The faint scent of jasmine in the still afternoon air brought back the memory of Chris and her shivering eleven-year-olds, and the slow, steady strokes of Sylvie's arms skimming through the water as she seemed to pace herself just behind the lead swimmer.

Sitting behind the wheel of his car, Mike wondered what had made his mind link the unfortunate Marsha with the happy memory of Sylvie—alive, in motion, in control. He shook his head as he recalled the words of Father Trent. "She was barely sixteen. . . ."

Mike flipped open the note pad to the next-to-last page to find another name: Angela Jackson—waitress. This one had said she knew the dead girl. "She talked with me once in a while" were her precise words. She knew her as Marsha—"just Marsha"—nothing more. Fuller tapped his thumb thoughtfully on the page as his eyes skimmed over the notes. Angela Jackson had been very upset after the killing last night. When he watched her in the booth with Chris, she was a little calmer, but she was also fairly drunk by then. By the time Chris left to drive her home, she had been pretty far gone.

"Perhaps the liquor and a good night's sleep have eased the shock," Mike thought aloud. He'd try her again, he concluded as he flipped the small notebook closed and dropped it into his coat pocket with the picture of Marsha. If Angela Jackson could not give him a last name, a street, or a clue to relatives or friends, he'd have to release the photo to the newspapers. "A helluva way to get the news," he brooded as he imagined a stunned mother looking down at the evening paper. "One helluva way," he repeated as he drove west across the city.

Lauri Taggert lingered on her front sidewalk long after the silver MG had disappeared into the steady stream of late Saturday afternoon shoppers and tourist traffic. The steep, curving stairway that led up over the high basement to the front door was almost identical to those of the six other entrances on the other dull brick three-story houses along the sidewalk. Each row house had been somewhat restored. One neighbor had had the bricks sandblasted to renew their color. Some folks had added bright shutters and had painted the metal grillwork to match. Ralph Taggert had converted the high-ceilinged basement of their 1854 townhouse into a rental apartment.

Reluctantly Lauri stepped up toward the front door. Usually Saturdays were safe. Her dad would be puttering around upstairs, turning the attic into another rental unit. Her mother would be at the dress shop till six. Her young brother would be stationed in front of the TV or playing in the backyard.

Inside the foyer Lauri paused. The house was silent. No hammering from above, no blare of cartoons from the living room. She stood very still. No sound from the attic. Quietly she tiptoed

through to the kitchen and peered down into the small yard. No Robbie.

From upstairs came the abrupt flush of the toilet. Then the unmistakable heavy tread of Ralph Taggert echoed down the wooden stairway. Lauri dashed toward the refrigerator. Hastily transferring bottles and Tupperware containers to the table, she braced herself.

"Hi, Dad. Boy, am I hungry. You want a sandwich?" Her words came rapid-fire. "I had a great time with Sylvie. . . ." She kept up a steady stream of chatter as her father reached past her and grabbed a beer from the refrigerator. "I like the lessons," she continued as she plopped four slices of bread on the cutting board.

"What lessons?" Taggert asked, popping open the can.

"Roller-skating," Lauri answered brightly. "Remember? Mom said I could take lessons Saturday mornings. Sylvie and I went this morning. Sylvie's aunt brought us home in her sports car. It was neat."

"I wondered where you were," Taggert muttered. "When I got up, you and your friend were gone."

"Where's Robbie?" Lauri inquired without lifting her eyes from her nearly constructed sandwich.

"With the Bakers—a birthday party. They all went to Forsyth Park for a picnic." He took a slow pull at the beer as he leaned against the doorjamb. Lauri slapped a piece of cheese atop bologna, concentrating intently on her creation. Already the cold, clammy sensation was beginning.

"You've been awfully busy lately, honey," the thick voice oozed around her. "Every time I turn around you're off somewhere—swimming, now skating. I don't get to see my baby like I want to."

Lauri consciously kept her breathing steady. Her

hand lifted the knife and sliced each sandwich into neat halves. Two pieces she placed on a paper napkin and slid them across the table. "Here's one for you," she announced with a smile. Deliberately she got a tall glass from the cupboard, filled it with milk, then settled at the kitchen table with her own sandwich.

"Your mom just can't make me feel good—like you do." Taggert eased into the chair facing her. "She's cold and hard and old. She don't love anybody."

Lauri kept her eyes riveted on her sandwich, forcing herself to chew and swallow each bite.

"With you away so much I really get to needing you bad, honey," he said earnestly. "You know it don't hurt you any to give the old man a little attention. You know I'd never hurt you, baby doll. I'd do anything for you."

Lauri put the half-eaten sandwich back on the napkin and stared glumly at the glass of milk. Taggert's own untouched sandwich lay on the napkin before him.

"No one's home. . . ." Taggert reached across and took her hand. "Come on upstairs with me, baby. You know how much I need you. I work so hard so you can have nice things. I'd go nuts if I didn't have my little honey Lauri, if I didn't get to be near you, baby." He had already eased around toward her, still clasping her limp hand.

"You wanted skating lessons—you got 'em," he breathed down on her. "You want skates—nice ones with boots—you can have them. You want a fancy outfit with a little skirt so you'll look great— you can have it. I'll give you anything to make you happy, honey. Come on—make me happy too, baby." He pulled her hand toward his crotch. "It

Lauri obediently got to her feet and padded off to the bathroom. She locked the door behind her. She reached out and turned on the shower. She stood in the center of the old bathroom with her arms crossed over her chest, rocking back and forth slowly, weeping softly as the shower spray pounded into the vacant tub. Abruptly she knelt over the toilet as a violent spasm sent the undigested bits of lettuce and bologna spewing into the still water. She crouched there, clinging to the cool porcelain bowl as dry heaves shook her. Finally, pale and shivering, she lay on the tile floor.

"You all right, honey?" The door handle moved slightly. "Lauri? Answer your daddy, baby."

The only response was the uninterrupted rush of water echoing in the high-ceilinged bathroom.

Mike Fuller knocked on the wooden door. Around the handle the thick brown paint was chipped and peeling.

"Who is it?" the female voice asked apprehensively.

"Sergeant Fuller, ma'am. Savannah police. You spoke with me last night at Sunny Jim's Bar." He waited while the key clicked and the door opened several inches. The wide brown eyes of Angela Jackson scrutinized him.

"Yeah, I remember you." The door opened wide and the young woman motioned for him to enter. "Excuse the mess." She hastily made a circle through the room, grabbing up scattered newspapers and a few items of clothing, then stuffing the garments into a half-filled laundry hamper. Patting her disheveled hair self-consciously, she flushed. "I guess your lady friend told you I passed out on her last night." She lowered her eyes. "She was such a

nice lady—I guess I must have had too much to drink." She shrugged apologetically.

Fuller was already shaking his head. "You were no trouble at all," he assured her. "You had a rough time, Miss Jackson." He failed to mention that he and Chris had not even discussed her.

"Well, tell your friend that I appreciate her bein' so nice to me, bringing me home and all." Angela motioned for him to sit down in the armchair. She sat on the unmade bed, staring at him expectantly. "You found that creep yet?" she asked.

"No, ma'am. The sketch is in the paper today— it may bring some results. What I came to see you about is the dead girl. I'd hoped you could come up with something to help identify her. If she has a family, they should be notified."

"I don't think it matters now," Angela said quietly. "It was their fault she ended up with that creep." A sudden chill in the brown eyes set Fuller's head bobbing in apparent understanding.

"She told you about her family," he led the woman.

"She told me her old man fucked her," Angela said evenly. "Fucked her *up* as well. Made her feel like a freak," she hissed. "But it was him who was the pervert." Her sallow face was solemn. "See, I know how she felt. I ain't never told nobody"—she seemed surprised at her own frankness—"but my old man fooled with me too."

She straightened her shoulders and stared at him wide-eyed. "I never thought I could say it out loud, but I'm sayin' it now. My old man was a two-faced bastard. He told me God made me from him—for him to teach. When I found out that other kids weren't gettin' the same lessons from their old man, I felt like shit. When I tried to tell my old lady, she

shipped me off to her sister. That's how come I'm in Georgia. My aunt kept me till I finished high school. Now I've got my job and my own place." Her dark eyes shifted to the stark, disorderly room. "It ain't much—but nobody fucks with me now." She fell silent and stared at her hands. She felt emptied out, but clean, clean way down deep. "I ain't much," she whispered. "But I ain't shit."

Mike let the silence hold the moment. Finally he spoke.

"About the dead girl. You said you only knew her first name. . . ." He paused.

"Her name was Marsha Barts—something like that. I knew her name," Angela confessed, "but there didn't seem much point in tellin' it. She was dead. Her troubles were over." Anxiously Angela looked up to ask, "I'm not in trouble, am I?"

"No trouble," Mike assured her. Angela shifted her eyes back to her hands as he scribbled in his notebook. "Anything else? Any other details you can recall?"

Angela expelled a slow breath. "She used to live out by Hunter Air Force Base with her folks and younger sister. She met this guy Butch hangin' around the joints up there. He told her she could make good money screwin', so he used to set her up with guys from Hunter. He moved her out this way so her folks wouldn't find her. He set her up somewhere in this area and pimped for her."

"Last night you told me she was sixteen. What was she doin' hanging out in a bar?" There was no accusation in his tone, only weariness.

"She had fake IDs sayin' she was older. Besides, she could hang around bars in the afternoon, pick up a few tricks, and keep the money for herself. This Butch creep only took her guys at night."

"So he must have had a daytime job somewhere," he surmised.

"Check Hunter Field," Angela suggested.

"I will," Mike said, nodding. "Look. I really appreciate your help." He leaned forward earnestly. "I'm glad you decided to open up."

Angela smiled wearily. "I think her dyin' really got to me," she said pensively. "Her dyin' and then your lady friend bein' so nice. That coulda been me layin' there. Just like Marsha. Nobody woulda given a damn. Your friend, Chris, she knew how scared I was. She was real nice. . . ." Her voice trailed off as she knitted her brow in thought. The memory of the previous night was quite fuzzy. "She musta cleaned me up and put me to bed," Angela said softly. "She took care of me, like I was somebody." She raised her chin confidently. "So I've been thinkin' that I *am* somebody—somebody good. It was my old man, not me, who was shit. He was forty years old and I was thirteen and I didn't even have tits." She managed a weak smile. "There ain't nothin' sexy about a thirteen-year-old kid with no tits."

Mike reached out and patted her shoulder. "You hang in there, Angela," he said, smiling. "And you let me know if I can help you out." He stood to leave. "And if you think of anything else—anything that might help me—just call." He jotted his name and office number on a piece of paper and passed it to her.

Angela accepted the paper, then looked up. "You tell your lady—tell her thanks for me," Angela reminded him. "She really made me feel good about myself. Tell her that," she insisted as she followed him to the door. "Really good . . ." she repeated as she closed the door behind him.

Mike wound his way down the narrow stairs of the old rooming house. Wearily he glanced at his watch. He'd check with his partner, then he'd call Chris. He remembered how she had sat in the small booth at the bar, with Angela's hand resting on her arm. Now he wondered what they had said to each other.

"She really made me feel good . . ." Angela's words made him smile. *Me too*, he reflected as he stepped out onto the street.

Two knobby-kneed black girls with rows of tight braids subduing their dark curls were crouched on the cracked sidewalk playing jacks. They stared with big curious eyes at the tall man in the pale gray suit. Men in their neighborhood didn't wear business suits. Mike nodded to them. "Afternoon, ladies," he said with a grin as he headed for his car. Glancing over the car roof at them, he remembered what Angela had said. "Nothin' sexy about a thirteen-year-old kid with no tits." The two youngsters on the sidewalk were now convulsed in giggles, hugging each other while their big eyes rolled toward the funny man in the suit. *Cute*, Mike mused, *but definitely not sexy.*

As he guided his unmarked car through the heavy traffic, Mike recalled a crude expression always heard around the squad room after some bizarre sex offense: "A hard dick has no conscience." He squinted into the low sun. "His own kid," he breathed. "Just a kid. No conscience." The words haunted him. So did the mental picture of the woman-child, Marsha, dead on the barroom floor.

"I sure missed you." Mike reached out and touched Chris's shoulder. Twenty-one pairs of wide eyes were riveted on the tall, curly-haired man and

his companion. Self-consciously he dropped his hand.

Chris turned to the girls. "You do a few warm-up laps," she said, grinning at them. "I'll be with you in a couple of minutes." The eleven-year-olds stood transfixed, still staring. "Now!" Chris pointed to the pool. Abruptly they scattered, giggling and glancing back to watch their coach and "that man."

"I missed you too, Michael." Chris slid her arm under his and walked him toward the bleachers. "But Sylvie really needed to get away for a short break. I'll have to give you my number at the beach, so that if you need to talk, you can call me there. Maybe next weekend you can get off and go with us. There's lots of room in my aunt's house. She'd love to have you visit."

Mike stared down at the oval face and cool green eyes. Her pale hair was twisted into french braids again, but the memory of it cascading down over him made his color deepen. Even through her warm-up jacket he could feel the pressure of her body against his arm.

"Are you listening to me, Michael?" Chris tugged at his sleeve. "I just invited you to the beach next weekend."

"Oh," Mike stammered. "I was just thinking—"

"I know what you were thinking," she said softly. Again he flushed. "Let's talk later," she suggested as her eyes shifted back to the girls in the pool. "I've got to get going. Just try to find a seat, make yourself at home." She waved toward the nearly vacant bleachers.

Burt Rambo sprawled midway up the stands. He raised a beefy hand in welcome.

"There seems to be a place available," Chris kidded. "See you later." She strode off.

"Good to see you." Rambo extended his palm and shook Fuller's hand. "Hell of a way to see her, ain't it?" He chuckled. "You'll get real good at holding towels and keeping score as the season progresses. With these gals you either pitch in or you spend a lot of time alone," he added philosophically.

"So I'll learn to help," Mike said, shrugging amiably. His eyes followed the blond woman to the far side of the pool. Chris unzipped her jacket and pitched it against the bathhouse wall. Mike leaned forward, propping his elbows on his knees, clasping his hands as he contemplated her long, lean body.

"Anyone in there?" Chris shouted into the bathhouse to roust the stragglers. "Come on, you slowpokes. Let's get started." Two young black girls scurried out; a blond kid with freckles and round brown eyes followed a few steps behind.

"Lauri . . ." Chris spoke apprehensively. "You're a little late, my friend."

The blond girl nodded, her face expressionless.

"Come on." Chris reached out so the child could slide up next to her. Lauri Taggert slipped her arm around the woman's waist as they proceeded in step toward the far end of the pool. Chris rested her arm on the child's shoulders. She could feel the tension beneath her fingers.

"How would you like to spend next weekend with Sylvie and me at the beach?" Chris asked as they walked along. "I'll talk to your folks and we'll leave Friday night, right after the meet."

"Oh, could I? Would you talk to them—ask them?" Lauri pleaded. The undercurrent of desperation made Chris jerk her eyes down to the pale upturned face.

"Sure," Chris said, forcing a cheerful smile. "I'll

call your mom," she asserted. "I'm sure I can take care of you."

Lauri Taggert sighed and managed a wistful smile in return. "I hope I can go." She tightened her grip around Chris's waist.

Up in the bleachers Mike and Burt were watching the small girl and Chris moving toward the far end of the pool.

"She sure has a way with those kids." Burt Rambo's words drew Mike from his preoccupied silence. "They flutter around her like moths on a light bulb," Rambo observed. "Around and around, then they touch base and flutter off again."

Rambo's eyes followed Mike's as Chris stood chest deep in the water, boosting each young swimmer through her flip turn. One hand would tuck the child's head under, the other hand would slide beneath her fanny, helping her spring and stretch out into the next lap. Always there was a child near Chris: resting a hand on her arm, touching her shoulder, leaning against her side. And Chris's slender hands moved from child to child—touching, patting, reassuring, guiding their motion.

Like a moth to a light, Mike mused. The waitress had been like that, he recalled. Chris had sat in the booth while Angela Jackson hovered—touching her, reaching out to her. Then Chris had rested her palm over the woman's hand. And Angela had been grateful. "Tell your lady thanks for me," she'd said. "She made me feel good about myself."

Your lady. Mike smiled at the words. *My lady*. He studied the sleek wet skin of the blond coach.

"Sylvie is Chris's niece?" Rambo asked without moving his eyes from the pool.

"Yeah."

"How come they got the same last name? Sylvie must be her brother's kid," Rambo speculated. "Does Chris have brothers?"

Mike shrugged. "I never asked."

"Well, the family genes are real heavyweights—powerful babies." Burt Rambo shifted his thick legs and leaned forward next to Mike. "Look at those two," he breathed as Sylvie glided up next to Chris. "That hair, those cheekbones, those eyes, even the set of the jawline." The two men scrutinized the features of the twosome in the pool. "They look like the same person at two different stages of development. Déjà vu. More like sisters, twin sisters even" —he nudged Mike—"or mother and daughter."

Mike turned to look incredulously into the big man's intent face. "You're letting your imagination run wild."

"Yeah." Rambo chuckled. "It comes from being shut up with computers all day. I start following angles and get lost in the maze. I didn't mean any disrespect," he insisted. "I just got carried away." His shy smile returned. "Still. . . ." A mischievous glint in his eyes made them both look back toward the water. "Sylvie's what? Eleven? And Chris is maybe twenty-four, -five?"

"Enough." Mike cut him off before the speculation could continue. "I doubt if she had a kid at fourteen—and if she did, it isn't any of our business." He stressed the "our."

"Yeah, you're right," Rambo said, resuming his easygoing manner. "No sense buttin' into someone else's business. Bad habit of mine," he apologized. "Comes from—"

"I know. From being shut up with computers all day."

Rambo chuckled.

"You program computers?" Mike asked, taking charge of the conversation.

"I set up systems." Rambo's eyes brightened with a new interest. "I design the programs. I have a crew of processors and programmers to key the data and run them through. So I spend a lot of time thinking—and waiting for printouts," he said, grinning.

"How did you get to know Traci?" Mike asked.

"She lives in my apartment building," he replied. "It was real romantic. We were doing our laundry —separately, of course—in the Laundromat downstairs. We each had some dirty tennis shoes, so we shared a washer. It went uphill from there." His round gray eyes shifted to the near corner of the pool, where Traci Callazo was poised over a twelve-year-old, tapping her fingers against the kid's knees for greater spring in the dive. "I forgot what fresh air smelled like till Traci started draggin' me to these sessions." The affection in his voice made them both smile. "She's a real nice person," Rambo added. "She really cares about those kids. Makes me feel good just to watch 'em."

"I know what you mean." Mike stretched his long legs into the empty seats before him. "Sort of like seeing how the other half lives," he remarked.

"Ain't often you meet a nice girl—I mean nice on the inside," Rambo said. "Makes ya kinda nervous." He turned to Mike. "Like you gotta take special care not to screw up." His wide, honest eyes scanned Mike's face.

"I know what you mean." Mike breathed the words.

"I thought you would." Rambo grinned. "Why the hell else would you and I be the only guys sittin'

on these damn bleachers?" His eyes returned to the pool.

Chris had gathered her girls together at the far end of the pool. One by one she guided them through their racing dives. Each child bent low, stretched out, hit the water, took a few strokes, then circled back to try again. "Like a moth to a light," Mike observed. He clasped his hands patiently and breathed in the sweet evening air.

"You're very pensive, Michael," Chris said from across the living room. Sylvie had finished her homework and was in bed, almost asleep. Mike had dried the dinner dishes and had stretched back on the long, low sofa with a mug of coffee. He had sat there listening to the tooth-brushing, toilet-flushing, and good-night routine as Chris got Sylvie settled.

In a loose lavender shirt and deeper purple slacks, Chris crossed toward him, folding her long damp hair over her hand and fastening it on top of her head with a gold comb. Easing down beside him, Chris rested her hand on Mike's chest and leaned her head on his shoulder. "How was your weekend?" she asked. "Did you identify that young girl?"

Mike hesitated. He hadn't planned on talking police business.

"Yeah," he said finally. "The waitress, Angela Jackson—she gave me her name. Marsha Barts, she told me, but it checked out to be Barth. Found it in the phone book. I went over Sunday morning and spoke with the father—her stepfather, actually. It was her, all right." Chris sat silent and intent as he spoke. "He just said, 'Oh,' and asked the name of the hospital. Then he sent a funeral home for the

body. Buried her this morning. The priest I talked to—Father Trent from Saint John's—he did the mass. She was Catholic." He paused, weariness making his shoulders droop. "You Catholic?" he asked. Chris shook her head. "Know much about it?"

"Sure," Chris replied cautiously. "I used to practice my Latin reading the missal. You can't teach Latin and Spanish without knowing something of the Catholic religion. Why?"

"Ever heard of Saint Maria Goretti?"

"Patroness of the young," Chris answered promptly. "She's a relatively new saint. Canonized in the 1950s."

"What else?"

Chris thought for a second. "Virgin. Martyr. Lived at the turn of the century. A neighbor boy tried to seduce her. She resisted and he stabbed her. She forgave him before she died of her wounds. He went to prison, eventually repented. After he was released he worked for her cause—for beatification."

Mike rested his cheek on her head and looked down to ask, "Worked for what?"

"Beatification—the state before sainthood. The ceremony was held at Saint Peter's in Rome. Her mother attended." Chris leaned forward and stared at him. "Why are you so curious about her?"

"Father Trent told me about her. She was Marsha Barth's favorite," he stated flatly. "They had a lot in common."

Chris nodded slowly.

"How old was this Saint Maria . . . when the guy killed her?"

"Not quite twelve," Chris replied.

"Je-sus," Mike groaned softly. Chris leaned back

against his outstretched arm. They sat side by side
in silence for several minutes. "Angela Jackson
wanted me to thank you for being so nice to her,"
he finally said. "She told me she passed out on you.
That right?"

"Sort of," Chris conceded.

"She tell you anything about that girl?" Mike
tried to sound casual.

"Just that she came into the bar in the afternoons
and that Butch character came in and found her.
She just repeated what she'd told you," Chris
asserted. "She didn't talk a whole lot. I just sat with
her and comforted her. She was too shaken up to
talk much."

"I went to see her Saturday," Mike said. "She was
really helpful and very grateful to you for being
with her. You should have seen her. She looked like
a different person. . . ." He groped for a fitting
description. "Real solid. Not hard, but just solid,
like she knew where she stood." He shrugged in
frustration. "I can't explain."

"I think I understand," Chris said quietly. She
eased him forward so she could massage his tense
shoulder muscles.

"Anyway, she loosened up and talked, about
Marsha and about herself. It seems they had a lot in
common too."

The slow, rhythmic motion of Chris's hands on
his back ceased momentarily. "Really?" Chris
asked. "What did they have in common, Michael?"
The steady massage resumed as she waited for his
explanation.

"Let's talk about something else," he suggested.
"I don't want to get into it." There was no repri-
mand in his tone, only fatigue—deep fatigue.

Chris slid away from him and quietly crossed the

room to a golden candelabrum in the shape of a hand. Mike knitted his brow in curiosity. He couldn't recall having seen this unusual item the other times he'd been in her apartment. Chris struck a match and lighted one slender taper. The pale flame flickered, then burned evenly. "Roll over and I'll work on your muscles," she said, smiling, as she returned to him. Obediently Mike spread out facedown on the long sofa. Chris paused by the light switch. Except for the single candle the room was suddenly dark.

"So tell me about you," she breathed against his shoulder as she bent above him. "How come you're not married, Michael?" He started to turn to face her, but she pressed against him and continued to massage his back.

"I was planning to interrogate you, Miss Martin," he protested.

"Answer my questions first, then I'll answer yours," she said.

"OK," Mike agreed. "But do you mind if I spread out on the floor so you can work on my back without twisting your own?" He eased onto the soft sea-green carpet and stretched out on his stomach with a contented sigh.

"Make yourself at home," Chris said, laughing. Then she crouched above him, methodically resuming the massage. The expert manner in which her strong hands unknotted his tired back, coupled with the darkness and the sweet smell of the candle, made Mike feel he could talk openly and without anxiety.

"I was married," he began. "Married a girl when I was in college."

"And . . . ?" Chris waited.

"And I became a rookie cop—not a college

student," he explained. "Cops work late and have weird hours. We get wrapped up in our jobs. She was a nice girl—wanted to have kids. I wanted to make detective. She didn't think a cop was a good risk as a father. Neither did I," he ended solemnly.

"So what happened?" Chris prompted as she squeezed his tense neck muscles.

"So we got a nice agreeable divorce. She moved back to her hometown, got married, and had some kids. She's happy—she's got what she wants."

"And what about you, Michael?"

"You mean do I feel bad about it? Not really. It's just somethin' I tried and didn't do very well. I'm happy for her. She'll be a good mother."

"And what will you do?"

"My job," he said simply.

"Does your job make you happy?" Chris moved beside him and stretched out on the rug next to him.

"Sometimes I feel real good." He rolled onto his side and propped his head on his arm. "Once in a while, when George and I get all the pieces to fall into place"—he closed a fist enthusiastically—"when we really get a solid case, I feel great. Like I really made a difference."

"That's what you want? To make a difference?" She looked up at his earnest expression.

"That's it," he breathed. "To really make a difference. Sometimes it's hard to feel it, at least in this business. But there are moments. . . ." He grinned at his sudden outburst. "Say, I was going to quiz you." He leaned one arm over her and gently kissed her upturned mouth. "So here goes. Have you ever been married?"

"No." Chris slid her arm over his neck to pull him nearer.

"Got any family?"

"A sister, several aunts and cousins." She kissed him: a long, lingering kiss that made his heartbeat accelerate. He intended to ask about Sylvie, why her last name was also Martin, where they were from originally—and . . . and . . . what about Chris's parents? But the wide green eyes looked up at him in the candlelight. A few strands of pale gold hair slid from the long teeth of the gold comb. The soft lavender shirt fell gracefully over her body.

"Where did you say you kept the life preservers?" Mike breathed hoarsely.

"You won't drown here on the carpet, Michael." Chris sat up and slid the pale lavender shirt over her head. Mike stared at her slender form, the golden tanned throat and the pale breasts below. His gaze shifted apprehensively to the hallway down which Sylvie's room was located.

"She's asleep, Michael," Chris whispered. "She'll stay asleep."

Michael lifted the gold comb from her hair and the pale curtain fell once more. It brushed across his cheeks and settled on his chest, softly closing out the city, the long, weary day—the world.

Once upon the sea there came a great storm. The sea creatures retreated to the deepest waters in search of a tranquil place to wait out the tempest. Along the shore seabirds huddled over their nests, covering their young with widespread wings. For two days a mother pelican sat without moving, her eyes closed against the strong winds, her feathered back resisting the torrent.

Then came the still, silent aftermath of the storm. The yellow white sun beat down upon the land and quickly dried away the moisture. The pelican flew out over the ocean in search of food for her young and herself. But the storm had driven away the small creatures on which the pelican fed. Farther and farther she circled out over the ocean amid flocks of other birds equally desperate for food. A few found some sustenance, consumed it ravenously, then, still hungry, searched on for more. The mother pelican was not so fortunate.

She returned to the nest without nourishment for her young. Panting and dying, they lay listlessly in the nest.

"We are lost," wept the other birds. "We will

surely see our young ones die before our eyes."

"There is nothing we can do," they lamented. They sat forlornly on their nests while the sun beat down upon their backs.

In desperation the mother pelican pierced her breast with her beak. She ripped open the flesh and let her blood trickle into the open mouths of her young.

"But you will die," protested the other birds when they witnessed this act. "You are so selfless," they cried in shame, for they knew their own offspring were dying and they would not sacrifice themselves as the pelican had.

The mother pelican looked from one hollow-eyed creature to the next. "Foolish wretches," she said, laughing. "I am most selfish of all. I refuse to accept the terms the fates have given me. This dying will be by my own choice. My young ones cannot yet make such a decision for themselves . . . so I do what I choose willingly. I have the pleasure of determining my own fate. They only have the means of surviving. The exchange, my friends, is not an equal one."

"What shall we tell them of your sacrifice?" asked one bird.

"Tell them nothing of sacrifice," gasped the dying pelican. "Tell them only that their mother refused to submit to despair."

CHAPTER 5

❖❖❖❖❖❖

I set her on my pacing steed
   and nothing else saw all day long
For sidelong would she bend,
   and sing a faery's song.

              —Keats

George Parsons straightened his tie as Mike rang the doorbell. The small woman who opened the door looked apprehensively at the two tall men on her doorstep. Her red-rimmed eyes narrowed suspiciously.

"I'm Sergeant Fuller, ma'am." Mike held his identification out to reassure her. "I spoke to your husband on Sunday, about your daughter Marsha." The woman's eyes shifted from the metal badge to Mike's face, then over his shoulder to the tall black man with him. "My partner, Detective Parsons, ma'am," Mike stated. "We would like to talk with you for a few minutes." Her dull eyes returned to the badge.

"Come in." The sound was little more than a whisper. The woman turned and walked along the narrow hallway. Fuller and Parsons looked at each other, then followed her.

"Mrs. Barth," Mike began once they were all seated in the dim living room, "when your daughter left home several months ago, did you make any attempt to locate her?" The woman shook her head. "Your husband said Marsha was sixteen." The

woman nodded. "You didn't report her absence to the police. Did you have any idea where she had gone?" She shrugged.

Parsons leaned forward and took over. "Mrs. Barth, did you know any of Marsha's friends? Anyone who may have kept in touch with her?" Again silence and a slow shaking of her head. "When she was in school, did she have any particular girl friend—or boyfriend? Anybody she mentioned?" The woman's gaze shifted toward the hallway door and the sound of footsteps coming from farther back in the house.

"What's goin' on?" the thickset man demanded as he stepped into the room. In a sleeveless undershirt, soiled jeans, and wrinkled socks he stood bleary-eyed, trying to focus on the two seated men.

"We're from the police," Parsons began as they rose.

"Oh, it's you." Jack Barth finally recognized Fuller. "Waddaya want this time?" He crossed to the big armchair and settled in it. "I told ya I'd take care of it—so I did. She's buried and done with."

"Yes, sir," Mike proceeded smoothly. "We're sorry to have to disturb you at a time like this, but we hoped you and Mrs. Barth could give us some information that might help us track down the man involved in your daughter's death. We just asked your wife if she knew the names of any of Marsha's friends, anyone from school who may have kept in touch."

"We don't know anything," Barth replied without hesitating to consider the question.

"Do you have any relatives or friends in the city who may have been in contact with Marsha?" Parsons tried again. "Perhaps a priest or a doctor?"

"Nobody," Barth insisted.

"Is there anything that occurred before she left home, anything she mentioned, that could give us a clue to her friends or places she frequented?" Parsons's low voice rolled across the room.

Mrs. Barth looked up as if she was about to say something. Jack Barth shot her a cold glance. "Mommy and me don't know nothin' about the little bitch," he said, speaking each word distinctly. Mrs. Barth dropped her gaze and crossed herself. "She was a troublemaker—hung around here tellin' lies and making trouble. When she took off it was good riddance." His calm, even voice was chilling. "I did what I said." He stood to dismiss the men. "We don't know nothin' and we want to be done with it."

Parsons and Fuller never moved. Mike stared across the room at Mrs. Barth. "Ma'am, do you know why Saint Maria Goretti would have a special significance for your daughter?" He ignored the impatient shifting of feet by Jack Barth. The woman slowly raised her pale face. Wide, tear-filled eyes moved from Jack Barth to the two detectives. "Was she a troubled child?" his soft voice prodded her.

"You guys better leave. You're upsetting my wife. Don't you cry, Mommy," Barth ordered her. His harsh tone seemed blatantly ill suited to the endearment *Mommy*. "You go take a nap," he barked like a drill sergeant. Obediently the thin woman withdrew from the room. "We had enough." Barth headed into the hallway and jerked open the door. "You don't have no right to put her through that," he declared. "The little bitch is gone. Leave it at that."

Fuller slid his note pad into his pocket and nodded for George Parsons to follow. "We appreciate your help," Mike said calmly as he stepped past

the man. Jack Barth stood staring after them as the
two detectives slid into their car and moved out
into the sparse traffic.

"We'll try her again when that surly bastard isn't
around," Mike suggested. "I think she knows
something—which is more than we've got now."
They drove in silence to police headquarters.

"You gotta testify at two," the desk sergeant
greeted Fuller. "You too, Parsons. At the court-
house." The two detectives nodded. Both headed
for their desks for the manila envelopes pertaining
to the cases coming before the grand jury.

"Simmons, Willie Joe: age 23. Charge: second-
degree murder. Four witnesses to a barroom fight in
which the accused stabbed LeRoy Clemmons, de-
ceased." Fuller skimmed the details. This was an
easy one. Clemmons died and Simmons was so
badly cut he was hauled off to the emergency room,
then on to jail.

"Someone wants to talk to you about the sketch
from the newspaper," the desk sergeant called,
interrupting Fuller's studious silence. He jerked his
head toward a slim fellow in fatigues.

"Send him over." Mike pushed aside the Simmons file and reached for his note pad. The artist's
sketch of Butch had been run a second time in the
Savannah *Post*. The young airman by the front desk
had a folded newspaper under his arm. He lifted it
out and unfolded it anxiously as he approached
Fuller's desk.

"I think this may be a guy who works with me at
Hunter," the man began. "I just hope I'm right," he
added anxiously. "He didn't show for work today. I
guess it's 'cause his picture is out."
Fuller kept nodding and gesturing for the fellow

to take a seat. Finally the young man noticed the extended hand; he promptly fell silent and sat down in the straight-backed wooden chair.

"What do you do at Hunter?" Mike asked, trying to relax the man.

"I'm a mechanic." He began supplying details. Mike fastidiously noted each detail. Halfway through he glanced over at George Parsons. Silently Parsons nodded and strolled to Fuller's desk, perching casually on a corner, listening intently to the account.

"This guy once told me he ran girls—said he had a bunch of 'em. Real young stuff, he called 'em. Tried to get me interested." The fellow shrugged. "I was interested all right, but I like 'em legal. No jailbait for me, if you know what I mean." He looked uncertainly from Fuller to the tall black man. Both detectives nodded calmly. "Well," the airman went on, "I just figured it had to be him. Looks like him in the drawing. Stabbin' a young kid—seemed to fit." He shrugged again.

Five minutes later Parsons and Fuller were heading down Bull Street toward Hunter Air Force Base with the name, rank, and serial number of Bertram Willis, also known as Butch. The sad wide eyes of "Mommy" Barth haunted Fuller. The words of Jack Barth echoed in his brain: "The little bitch is gone. Leave it at that." Slowly he shook his head, trying to loosen the image of the Barth woman from his mind. She had scuttled off like a cockroach when Barth ordered her to leave.

"She's buried and done with," Barth had said of his daughter.

"Not by a long shot," Fuller sighed as the entrance to Hunter loomed ahead.

* * *

"Looks like you're having a pretty good week." Chris stood in the open doorway smiling at him. Fuller nodded absentmindedly as he looked at her.

"Almost a week," she corrected herself, since it was only Thursday. "You still plan to go with us for the weekend?"

Again he nodded.

"You want to come in or shall we go?" She stepped back and waited. Chris had twisted her blond hair into a spiral, secured with an oval barrette of mother-of-pearl that gleamed in the light. Her pale ivory knit shirt was slit low at the front and a long slender chain held a golden seashell in the tanned hollow between her breasts. With difficulty Mike lifted his eyes from her neckline to her cool green eyes.

"I was . . . admiring—" he stammered.

"My shirt? My necklace? My muscles?" she chided him.

"All of the above," Mike conceded. "You look great," he concluded with a broad grin.

"Then we'd better go now." Chris grabbed a light jacket from the back of the chair. "The boat leaves in twenty minutes and—"

"—and no quickies."

"—and I don't want to miss the cruise." Chris arched her brows in exaggerated disapproval.

"Oops." Mike chuckled. "Pardon me while I take my foot out of my oversized mouth."

"Sylvie!" Chris called toward the hallway. A few seconds later the robed form of the youngster flashed across the room. "We're leaving," Chris explained. "We'll be back in a couple of hours. You be ready for bed. Call the neighbors if you need anything. And don't stay on the phone for the whole

time." Sylvie responded to each comment with a polite nod.

"She'll be all right alone?" Mike asked as they entered the small elevator.

"I left her dinner. The neighbors will check on her. The door is locked. No one can go skulking about the building without attracting attention. Besides, she's a smart kid. She wouldn't let anyone in—and this gives her a chance to feel a little independent." Her calm, rational assessment reassured the detective. "We'll be back a little after dark," she added a bit uncertainly.

"I gather you're a bit nervous about it." He slid his arm around her shoulders.

"When she's too old for a baby-sitter and still too young to be on her own, it makes one slightly uneasy," Chris acknowledged.

"You're sure you want to go?" he questioned her.

"It's taken us two weeks to agree on a time and a night and to get tickets. We're going," she said, grinning. Arm in arm they crossed the grassy park, winding among the sightseers, moving toward the waterfront. The low white tour boat, the *Waving Girl*, was already loading passengers for the twilight cocktail cruise. They headed to the upper deck and settled into seats by the railing. Already a gentle evening breeze swept over the river, sending ornate patterns of ripples across the surface of the water.

Mike eased his chair closer to Chris so his arm could rest along the back of her shoulders. In companionable silence they sat gazing out over the river while other passengers strolled the deck. A low squat tugboat with black tires cushioning its blunt front chugged by on the far side of the wide river, laboriously guiding a massive Algerian tanker

upriver toward Elba Island. On the near side a second ship, low and gray with a rust line showing above the water, moved toward the ocean. Ahead the *Barba Negra* bobbed at its moorings.

"Blackbeard," Chris whispered in his ear.

Mike looked at her curiously.

"*Barba Negra.*" She pointed at the old ship. "It means 'Blackbeard'—after the famous pirate. He actually sailed these waters. I guess you knew that," she apologized.

"Hmm, I never really thought about it," Mike answered quietly. "I guess I miss a lot." His dark eyes looked back toward the tanker gliding by. "I always seem to get wrapped up in another case before I finish up the one I'm on. I stay pretty involved with my work. It just keeps on coming."

Chris leaned against him, threading her fingers into his. "How about some cool white wine?" she suggested. "And you can tell me about your latest cases while we cruise along. Then I'll take you home and feed you."

"And then . . .?" He brushed his lips against her ear.

"And then you can rest up for the weekend. We're taking two girls with us."

"Two?" he asked, surprised.

"Sylvie invited Lauri Taggert, so that means *two* girls with whom you can throw Frisbees, fish, swim, steam crabs, and cook marshmallows. Michael, my friend, you'll need your rest."

"I thought this was to be *our* weekend together." He sounded mildly distressed.

Chris turned her deep green eyes up to meet his. "That's also why you'll need your rest now." She pressed a soft kiss against his lips. "You just sit

here." She leaned back and smiled. "I'll get the wine."

Mike watched the graceful sway of her body as she strode toward the bar. The low rumble of the boat motor made the *Waving Girl* shudder as she prepared to move out into the river traffic.

"The *Waving Girl* is named in honor of Florence Martus, Savannah's fabled Waving Girl whose statue stands at the east end of River Street," the pleasant voice of the tour guide intoned through speakers at the rear of the boat. "In the late 1800s, when her fiancé went to sea, Florence Martus vowed to wave a greeting to every ship passing her home at the lighthouse on the riverbank. For more than forty years the faithful woman waved a scarf by day and a lantern by night at each passing ship. Every seaman from every port knew the story and waited to catch a glimpse of her. After forty years Florence died. Her beloved had died much earlier —lost at sea."

Mike's eyes lingered on the lovely oval face above the proffered wineglass. The voice of the tour guide faded into the steady hum of the motor and the soft rush of evening air. Mike felt only the warmth of Chris's body as she leaned against his shoulder, sipping her wine and looking out over the harbor. When he looked down and felt the deep green eyes meet his, he lost all interest in the passing sights. "Lost at sea. . . ." the microphone echoed as the cool greenness enveloped him.

"Chris, you'll have to go without me. Something's come up," Mike's low voice announced through the telephone. "I just can't leave town right now."

"Something good or something not so good?"
Chris asked.

"The kid we've been looking for—the one who
shot the woman in the spine, the shopping center
murder—well, he's shown up on the east side.
Parsons got a tip. So we're taking some guys in
plain clothes out there. We're hoping to grab him. A
couple of likely places are being staked out."

"So go," Chris insisted. "I understand. Just be
careful, Michael. Please don't get hurt."

"Yeah," he answered quietly.

"If you get him—and finish the paperwork—
maybe you could come out by yourself. Tomorrow,
or even Sunday, just to get away for a little while,"
she suggested.

"I don't know, Chris," he groaned. "I may be
sitting in the corner of some joint the whole damn
weekend."

"Well, let's just leave it this way. If you finish,
come on out. Here's how to get there. Take
Seventeen-A to Hilton Head. . . ." She dictated the
directions to him. "I mean *whenever* you're
through. Even if it's two past midnight, Michael.
You *need* to get away, my love," her soft voice
asserted.

"Sure," Mike responded. "I'll see you, Chris—as
soon as I can."

The red orange sun crouched low behind the
distant pine fringe in the west as Mike left Savannah heading north. By the time he reached the
Hilton Head causeway, the last glow was leaving the
sky.

He'd spent most of Friday night waiting for the
kid to show. At 4:00 A.M. the guy had ambled into
the all-night pool hall. George Parsons had been

shooting a four ball into the right side pocket. Before the ball dropped, Parsons had pinned the wiry kid against the wall with the cue stick and held him there while Mike lifted the .22 pistol from the boy's belt and read him his rights.

After three hours of interrogation and processing, Fuller and Parsons had had what they needed.

Wearily Mike had gone back to his apartment, gulped down a cold beer, and collapsed across his bed. When he'd finally woken, he'd lain staring at the bedside clock for several seconds, focusing his eyes on the slim golden hands. Then he'd flung his feet to the floor and shifted into high speed, carefully shaving, shampooing his thick hair and blowing it dry, then yanking on his faded cutoff jeans and a loose red knit shirt.

Staring in the mirror, he'd sucked in his stomach and studied his image. "Hilton Head ain't for beach bums," he'd grunted in dissatisfaction, then switched the cutoffs for khaki chino slacks rolled at the cuff. "Better," he'd decided. Fastidiously he'd tucked his bathing trunks, a change of clothes, and his sandals in a small satchel with his toilet articles and headed for the car.

Mike drove past the hedge-lined driveway twice before he finally decided it must be the right place. He'd expected a nice enough house . . . but something beachy. The two-story Spanish-style stucco building at the end of the winding driveway looked more like a resort hotel; it had curving archways, covered walkways, and iron grillwork balconies. Clumps of white azaleas and thick green shrubbery rimmed the circular front drive. With a sigh of relief Mike spotted Chris's silver MG parked beside the house. After an apprehensive glance down at his scuffed tennis shoes protruding beneath the cuffs of

his slacks, he grabbed his satchel and strode up the front steps of the hacienda.

"You must be Michael." The greenish-gray eyes looked up at him. "Please come right in." The slender woman with almost white hair hastily took his satchel and set it aside, then linked her arm under his. "I'm Elena," she told him, "Christina's aunt. I am so pleased you were able to get away and join us. We've heard so much about you." She spoke cheerfully, without pausing, as she guided him from the marble-floored foyer through a long hallway toward the rear of the house.

"Michael!" The high-pitched squeal made him jump as Sylvie lunged across the room to greet him. Behind her, sandy-haired Lauri Taggert looked up and smiled shyly.

"Hi, short stuff," Mike said, hugging Sylvie. "Hi, Lauri." He nodded to the other youngster, who sat cross-legged on the floor with an unfinished game of Chinese checkers, waiting for Sylvie's return.

"Hello, Mr. Fuller," Lauri politely replied.

"Have you had your dinner?" the white-haired Elena asked, reclaiming him. Mike suddenly realized he'd forgotten to eat.

"Come in the kitchen and we'll see what we have. Christina is out on the beach somewhere. She'll be back"—the gray-green eyes sparkled—"well, whenever she chooses." Her soft laughter eased his awkwardness. Mike followed the slender woman through the doorway. Two pairs of deep green eyes turned to appraise him. Mike stopped in mid-step, stunned by the twosome. Both blond, like Chris. One perhaps eighteen; the other, vaguely familiar, closer to thirty, maybe thirty-five.

"Alicia, Katherine, this is—"

"Michael," they chimed as broad smiles greeted

him. Fuller felt his color deepen as he returned the smiles.

"Nice to meet you," the older of the two said. "I missed you once before—at the hospital." She waved him toward a high stool across the counter from her. "Chris said you had coffee together, after I left."

Mike vaguely remembered that Chris had been talking with a white-clad nurse before he'd even spoken to her. "Savannah General," he said, nodding.

"Intensive care," Katie added as Mike's eyes brightened with the recollection.

Mike nodded again. "We picked up the guy this morning," he noted.

Katie understood. "Good," she said quietly.

"How about a beer?" Alicia, the younger one, was holding out an ice-cold, dark brown bottle.

"He needs food." Elena's soft hand rested on Mike's shoulder. "We do have plenty of soup left."

"I'll get it." Alicia sprang from the stool. Within a minute she slid a large bowl before him: steaming bouillabaisse, thick with lumps of crabmeat, pink shrimp, onions, and herbs. Elena moved around the kitchen, efficiently supplying hot rolls, a spoon, a napkin, and a frosted mug from the freezer for the dark beer.

"Christina said you have been working hard and you need a change of pace." Elena sat on the tall stool next to Mike. "So we are not going to discuss business," she declared. Across the table Katie and Alicia nodded sympathetically, watching him with obvious interest as he ate.

"This is incredible," Mike said. "Who's the cook?"

"Me." Both pairs of green eyes across the table

flashed mischievously as Katie and Alicia answered together.

"It's a group project," the elegant woman explained from beside him. "The girls each add something. The more times someone passes through the kitchen, the better the brew becomes."

"It's sort of fend-for-yourself here." Katie laughed. "We don't do anything at any certain time—so if you're hungry, you feed yourself. If you're tired, go to bed. If you feel like swimming, you go. That's where Chris is," she noted.

"In the dark?" Mike's eyes shifted from the golden glow in the kitchen to the slate sky outside.

"You have to try it before you knock it," Alicia insisted. "Nothing like a cool plunge in the ocean with only the stars and the surf to keep you company."

"I'd be more concerned about the sharks and jellyfish," Mike replied.

"No problem," Alicia pronounced with a grin. "Just ask them for a little privacy. They're very cooperative."

"I'll try it," Mike promised. "I'll tell them you said it would work." He spooned up the last lump of crabmeat and sighed with contentment.

"You can take your beer and go down to the beach if you want," Elena suggested. "Christina is out there somewhere. Just shout." She patted his arm. "We won't feel rejected if you leave us."

"You're sure?" Mike asked, hesitating.

"Go," Alicia and Katie chorused. "Chris will be relieved to see you," Katie added.

"I'm going." Mike grabbed the cool mug on his way out the door. "Thank you for the soup, the beer, and the company." He backed across the room.

"Go!" the women repeated, laughing.

"Try the pier—off to the right," Katie called after him.

After the back door slammed closed, the three females looked at one another in silence, then sat around the table.

"What do you think?" Elena's soft voice broke the silence that filled the room.

Katie took a deep breath. "He's very nice," she said thoughtfully.

Elena nodded. "He looks big and tough, but he is very gentle. There's a softness in the way he looks at Sylvie—the way he hugged her."

"He is a policeman," Alicia cautioned them. "I don't like that part." The other two pale-haired women nodded. Slowly the three extended their hands until their fingertips barely touched in the center of the table, forming an intricate lacework of fingers. For the next several minutes their communication was wordless . . . ancient.

Finally their hands pulled apart and they opened their eyes.

"But Chris will be the one to decide," Elena noted quietly. "We will give her time. Plenty of time. I can see in her eyes that she loves the man Fuller. Let her discover that for herself."

Mike followed the weathered wooden walkway down toward the beach. Clumps of sea grass and rolling mounds of pale sand formed a buffer zone between the low flat beach and the higher, smoother green grass surrounding the house. Mug in hand, Mike sat on the far end of the walkway staring out along the beach. As his eyes became accustomed to the darkness, he could see the foamy ruffle of white where the waves collapsed near shore. Gradually

the pale moonlight outlined the chocolate-colored pier jutting out over the dark sleek surface of the ocean. A twenty-foot sailboat and a small skiff secured to the private pier bobbed side by side in companionable harmony on the rippling water.

At last Mike saw a figure striding out toward the end of the pier. Her long hair, almost white in the moonlight, hung below her shoulders. Mike narrowed his eyes and peered at the figure, unable to determine whether the body beneath the hair was clothed. Silhouetted against the water, Chris poised at the end of the pier, then dove silently under the inky surface. Mike stood, looking out beyond the dark pier, watching for the water to break when she surfaced. Slowly he crossed the beach, keeping his eyes fixed where she had dived.

The only sound was the slow, even rush of the waves, one after the other, rolling over near the shore.

Apprehensively Mike quickened his step, loping along the beach to the near end of the wooden pier. He plopped the glass mug into the sand, kicked off his shoes, and thudded down the pier toward the spot where Chris had stood.

"Chris!" he yelled over the water. "Chris!" he screamed into the soft ocean breeze as his heart thundered in terror. "Where are you? Chris, where are you?"

Pacing from side to side on the wooden structure, he scanned the water, stripping off his shirt, socks, and watch and dropping his keys and wallet on top of them.

"Chris!"

The scream went unanswered.

In helpless frustration he stood staring down into the water while the seconds turned into long min-

utes. "Jesus Christ," he groaned at the unbroken surface that shimmered before him. "Chris. . . ."

"Michael?" The familiar voice came from way behind him. Fuller jerked around, his dark eyes searching the vacant pier. "Michael?" The voice came from the water, near the shore.

Racing back past the moored boats toward the beach, Mike saw the sleek hair and pale shoulders just above the breaking waves. Vaulting off the side of the pier, he landed thigh deep in the water, then lunged toward her.

"Chris!" He collapsed into the water beside her, enclosing her in his arms. "I thought you'd drowned," he gasped, covering her face with kisses. She laughed and fell on top of him as they tumbled into the foam. "You scared the hell out of me," he grumbled, half-angry, half-relieved. "I didn't see you surface." Then he froze, realizing that the lady in his arms was completely naked.

"I have a towel on the beach," Chris said. She lay submerged up to her neck as the waves rippled over her shoulders. "You want to get it for me?" she asked.

"Yeah, sure." Mike lurched in the direction Chris had pointed. He grabbed the huge towel atop the blanket and waded back into the water, holding it outstretched so she could stand and let him wrap it around her.

"You sure scared me." He hugged her shoulders as they strode onto the beach. "I yelled but got no answer."

"I didn't hear you call," Chris apologized. "But I'm glad you're here, Michael." She reached down to the blanket and lifted a soft sweat shirt. She tugged it over her head, pulling the towel out from under it. Only her bare legs showed below the long

shirt. "Here," she said softly. "You wrap up, Michael. You're shivering."

Gratefully Mike flung the big towel around his bare shoulders. "All my stuff is out on the end of the pier," he explained. "I thought you'd got a cramp or hit your head or something. I was goin' in after you. Where in the hell did you go? You musta been under for five minutes."

Chris ducked under the towel and snuggled close against his bare chest. "It's hard to see at night." She slid her hands up his back. "You must have missed me. You don't think I could stay under for five minutes, do you?" she chided him. "I'm sorry you were worried." She pressed a gentle kiss against his throat. "Come on, sit down on the blanket and let's warm each other." She wriggled close to him inside the giant towel so they could sit side by side.

After almost a minute of silence Chris spoke again. "I gather you met my aunt and my cousins."

Mike and Chris were lying back on the blanket, gazing up at the stars. "Katie and Alicia are Elena's daughters?" Mike asked as he realized the connection. "Who does Sylvie belong to?"

"To all of us," she replied. "We had to take over shortly after Sylvie was born. Her mother—my sister—has to work. Her job requires a lot of travel. We all became Sylvie's guardians."

"And her father?"

"He died. Sylvie never knew him," Chris answered solemnly. "So we share her. Mostly she's with me."

"She looks like you." Mike rolled up on one arm to gaze down on her serene face. "You *all* have a striking family resemblance," he noted in a low voice. "What happened to the men in all these relationships? The poor devils must have had very

weak genes," he joked. "No dark-haired, brown-eyed cousins or sisters lurking in the family background? No brothers with—" He suddenly pulled upright. "Say, what about the males? Aren't there any uncles or fathers or brothers?"

Chris looked up, her green eyes luminous, beautiful, in the moonlight. A slight smile played about her full mouth. "It just worked out this way," she replied, her voice much more solemn than her pleasant expression. "We do pretty well without them." There was no defensiveness in her voice. "We do like men." She walked her fingers up his bare chest.

Mike cleared his throat. "It just makes me a little uncomfortable now that I think about it," he confessed. "All those females. It's just a bit peculiar."

"Michael, we're not peculiar—if you're thinking about lesbianism or anything kinky. Of course, I love females. I'm one of them. I have a special sympathy for them—but I don't make love with them, Michael. I'm very selective." She pulled him down to her. "And I choose to make love with you, if you choose me." Michael slid his hand from the soft warm sweat shirt to the cool smooth flesh beneath it. "Warm me, Michael," she whispered against his lips.

The pale moon retreated behind a misty mask of clouds. The dark night sky glimmered with only a few distinct stars.

"Out here?" Mike glanced up the abandoned beach, then reached for the front snap on his tight wet slacks. Chris slid the thick sweat shirt up over her hips and shook her head so the long damp hair fell over her shoulders.

"Would you prefer to go inside?" She knelt

beside him. "No one will disturb us here," she
assured him. A cool breeze from the ocean sent a
soft ripple through her hair. Her wide green eyes
gleamed like dark emeralds against her skin. Michael yanked the wet slacks off and wadded them
and his shorts into a lump. He slipped beneath the
slightly damp towel and their cool flesh touched.
"Warm me, Michael." She slid her fingers over his
neck and up into his thick damp hair. She opened
her lips and nibbled his ear, her breath warm
against his neck.

"Chris," he sighed. "Christina. . . ." The sound
floated from his lips like a prayer. "Christina," he
repeated as the slow, steady rhythm of the waves
echoed the languid motion of their bodies. Their
words were lost in the whisper of the pale sea grass,
swaying in the gentle ocean breeze.

Stately, white-haired Elena struck the match,
then slowly moved the flame from taper to taper.
Two candles burned evenly.

"Our guests are asleep," she noted. Then she
turned to the green-eyed, blond-tressed females
seated within the circle of seashells. Each mature
female was naked except for a slender gold chain
about her neck from which a spiral-shaped seashell
was suspended. The youngest one wore instead a
tiny milk-white coral fan—five-pronged—in the
form of an open hand, for she was still among the
protected.

"Tell us of your young friend." Elena directed the
question to the youngest one.

Sylvie clasped her hands on her lap as she
replied. "I fear she is in great danger," she began.
"Lauri's father has coerced her into frontal contact.
He did not attempt penetration; however, she is

terribly upset. I can feel the tension in her body from across the room. If I touch her, I can hear an inner wail, a desperate lament from deep within her."

Chris reached out a hand, resting it in comfort on Sylvie's shoulder. Elena's green eyes shifted to Chris.

"You felt it too?" Sylvie asked. Chris nodded.

"What do you recommend?" Elena turned to the others.

"Eliminate him before he harms her further," Katie said.

"Try to break the pattern—a dream of warning—" Alicia suggested, voicing another possibility.

"And you, Christina, what do you recommend?" Elena asked.

Chris's eyes slowly swept around the circle to Elena. "It has only been three weeks since the last one," she replied. "I have to decide about my other responsibilities. I care very much for this human, Michael Fuller, but I also have great apprehension about leaving the Taggert child unprotected. I cannot recommend anything," she said wearily. "I will simply do as you say." She lowered her head in silence.

"And you, Sylvie?" Elena's deep rich voice rippled across the circle. "What do you suggest?"

"I want to take my place among you," Sylvie asserted. "I wish to be more than a mediator. I wish to share the task of protecting. If one of us is to eliminate Ralph Taggert, I want to be the one." Her cold green eyes stared evenly at the eldest among them.

"So you must want him eliminated," Elena noted.

"I want Lauri to be safe," Sylvie replied. "I do not presume to dictate the method. But—if it is to be done . . ."

"You want to do it," Elena acknowledged evenly. "Christina." The elegant woman eyed the bowed head intently. "Is Sylvie ready?"

"I have taught her carefully," Chris replied. "To them she is a child. They have no idea of her true age. To me she is almost an equal. Like the humans she is maturing much earlier than our previous generations. Already she must concentrate to pass among them without revealing her abilities. I believe she is ready to advance."

Elena solemnly regarded the oval face of the youngest member. "In human years you are only eleven," she said softly. "You have served well as our contact with the young girls whose situations were not advanced. Once you have used your full powers you will have to move on to the next center."

"Will I be with my mother?" Sylvie asked hopefully.

"There is an excellent chance that that is precisely where you will go." Elena smiled. "Your mother would enjoy your companionship—as well as your assistance."

"Then may I be Lauri's protector?" Sylvie asked.

"We will help you through the transition," Elena agreed. "You will begin tonight." Elena stood and crossed the room, moving aside several seashells so she could leave the confines of the circle. She returned with a rectangular lacquered box, the top of which was inset with iridescent white and gray mother-of-pearl. Kneeling before the girl, Elena opened the box, placing its contents on the pale green carpet.

"You must surrender the coral as you assume your station in the sisterhood," she announced.

Obediently Sylvie undid the clasp of the gold chain and placed the coral amulet on Elena's outstretched palm. Elena put it aside, then threaded the replacement—the spiral seashell—onto the chain and secured it around Sylvie's neck. She intoned, "As the shell curves outward, each spiral building on the one before, so shall you prosper and serve. Your gifts arise from those who preceded you; they will be passed on to those who follow."

Next she passed Sylvie an ancient gold comb, long-toothed and crescent-shaped. "This belonged to your mother—and her mother before her—and so on through the ages."

She held out her hands to receive the gift. "It will restore you when your strength ebbs," Elena explained. "And this ring of pearl represents your link with the sea, the tides, and the moon." Elena slid the finely wrought gold ring on Sylvie's finger. "Now, these you may also have—but you must not use them until we all agree you are ready." She placed a large amethyst-throated seashell and a serpent-shaped golden bracelet back into the rectangular case. "First you will warn the father of your young friend—warn him with the dream of the green serpent. This man's actions are heinous, but we may be able to spare him—and save his child. We are compelled to try."

"I will try, Elena," Sylvie promised solemnly as she accepted the closed lacquered case from the older woman.

Elena moved backward, taking her place again within the circle, sitting between Sylvie, the youngest, and Katie, the eldest except for herself.

"Generation to generation, we are linked," Elena

proclaimed as they all clasped hands. "To protect the children, to ease the grief, to reproduce and nurture our kind—until our souls return to the vast ocean from which we arose."

The five pale-haired female creatures swayed in the moonlight, chanting an ancient, wordless melody of seas and tides, of birth and death, of unending cycles within cycles—a sea song from a time before human memory.

The slow, steady pounding of the ocean waves against the shore echoed their melancholy song.

From deep in the Caucasus a tribe of female warriors migrated to the banks of the Thermodon to found a state ruled by a queen. From there they extended their colonization to the islands of Lesbos and Samothrace. Beautiful to behold, these tall fair-haired females were transformed in battle into ferocious, cunning warriors who screamed like demons from the underworld. They bared their bosoms, both to free themselves from encumbrances and to terrify their foes with the disfigurement on their right torsos. Some said that before the onset of her menses, each of these females was seared across the right breast with a red-hot sword blade, thus preventing that breast from developing. The awesome network of scar tissue would remain as mute testament to their courage and endurance. The prowess of these females with bow, ax, and spear is attributed to the added strength in the arm and shoulder of the right side that did not need to support a breast. Others said that this disfigurement appeared only in the frenzy of battle, when the flesh of the right torso seemed to melt away, revealing a warrior's chest bones and the thundering heart within.

These females took no husbands, a characteristic echoed later in the tales of Amazons and Sirens who traced their source back to this warrior band. Instead each chose a strong and courageous male for a mate and lay with him until a child was conceived. Then the male was exiled or executed, for no man possessed authority over the warriors or their young. Only female children remained within the warrior sisterhood, and the women cared with equal tenderness for the offspring of their kind.

Serena, a beautiful warrior maiden, aroused the passion of one particular suitor who did not accept the customs of her tribe. One night he stole her away and carried her across the sea to his homeland to be his bride.

Vowing to rescue Serena, the warrior women followed in their ship. On the rocky shores of the distant land a great battle ensued.

Outnumbered and on unfamiliar terrain, the women were ultimately defeated and driven back to their ship. In despair, Serena, who had witnessed the battle from a citadel high above the sea, threw herself from the walls into the surging waters. Unwilling to abandon their kinswoman even in death, the warriors sent two from among them to swim beneath the sea and recover her body. They bore the dead Serena to the waiting ship, then set sail across the dark waters.

The story spread of the defeat of the warrior women. No longer known as such formidable adversaries, the sisters in the nation of women sought sanctuary in other lands. They separated into small bands, some moving inland to secluded valleys and hillsides. Others ventured westward, following the sun into uncharted waters.

CHAPTER 6

❖❖❖❖❖❖

His soul shall taste the sadness of her might,
And be among her cloudy trophies hung.
—KEATS

"We got an indictment," Mike said into the telephone mouthpiece while he shoved a stack of papers back into their manila folder. "First-degree murder for the shopping center shooting."

"Good," Chris replied. "What happens now?"

"Trial is set for six weeks from now—late in June. There's no bail, so the guy will just sit while his lawyer does his thing."

"Well, at least you and your partner did your share. Was it Detective Parsons's case or yours?"

"George had this one," Mike answered. "He sure looks good on it," he added with a chuckle. He leaned back and stretched his legs out to the side of his desk. Except for two other men the squad room was abandoned. "I really miss seeing you," he said, lowering his voice abruptly. "This evening shift stinks and I'm only on the first week. Why don't you stay home next weekend and we'll see each other?"

"OK." Her rapid reply made him smile.

"You think you'll be coming back early this Sunday?" he asked hopefully. "We could have dinner or go for a walk or something."

"Sylvie and I have a few things to do here at the

beach," Chris replied in her matter-of-fact tone. "We won't be coming back to Savannah till Sunday night—then Sylvie goes straight to bed to get rested up for school. You want to share a late dinner?"

"What time?" Mike responded instantly.

"How about nine, nine thirty, Michael?" Her soft voice said his name with a special warmth.

"What about school? I mean, you have to teach Monday. I don't want to impose on a school night," he blurted out.

"Michael," she said, cutting him off, "that was this past week." She laughed. "I was tired and had some extra work to do. This weekend I'm getting a lot of rest. Elena and Sylvie and I had the house to ourselves. I've been going to bed when Sylvie does, so I'll be able to stay awake. Just come over about nine. Sylvie will be sound asleep and you and I can listen to some music together. If you want, bring a change of clothes. You can sleep over. It will save you a trip."

"Fine," Mike finally breathed. "I sure miss you," he concluded lamely.

"I miss you too, Michael. See you Sunday." She paused, waiting for him to say something.

"Yeah—well, good-bye, Chris," he said reluctantly.

"Bye, Michael," she whispered. Then the phone clicked and there was silence.

Fuller slowly put the receiver back on the cradle and stared out the window at the dull black sky. It was nearly starless, like the night a week before when he and Chris had lain on the beach holding each other as the pounding surf had nearly lulled him to sleep. Chris had tugged him to his feet and wrapped the damp towel about him sarong-style, then led him back to the hacienda. Mike remembered following her up a stairway to the guest

bedroom, where someone had hung his clothes and placed his satchel on the footlocker by the end of the bed. He remembered sliding naked and alone between the cool sheets. The next thing he'd been conscious of was the steamy scent of hot coffee from a mug on the bedside table when he awoke the next morning. His watch, keys, and wallet—reclaimed by someone from the pier where he'd put them—had been placed neatly beside the mug. He had slept soundly for only five hours, without dreams, and had awakened more rested than after nights when he'd slept eight hours or even more.

Sighing, Fuller shifted his attention from the bleak sky to the paperwork strewn across his desk. "Barth, Marsha," the file to his left read. He picked up the top page and stared at the photo beneath it. "Willis, Bertram" was the label on the picture. This was the military file photo that Angela Jackson had picked out as Butch, the same man who'd stepped into the back hall of Sunny Jim's Bar with Marsha Barth. Ten minutes later Marsha had stumbled back through the swinging doors and bled to death on the dirty wooden floor. The picture of Willis had been in the newspaper that week, along with the earlier police sketch and a description: age early to mid-twenties, height five-nine, weight 150 to 165, sandy hair, mustache.

The article was headlined, BARROOM SUSPECT IDENTIFIED BY POLICE, and ended with Fuller's desk phone number and a request for any information on the case. Bertram Willis had not reported to work at Hunter Air Base since the photo had first appeared eight days earlier. He had stripped his quarters of all personal belongings and had simply disappeared.

Fuller sat staring at the photo for several moments. The flashing red button on his desk phone

finally drew his attention away from the slick black-and-white image.

"You better come down here, Sergeant," the first-floor night receptionist greeted him. "There's a man here who wants to see you about the picture in the paper." Fuller slid his feet under his chair.

"I'll meet him at the elevator," he directed the woman. "Send him up."

A long pause made him frown impatiently. "What's the matter?" Fuller asked sharply.

"I think you'd better come down, sir," the woman repeated.

"Why not send him up?" Fuller demanded.

"It's him, sir," the woman explained in a whisper. "It's the man in the paper—the Barth case. He says he wants to give himself up."

Mike slammed the phone down and lurched forward, loping across the room as he checked his side holster for his gun. "Jesus Christ," he muttered as he waved for the officer at the corner desk to assist him. "The guy's downstairs. Willis, my murder suspect. Come and back me up, Lindsey."

The second man grabbed his coat and galloped after Fuller, whose finger was already pressing the elevator button. "Just keep cool and watch his hands," Mike said in the elevator as he straightened his tie and ran his hand over his hair. When the door opened, Fuller hesitated, then stepped out calmly and stared at the young man waiting in the reception area.

Hollow-eyed and unshaven, Bertram Willis glanced apprehensively at the tall, solemn, neatly groomed detective who approached him. The second suit-clad detective stayed behind near the elevator, casually noting the encounter from a distance.

"I'm Sergeant Fuller," Mike said, deliberately

easing to his left so that Lindsey had an unobstructed view of the seated man.

"I'm Bertram Willis," the young fellow replied. "I'm tired of hidin' out. I guess you've been lookin' for me." He bolted to his feet as Fuller jerked his thumb up. Following Fuller's directions, Willis leaned against the counter, spreading his feet apart so the detective could check for weapons. "It ain't like you think." Willis said the phrase twice. "She pulled a knife on me. I was scared and took off." His explanation poured out in a torrent of words.

"Hold it, hold it," Fuller said, trying to calm the fellow. "Lemme get a few things straight before you start talking. Lindsey," he called to the officer by the elevator, "get the interview room ready."

Methodically Mike checked the man's pockets as he recited the statement of rights for Willis. After each phrase Fuller paused. "You understand?"

"Yeah," Willis responded each time. Satisfied that the fellow was unarmed, Fuller escorted him to the first open door down the hall—a nine-by-nine-foot office containing only a desk, two chairs, a lamp, a telephone, and Detective Lindsey.

Bertram Willis sat in the straight-backed chair facing Fuller, who relaxed in the desk armchair, stretching out his legs and staring at the suspect. Lindsey backed out the door, pulling it shut behind him. After gazing at the nervous young man for over a minute, Fuller lifted a tape recorder from the desk drawer and set it up. He adjusted the microphone toward Willis, then leaned back. He droned a brief preamble into the microphone, stating the date, the time, and the location of the interrogation. Then he gave his name as he looked up at Willis. "Please state your name," he directed.

"Bertram Warren Willis," the tense man responded.

"How many years of formal schooling have you completed?"

"High school," Willis replied, then paused as he silently calculated the years. "Twelve years of schooling," he concluded.

"You are a high school graduate?" This would establish for the record that Willis was sufficiently able to understand the procedures and questions.

"Yeah," Willis answered flatly.

"You have been advised of your rights. . . ." Fuller paused.

"Yeah. . . ."

"And you are speaking to me, without an attorney present, by your own choice," Mike said, pressing each critical point.

"Yeah."

"And without coercion of any kind."

Bertram Willis stared at him blankly.

"We are not forcing you or threatening you in any way," Fuller clarified.

"Ahh, no. I just came in to straighten you guys out."

"About the death on April thirtieth of Marsha Barth?" Fuller asked.

"Yeah, about her. I didn't murder no one. She came at me with a fuckin' knife, so I fought her off."

"Just hold it a minute." Fuller slid a printed form toward Willis. "Please sign here and here," Fuller said, touching the pen to two solid lines and then passing it to Willis, "to verify what you just said— about knowing your rights." Willis glanced over the form and signed both places. "Now could you begin slowly, Bertram?" Fuller leaned forward in his armchair. "Now, did you see Marsha Barth on Friday, April thirtieth?"

Carefully Fuller questioned the young man while the reels of the tape recorder slowly revolved. By 8:22 P.M. Fuller had the statement and booked Bertram Willis for murder in spite of Willis's protest that he'd only acted in self-defense.

At 8:42 Mike turned to walk away from the holding cell where Willis was being fingerprinted. Willis called after him, "You're makin' a big stink outta nothin'." When Fuller kept walking, Willis grinned at the nearest officer, shrugged, and said, "All this crap over a whore."

The dapper gray-haired fellow in the crisp gray uniform stood in his glass-walled office overlooking the sprawling dockside warehouse. The pale yellow and silver shoulder patch—Steinlach Pharmaceutical Company—glimmered in the fluorescent light. Efficiently the man scanned the console, flicking on the buttons of each video unit until all six bore images in shades of gray of the various exits and hallways of the massive complex. At precisely eight thirty the uniformed man picked up the phone and dialed.

"All set here," he said calmly. "Not a mouse in the joint. You gu take off. I'll take it from here." In the far left m itor another uniformed security guard stepped in o camera range, grinned, and shot a finger at the lens.

"Tell Hicks not to wave his IQ at me," the fellow snorted into the telephone. "And tell the asshole to wear his tie when he's on duty."

The telephone clicked and another uniformed figure appeared on monitor number one, joining the grinning security guard who had already turned down the hall toward the exit. The man at the console watched closely while the two armed men

paused at the heavy Plexiglas security door. He pressed a button and the door opened, allowing them to pass through. One man inserted his key into the outside door lock. Again the man at the console pressed a button, and the exterior door opened. When the outside door closed again, the Steinlach Pharmaceutical warehouse was secure for the night and Andy Russell was alone with six television sets silently monitoring the building.

Russell lifted a cigarette from the pack in his chest pocket and tapped it on the Formica desk top as he scanned the sets. He struck a match and puffed until a thin cloud of smoke floated above his head. Quietly Russell crossed to the file cabinet by the desk, unlocked the lower drawer, and lifted a video cassette from the back. He disconnected the last unit from the surveillance system hookup, then clicked the cassette into the video recorder below set number six and rocked back in his chair.

The image of the vacant loading dock door was displaced by a series of flickering lines and flashes, then a curtained window and the foot of a queen-sized bed.

From the right side of the picture Andy Russell's own form stepped into view. Slowly he disrobed before the stationary camera until he stood in leopard-print Jockey shorts. He beckoned to some-one offscreen. His smile wavered as he gestured again. Then she came forward. Clad only in a two-piece swimsuit, the young girl kept her eyes turned from the tripod-mounted camera. Grinning widely, Andy slid his arm over her shoulders and pulled her close. His right hand clasped her waist, tugging her around so her belly pressed against his crotch. He dropped his hands to her buttocks, cupping his palms under the rounded cheeks as he

eased her to her tiptoes and thrust his crotch rhythmically against hers, whispering into her ear.

Russell sat motionless, his eyes riveted to the two figures on the screen. There was no sound with the black-and-white picture, but Russell remembered what he had said. He had called her his pretty pussy, his special pretty pussy. He had begged his pretty pussy to kiss it.

Russell was sweating now as he stared at the girl, who dropped to her knees before the man on the screen. He let the cigarette fall from his fingers, then moved his hand toward his crotch as the girl on the screen pressed her face against the leopard-print Jockey shorts. Her mouth moved. Russell knew what she was saying. "Come out and play." He knew it word for word. "Come out and play"— just like he'd taught her to say. The man on the television set reached for something off camera and the screen went gray.

Russell unzipped his pants and clutched his bulging member. "Come out and play," he breathed hoarsely, supplying the unheard dialogue for the videotape. "Come out and play—come, come, come," he gasped as his hand moved rapidly. He remembered every detail of what she had done after he'd turned the camera off. She had pulled down his Jockey shorts and put it in her mouth. Eyes closed, Russell kept playing the scene over and over in his mind. Then the spasm hit, stiffening his legs and drawing a half scream of release from his parted lips as the whitish fluid arched into the air and splattered silently onto the dusty linoleum floor between his feet.

That few minutes of tape had cost him dearly, Russell acknowledged as he fell back in his chair. She hadn't wanted to do it—especially not on tape.

But he'd known how to make her cooperate. And afterward he'd bought her off—big time. Ten days in Europe over the Easter break with her high school class. He was still putting in overtime to catch up with the payments to the finance company. But it was worth it. Now he could play the tape whenever he wanted. Any night at work when the office was empty. And it sure did the trick for him. Even without the last part, which she wouldn't let him tape, even without actually seeing it all, he could get a red-hot hard-on. When he read her lips he could feel his crotch tense just like when she really did it. And if he closed his eyes, he could do it all, and he was Superman—any time he needed it.

Russell sat staring at the slick substance on the floor. Gradually his pulse settled back to normal and he crammed his limp member back into his pants. He removed the cassette from video six and replaced it in the lower file drawer, scrupulously locking the cabinet. Next time, he promised himself, he'd get her to lay out on the bed and let him tape his part—easing his face down on it. "Pretty pussy," he murmured as he scanned the sixth screen, which once again showed the loading dock door. "When her ma is out—and we're alone. This time I'll be doing it—and I won't have to turn the fuckin' camera off."

"Did you say this?" Chris thrust the folded newspaper under Mike's nose once she'd closed the door behind him. Her deep green eyes regarded him cautiously as she waited for his reply. Mike took the newspaper and scanned the article below TEEN DEATH CLAIMED SELF-DEFENSE. Savannah attorney Ed Ingram had taken the case for Bertram "Butch" Willis. In characteristic style he had re-

leased some of Willis's statements to the press: "I didn't know she was sixteen. I loved her, I'd've done anything for her. She paid me to bring her some men; I worked for her—she didn't work for me. She acted real sweet at first, then she turned mean. We argued and she pulled a knife."

The three-column article had run in the Sunday paper, complete with a picture of Butch Willis appearing as helpless and remorseful as his lawyer could coach him to look. At the end of the third column was the section involving Fuller.

"Detective Fuller, who has been leading the investigation in the death of Marsha Barth, said that Bertram Willis turned himself in Friday night at police headquarters. Willis volunteered details about the case and has cooperated with investigators. 'Street life is tough for runaways,' Fuller stated. 'Most of them are underage. They can't get a regular job. They have to become ruthless to survive. It seems that a lot of young girls who run away from home end up this way.' "

"So?" Mike looked down at Chris. "What's wrong with what I said?"

"You imply that Marsha Barth was ruthless. You sound as if her death were nothing important—just another piece of paperwork." Her eyes narrowed in anger.

Fuller looked down at the article again. "I didn't say anything of the sort," he protested quietly.

"You hang the threat of death over the head of any girl who wants to run away from home." Her low voice hissed out the words ominously.

Fuller stood in the dim living room with one arm resting on the doorjamb, the folded newspaper drooping by his side as Chris glared at him.

"Now, wait a minute." He pulled himself erect

and reached out to touch her shoulder. "Just calm down and we'll talk about this." His eyes shifted over toward the hallway and Sylvie's room.

"Do you realize what you did?" Chris's voice rose in indignation. "You told every kid who is desperate to get away from a bad situation at home that she's doomed, so she'd better shut up and stick it out where she is."

Mike's mouth dropped open as he stared in bewilderment at Chris.

"You make it sound like the girl is to blame—like Marsha Barth or any other girl is responsible. Like she was asking for it." Chris twisted her shoulder out of his grasp. "You'd better do your homework, Michael." She leveled cold green eyes at him. "You're on the wrong track."

"Hold it." Mike grabbed her arm as she turned toward the kitchen. Chris stopped in mid-step, slowly turning to glare at the hand enclosing her upper arm. Something awesome in the tension of her body at that moment stunned him. Fuller jerked his hand away. Chris took a slow breath, as if she was deliberately subduing some impulse to retaliate. Only then did she raise her eyes to meet his. They were bright, distant.

"Sorry." Mike held his hands palms out. "I didn't mean to grab at you like that," he apologized. "You're not being fair about this, though. You blast me and stamp off without giving me a chance to answer. Just hold on and let's get this ironed out."

Chris turned to face him, her arms crossed unsympathetically across her ribs.

"In the first place, what you read was only part of what I told the reporter. But it is true: street life is tough and girls do die. You may not like it, I don't

like it, but it's the truth. And I have done my homework," he said angrily. "I wasn't making any threats—I don't think Marsha Barth is only a name on a report. But she isn't unique and neither is what happened to her."

Chris stayed remote. Her green eyes seemed to stare right through him.

"I'm a homicide cop," he said, his tone softening. "Not a preacher, not a social worker. . . ." He blew out a long breath. "By the time I get 'em it's a little too late. I'm just the cleanup committee," he muttered.

Her eyes shifted suddenly, refocusing on the distressed face of Michael Fuller. Gradually the tension eased from her stance. Chris began to shake her head sympathetically. "So you are . . ." she said, barely breathing the words. Her arms uncrossed and dropped to her sides.

"Whew." Mike whistled through his teeth. "You're pretty frightening when you're angry." He watched her intently, still keeping his distance. Then one corner of her mouth tilted up in a rueful smile.

"Sorry . . ."

He stepped forward, resting his arm over her shoulders. "You come on like a steamroller."

"I can't help it," Chris muttered. "The article makes this Butch character sound like a misguided, innocent schmuck that Marsha Barth used and discarded. Parasites aren't misguided or innocent," she hissed.

"His lawyer is trying to make a case for him," Fuller conceded. "They're going for self-defense."

"But you seem to be agreeing," Chris said, dropping her eyes to the paper Mike still clutched.

"The reporter interviewed me yesterday. I just

answered some questions. I can't help it if he stuck it in after Willis's comments." He tightened his arm about her. "The newspapers aren't trying Willis—a jury will," he reminded her. "Don't let it get to you."

"It's not me I'm worried about," Chris replied grimly as she raised her hand to cover his on her shoulder. "When the kids who need help read a thing like this, it will scare them. They won't follow up and find out what happens in the trial. They'll only know that one girl left home, got killed, and no one really blames anybody but her."

"I'm afraid this case may get worse before it gets better," Fuller cautioned her as they walked toward the kitchen. "Willis met with his lawyer late this afternoon. Big powwow over the next move. With an attorney like Ed Ingram you can bet there will be some real crap floating to the surface. This time I'll keep out of it," he promised.

"Just what do you think they'll pull?" Chris asked as they stopped at the kitchen counter. The scent of hot, buttery oyster stew greeted them. A carafe of pale greenish white wine was on the small wrought-iron table in the corner.

"I'm afraid they'll really go after her—try to make her seem no-good. No one actually saw him kill her, so it comes down to circumstantial evidence and his word. The district attorney thinks we've got a good case—we just have to wait and see what charge is set by the grand jury."

"Michael, what did Angela Jackson have in common with the Barth girl?" Chris asked over her shoulder as she ladled the soup into bowls, then settled across from him at the table.

"I don't want to get into it." Mike avoided her eyes.

Chris sat silently staring at him. Finally she picked up her spoon and slowly made a circle in the creamy liquid. "Do you know that many runaways are simply desperate kids escaping from abusive parents or stepparents?" she asked solemnly. "Do you know that over eighty percent of women who become prostitutes have been sexually abused children?" She continued to stir. "They have been manipulated, fondled, coerced, violated, and traumatized by someone they loved and trusted—a father, a stepfather, a not-so-funny uncle. You know where they learn to be ruthless. You know how they learn to get by. They've been taught by real slick operators."

"I told you, Chris. I do my homework." Fuller leaned on his elbows and rubbed the stubble on his chin.

"Who can one of these girls turn to, Michael?" she raised her eyes to ask. "Her mother, if she's got one, is too weak or too scared to believe her. The man who's using her keeps telling her it's all right—or he reminds the child that it's their secret, or he says he'll go to jail and the family will be broken up and shamed if it gets out. He tells her that if she loves him, she'll do it. If she loves him, she'll keep it quiet. If she loves and cares for her family, she'll protect them by complying with his demands. And once she's done what he wants and has kept silent, he convinces her that she's an accomplice, not a victim."

Mike looked down at his untouched meal.

When he looked up, Chris gently held his gaze.

"Michael, what about Marsha Barth and Angela Jackson? Is that what they had in common? Were they both victims of sexual abuse?"

"Look, the girl is dead. We've got the guy who did

it. We're doing the best we can. We'll get a conviction," he insisted wearily.

"But it won't help Marsha Barth. It's too late for her," Chris countered. "And if the abuse she suffered is never mentioned, that won't help any other kid out there who is scared and mixed up and feeling dirty."

"My job is solving crimes. I can't prevent them from happening. No one can do anything about this stuff until a crime occurs. That's just the way it is. Come on, Chris. Let's just let it drop for a while."

"All right," Chris conceded as she looked at the deep hollows beneath his eyes and the traces of a beard from a full evening shift. "Let it drop. You're doing what you can." She poured them each a glass of wine and smiled up at him. "To justice." She lifted her glass and smiled more broadly.

"Justice," Mike echoed, nodding, and turned his attention to the tepid oyster stew. Chris took one taste of hers and wrinkled her nose.

"Let me zap it." She stood and confiscated his bowl. Efficiently she touched the computerized controls on the microwave oven. After a steady fifty-second hum the soft bell signaled that once again their late dinner was ready.

"You zap good," Mike kidded her as he savored the first mouthful.

Only a trace of a rueful smile flitted across her solemn face as Chris lowered her green eyes to the spiral of golden butter turning counterclockwise on the surface of her soup.

The two sat face to face within the circle of seashells. The timeless moan of sea wind in the throat of the conch shell ebbed and flowed with the night breeze.

"It is time." The taller of the two stood and moved outside the circle, her naked body catching the diffused candlelight. "You must do this alone."

The younger one placed the ring of pearl on her right index finger. On her left wrist she slid the golden serpentine band that held a spiral shell like the golden pendant between her breasts. Silently she crossed her left arm over, pressing the bracelet above her right breast. Her young voice wavered at first as she repeated the low chant with a regular wavelike rhythm, swaying forward and back, eyes closed in concentration. The older one with golden hair—the mentor—stood watching from the shadows as the swaying body and sighing voice united in the hypnotic ritual.

Ralph Taggert stood on the stairway, peering down into the darkness of the rooms below. He stepped soundlessly down to the landing, then proceeded farther toward the pale glow in the living room.

Lauri stood alone in the hazy shaft of light. She was naked. Her small breasts were cupped by half-moon shadows in the peculiar light and the triangle below her stomach was indistinct and dark. Her open eyes seemed to stare through Taggert, past him into nothingness.

"Lauri—" Taggert stepped toward her cautiously. "Lauri, baby, what are you doing down here?" The child did not move. She did not register any response to his presence.

"Lauri, honey." Taggert inched forward. Something moved in the triangle below her stomach. The shadow stretched out over her hips, then moved in a dark coil around her body, like a serpent slowly encircling its prey. It slid behind her left shoulder,

leaving thick dark bands from chest to hips. When it emerged and rested its head beside her throat, serpent eyes blinked open—clear and green and uncompromising. The eyes stared at him, daring him to reach out, challenging him to touch the child the snake embraced with its coils. It changed color gradually till its looping form was encased in iridescent scales in shades of green—crescent shapes that rose and fell with Taggert's strained breathing. The creature opened its mouth; its blood red ribbon tongue flitted in and out. Taggert felt the beginning of an erection as the tongue flicked again and again. The inscrutable green eyes were riveted to his.

"Oh, no," Taggert muttered, and clutched at his crotch. "No—" He couldn't let the creature see him like this. But the bulge grew, pushing at the fabric of his pants. Then he heard the ripping as the enormous erection broke through its restraints. Taggert stared down in horror as the dark cylindrical form emerging from his pants twisted and coiled around his thigh and spiraled slowly down his leg toward the floor. It eased onto the carpet, gliding sinuously across to the feet of the child, its iridescent scales catching the light as it moved. Then it encircled the feet of the young girl and coiled around her protectively, its eerie green eyes staring at him.

Taggert grabbed with both hands at his genitals. Nothing remained. The ripped cloth drooped limply against his body. "Oh, God—oh, no!" Taggert screamed, clutching the unfamiliar smooth curve of his body. "Please, no," he moaned, springing upright in bed as he stared wide-eyed at the darkened bedroom. Drenched in perspiration, Taggert whimpered as he comforted himself, relieved to once

again touch the warm soft flesh that hung between his legs.

"Ralph?" the voice mumbled from the next bed. "Ralph, you all right?"

Taggert held his breath, forcing himself to be silent. "Muscle cramp," he said with difficulty. "Just a cramp," he reassured his wife.

Sylvie's pale form swayed more and more slowly. Her slender wrist slid downward, finally resting on her crossed legs. Her long lashes fluttered as the to-and-fro rhythm of her young body gradually halted. Solemn-faced, she gazed upon her mentor. "It is done," Sylvie whispered at last.

"Now you must rest," the taller one replied. She stepped into the circle, lifting the young one easily into her arms. Cradling the initiate, she took her to the far bedroom and placed her beneath the covers. Retrieving the golden comb that had been passed down through the ages, she sat beside her ward, singing and drawing the long-toothed comb through the young one's hair until the green eyes closed once more.

"You have done well." She patted the sleeping form. "You have done well." Placing the comb back in its lacquered case, she sighed. Now they could only wait—to see if the warning was sufficient.

Wearily she returned to the circle of shells, lifting each one and returning it to the wicker basket. As she placed the basket on the mantel, her gaze lingered on the alabaster pelican, perched atop the driftwood.

"Protect the children," she whispered, smiling at the motionless bird. "Save the young."

When Zeus, the all-powerful, seduced Lamia, the beautiful Libyan queen, his consort-sister Hera flew into a jealous rage. She commanded the destruction of the children of Lamia. Only Scylla, the yet unborn product of the illicit union, escaped death. Lamia withdrew to a distant island, where she awaited the birth.

When Scylla was born Lamia returned to her own lands but left the child and an aged nurse secreted on the island. Scylla grew into a lovely maiden. The creatures of the sea encircling the island and the seabirds that nested there witnessed her great beauty and spread tales abroad of the golden-haired maiden who must surely have been sired by a god.

Poseidon, the sea god, brother of Zeus, came to pay court to the fair Scylla, but she resisted his advances. The crafty Poseidon persisted. He gave her gifts of rare beauty from the sea—corals, pearls, shells of great excellence—and won her over slowly, confusing her inexperienced young heart with his guile. Finally Scylla gave herself to him.

But Amphitrite, Poseidon's consort, was jealous

and sought to punish her rival. In the cool waters of the bathing place where Scylla went each day, Amphitrite put magic herbs obtained from the sorceress Circe. As Scylla stepped into the pool of spring water and was submerged to her chest, the portion of her body beneath the surface was slowly transformed into the monstrous iridescent scaled coils of a serpent of the sea. Terrified, the maiden grasped reeds from the shore. She pulled herself out, then lay weeping forlornly upon the shore.

Queen Lamia learned of her daughter's plight and interceded on Scylla's behalf, begging Zeus to undo this wretched spell. Lamia argued that Poseidon had seduced fair Scylla just as Lamia herself had been seduced by Zeus. She insisted that the maiden should be neither blamed nor punished— she was merely a victim of the lust of a god.

So convincing was her tearful plea that Zeus called Amphitrite to him and let her witness the defense made by Lamia. Amphitrite was likewise moved to tears and agreed to mitigate the punishment. As long as Scylla bathed each day in seawater and remained chaste, she could retain her beautiful form. But in the presence of any seducer, the repulsive serpent form would reappear, each time becoming more monstrous in aspect.

So Scylla remained chaste on her island abode, content with her companions the sea creatures and seabirds. And Lamia scoured the earth, snatching away innocent young girls whom she sent to Scylla to protect and nurture until they matured. When the mothers of these children protested to Hera, accusing Lamia of great cruelty, Hera transformed Lamia into a sinuous monster and exiled her to a dark, odorous cave to dwell with the wild beasts.

Scylla continued her quiet existence according to the terms of her agreement. Only when a ship passed too close to her island and some seafarer cast a lustful eye upon fair Scylla or one of her innocent charges did the serpent coils reappear. Scylla would then extend her awesome form and snatch the man to certain death.

CHAPTER 7

❖❖❖❖❖❖❖

Seductive siren of the sea,
   sing your ancient song to me.
Sing of tides, of time, of memory—
   sing of immortality.

—GRAY

"Where's Sylvie?" Traci Callazo clutched her clipboard to her chest as she paced along the side of the pool toward Chris.

"She couldn't make it today. She's working on a project and she just had to put in extra time. She'll be here Friday for the meet," Chris assured the dark-haired coach. "I promise."

"That's all I need to know," Traci said, grinning. "Say, where's the cute cop been lately? You still seeing him?"

"Michael is on the evening shift—four till midnight—all this month," Chris explained. "But we're still getting along fine."

"Good," Traci said with a nod. "Does this mean you're free for dinner? You and Burt and I could grab a bite after practice."

Chris hesitated. She had turned down all of Traci's invitations lately. "Sure. I'd like that," she replied brightly. "I rarely get a chance anymore to sit and visit with you off duty. It's high time we got together." Traci grinned again and strode off to her end of the pool.

Chris turned her attention back to the cluster of young girls at her end. "OK, let's do a few laps." She waved them off the edge. "Nice long strokes, and don't roll your body so much when you take a breath," she reminded them. "Come on, stretch those legs—kick from the hip." She paced the length of the pool, keeping abreast of the swimming girls. "Stretch, dig. Use your arms to pull you along. Stretch, dig . . ." she repeated as the youngsters swam the even lanes. "Ride the surface." She knelt at the end where they all clung, panting, to the side. "Skim the top of the water. The higher you are, the faster you can travel." Heads nodded dutifully as the girls turned again to face the distant end.

"We'll try it one more time," Chris insisted. "This time . . . skim the surface."

Burt Rambo eyed Traci with concern as the threesome settled into rust-colored wrought-iron chairs around a table outside the River Street Restaurant. "You cold?"

"I'm fine," Traci assured him. "A bit water-logged, perhaps, but otherwise fine." The flaps of the red and blue sectioned umbrella over the table fluttered in the breeze as deep shadows spread across the patio and onto the old gray ballast stone roadway.

"How about you?" He turned to Chris.

"I'm fine too," Chris asserted. Rambo's round eyes shifted from her to the newspaper in his hand.

"I see your friend Fuller has been busy," he said, tapping the column he'd been reading while he waited in the bleachers until swimming practice ended. "The newspaper is having a big time with this Lolita case." He turned it around so Chris could see the large black letters.

Chris frowned at the caption: LOLITA MURDER DISPUTED. The article focused on statements to the press denouncing Marsha Barth. *Prostitute*. The word was used twice. "Preferred contacts with older men." "Willis alleges that he paid the rent on her room as an attempt to keep her off the streets."

"Sure he did," Chris murmured. She continued to scan the article. Then she saw that Fuller was named as the officer in charge of the case. There was no statement by him.

"That's just awful." Traci had been leaning over and reading the article along with Chris. "This Willis guy turns her into a prostitute, makes money off her, then kills her when she steps out of line. Now he tries to make it all look like it was her fault." She wrinkled her nose in disgust. "This Lolita business is disgraceful. They make the girl sound like a sick, nasty, predatory creature. Poor Willis was just being a good samaritan."

"It's easy to take shots at a dead person." Rambo shrugged. "Who's around to defend her?"

"The family just wants to be left alone," Chris noted solemnly. "No one wants to be reminded that a child of theirs—or a friend of theirs—died in horrible circumstances. They'd rather just forget." Her oval face was expressionless. "If they start thinking about it, they may come up with some very tough questions and some unpleasant answers."

The waitress circled the table, placing menus, silverware, and glasses of water before the trio. Momentarily they all fell silent. Traci and Burt scanned the menu while Chris watched the plain-looking waitress walk away, then she spoke once more.

"Marsha's school records are quite good—

better-than-average grades, praise from teachers for her cooperation, and good conduct. Angela Jackson, the barmaid who witnessed the incident, was an acquaintance of Marsha's. She said Marsha was always quiet and polite. Then the papers describe this defiant, cynical, hard sixteen-year-old hustler." She hesitated. "It's as if there were two Marsha Barths—the one on the barroom floor and the nice kid who went to school and did her work. Willis killed both of them, not just the one they call Lolita."

"The papers seem to think that the first one, the hustler, makes better news," Rambo remarked. "Since you've taken such an interest in the case"— he arched his brows questioningly—"have you got any theories about what made the kid schizophrenic, with one face for business and one for friends?"

Chris opened her mouth to reply, then checked herself. "I guess I really shouldn't go on about it," she said, shrugging cautiously. "Michael said the trial will bring out all the facts—so maybe we should just drop it."

Rambo regarded her intently, then finally echoed her shrug. Promptly he lifted the newspaper from the table and tucked it away, out of sight, beside his wide leg. "So what do you want to eat?" Burt asked. "Name it and it's yours," he said, forcing a lighter tone. With deliberate effort they concentrated on the menu and made their selections.

Less than an hour later the pale lanterns along River Street were turned on and the trio stood and ambled out amid the light flow of passersby. Burt held Traci's hand as they passed from shop to shop, peering into the windows, pointing out curios that caught their attention. "Let's go in here," Traci suggested as she gazed at a music box with a

scrimshaw inlay on the lid. "Just to prowl." She looked eagerly from Burt to Chris.

"I've got thirty minutes till Sylvie is due home." Chris glanced at her watch and smiled. "So let's take a look around."

The display shelves in the small shop were laden with seashell jewelry, sand castings, scrimshaw items, pale white sand dollars—some broken open, with clusters of dove shapes spilling out. Thick ships' ropes were looped along the walls where circular porthole display cases illuminated from behind held nautical items of brass and gold.

"This looks like yours." Rambo pointed a thick finger toward a small nautilus shell perched on a brass stand. Chris touched the gold spiral shape on her necklace and glanced at him with surprise. "You didn't think I'd noticed. I did—I like it. Very pretty," he said as they both smiled. "You wear it a lot," he added, obviously pleased with his astute observation. "Does it have some special meaning? Good luck or something?"

"Something like that," Chris acknowledged, then eased on to another display window. Traci was on the far side of the shop, still entranced with the small music box that the clerk had retrieved from the front window.

"Sylvie has one now, I noticed," Rambo said from behind Chris's shoulder. "She used to wear that little white coral thing; now she has one like yours."

Again Chris looked at him in surprise. "You are observant," she said, managing a quick grin. "Yes, Sylvie liked mine so much, she just had to have one of her own."

"You know, shells are kinda symbolic," Burt went on. "Especially the ones that coil, like yours."

Chris turned deliberately blank green eyes upon him. "Really?"

"Sure," Rambo persisted. "Endless cycles: birth, life, death, rebirth through generation after generation. Immortality." His round eyes sparkled with enthusiasm as his thick hands rotated one over the other, making a continuous circle in the air. "All that good stuff." His broad face broke into a satisfied grin.

"So you're a philosopher." Chris smiled politely as she watched Traci Callazo approaching from the opposite side of the shop. "Burt's been telling me about seashells," she said to her.

Traci nodded. "You'd be surprised what the guy comes up with. He's a master of trivia. He knows something about everything."

"Almost everything." Burt laughed loudly, causing the blinking saleslady at the front to stare. "I'm a little weak on psycholinguistics and biogenetics," he joked, "and I still haven't gotten my Grand Marnier soufflé to work."

"He reads a lot," Traci told her, ignoring the big man's comment. "He sits up late at night reading peculiar things and somehow comes up with computer programs and systems. He's what our education professors would call a habitual divergent thinker. I just tell him he's weird." She slid her arm around Rambo's wide waist and gave him an affectionate squeeze. "Weird but harmless," she added with a smile.

Chris shifted an uncertain gaze from Rambo's half smile to the nautilus shell on the brass stand, then back again to the intelligent eyes that seemed to catalog her reactions. "Very interesting," she said cheerfully as she cast a parting look at the seashell. "I'd better get home. Sylvie will be in

soon. See you tomorrow, Traci. Bye, Burt."

"Let us walk you home," Burt said.

"No, don't bother," Chris protested. "It's just a block. I'll be quite safe. Besides"—she flashed an impish grin—"Traci may want another look at that music box." Backing toward the door, she waved and stepped out into the warm night air. Earlier she'd considered asking them up for a drink, but something about Rambo distressed her, and taking him into her home would be inviting an unnecessary intrusion.

Chris turned toward her building, breathing in the bracing sea air, letting it sweep through her lungs, refreshing her spirit.

Once inside her sanctuary she felt the tension ease from her shoulders. Slowly she moved from room to room, pausing to touch some memento or contemplate a prized possession. Many had been handed down from one generation to the next. The hand upon the mantel had been her mother's hand. Before the sisters had let the pallid form of Serena slip beneath the ocean surface for the final time, they had taken the hand, as was their custom. Encased in gold, it possessed a power that sustained her child Christina—a power that prevailed beyond death.

Protectively she lifted the hand from the mantel and clasped it to her bosom. With silent steps she carried it down the hallway, unlocking the end door within which Elena had stored her possessions. She placed it in a glass-fronted cabinet, no longer in use now that Elena had taken up residence in the house by the sea.

Chris locked the door once more. In silence she returned to the living room and sat, surrounded by

her aquatic paintings, waiting for the return of her companions. Closing her eyes, she leaned against the soft cushioned sofa. Her head tilted to the side as her breathing became slow and steady like the waves upon the shore. Only when the sharp sound of the key in the outside lock broke the silence did she wake.

"How about a little light on the subject?" Katie reached over and clicked on a lamp. Groggily Chris sat up to greet the twosome. Katie rested her hand on Sylvie's shoulder.

"How did it go?" Chris inquired.

"We tried," Sylvie began apologizing.

"Let's just feed you and get you to bed," Katie interrupted.

After a brief, halfhearted protest, Sylvie retired to her room.

"I don't know about this one." The pale-haired nurse sat across the kitchen table from Chris in the circle of light cast by the leaded glass lamp. "We waited near the Barth residence for almost an hour after school before anyone showed up. The girl came home from school, let herself in, and stayed in. If the mother was home, we saw no sign of her. The father came in around six. Sylvie and I sat there in the car the rest of the evening. Nothing. I just don't know how to make contact."

Chris nodded sympathetically. "I know it's hard, Katie, just waiting, but we have to reach that child. Marsha Barth died trying to get away from whatever goes on in that house. Her sister is twelve. She's too young to leave and too vulnerable to defend herself. I think someone owes it to Marsha to save the child like she wanted to."

"I'm not arguing," Katie asserted. "I'll help all I can. I'm just not sure Sylvie will hold up very well.

She's teetering between two roles—the guardian of Lauri Taggert and now the mediator in the Barth case. We're training her to move into full sisterhood, yet we're using her once more in the other capacity." Katie's pale, high-cheeked countenance seemed unusually weary. "I hope we're not expecting more of her than we should."

Chris reached across the table and interlaced her fingers with Katie's. "We have very little choice," she sighed. "There are so few of us." In somber silence the two passed the evening until midnight. Then the mentor proceeded to Sylvie's bedroom.

"It is time," she whispered to the sleeping young one. Sylvie stirred, then abruptly opened her eyes to stare at the one who summoned her from sleep.

Wordlessly Sylvie padded barefoot along the hallway into the living room, where the circle of seashells waited. Methodically removing her warm gown and donning the ring and bracelet of her kind, the young girl sat cross-legged, chanting the dream song. With eyes closed, wrist pressed above her bossom, she rocked to and fro, issuing once more the haunting warning to the manipulator of the young one. Once more Ralph Taggert writhed in tormented sleep and awoke, staring into the dark room while the thunder of his pulse echoed in his ears.

Chris pushed the gleaming metal shopping cart between the tall rows of multicolored cereal boxes. Ahead a short woman with slightly stooped shoulders hesitated and peered at the lower shelf. Chris moved beside the woman, then balanced on one foot, stretching upward to a far box on the top shelf. With a sudden gasp she teetered sideways.

"Oh!" The smaller woman reached out, grasping

the flailing arm and steadying her fellow shopper. "Are you all right?" She stared anxiously into the wide eyes of the woman whose stumbling fall she had prevented.

"I'm fine." Chris breathed rapidly. "I guess I'm not as tall as I thought I was." She smiled. "I really appreciate your help."

The shorter woman simply nodded and started to turn back to her cart, but contact had been made. The human had touched her first.

"My name is Chris Martin," she continued smoothly. She spoke pleasantly and stepped after the woman. "Please, tell me who you are so I can thank you again." She stood with hand extended.

Just as Chris knew she would, the graying woman turned to face her. She glanced at the extended right hand, then slowly offered her own. "I'm Caroline— Caroline Barth," the woman said shyly. Again she gazed into Chris's clear green eyes.

Side by side they pushed their carts up one aisle and down the next. The taller blond one would smile and speak occasionally. The slightly graying woman replied quietly, her eyes, like the bright shaft of a lighthouse, scanning the horizon, but always returning to make contact with the piercing green eyes that fixed on hers. Occasionally the twosome would pass near another shopper, and then they would fall silent. They would speak again when they had moved out of earshot of passersby.

At last they returned to the tall rows of multicolored cereal boxes. Again the blond one reached out her hand and the other woman returned the handshake.

"Caroline—Caroline Barth." She spoke the name as if for the first time.

"Well, thank you, Caroline Barth," Chris replied

brightly. "Perhaps one day I can come to your rescue." Quietly the tall blond turned and walked away toward the checkout counters.

The Barth woman's smile wavered uncertainly as she scanned unfamiliar items in her shopping cart. Bewilderedly she sifted through the bright cargo, trying to recall how the canned goods had gotten there when she had only come up the condiment and cereal aisles.

Caroline Barth took a yellow cereal box from the shelf and plopped it at one end of her cart. It had been a difficult few weeks, she reflected, excusing herself. Perhaps the newspaper articles about Marsha's death had troubled her more than she had realized. Finally she shrugged and continued on her usual course through the A & P, past the flour and cornmeal, methodically filling the gaps on her shopping list. At the front of the store Chris stepped onto the black rubber mat, causing the glass doors to soundlessly part as she strode out into the late afternoon sun.

She had read the familiar story in the face of the woman. She had felt the undercurrents to the woman's words, and she had heard the desolate wail of pain within when the sad-eyed woman touched her skin. Caroline Barth had sensed her oldest child's plight—but she had been too frightened to pursue it, too dependent on her husband to intervene. So Marsha Barth had struggled alone with the passions—natural and unnatural—that had led to her death.

"And now there's Jenny Barth," Chris said as she slid behind the wheel of her little MG. "But now there's also us. And we won't let the child be manipulated."

With deliberate caution Chris eased out of the

parking lot onto the main road. Her chest expanded and contracted rhythmically as she forced her rage to subside. One of them had to contact the child. One of them had to be led by that child to the perpetrator. Only then could the warning dreams be sent.

"Sylvie." Chris frowned as she breathed the name. The child would have to serve as mediator once again. "Poor Sylvie," Chris sighed. "But there is no other way."

It had taken Katie three afternoons to catch Caroline Barth going to the supermarket. Chris had still been at school when Katie called. But the contact had been made. There was no doubt now that something sexual had transpired between Jack Barth and his stepdaughter. Now it was up to Sylvie to make the final connection.

Wearily Chris drove toward the Savannah waterfront. Alone, she strolled the bridgelike walkway that vaulted over the old cotton warehouse storage bays, carrying pedestrians into the converted buildings that lined the river. Finally, seated crosslegged before the open French doors of her apartment, she drew the golden comb through her pale hair and wept.

"Why don't you shower now and get the sand out of your crevices while I pick up Sylvie at the roller rink?" Chris grinned and looked up at the sunreddened face of Mike Fuller. "I'll take my turn when I get back."

Involuntarily Fuller dropped his eyes to the hollow between her breasts where the spiral shell rose and fell with her breathing. The top of her swimsuit had shifted enough to reveal a sliver of pale white skin next to the deeper tanned area.

"I had sorta hoped we could do it together." He bent down and pressed a gentle kiss on her bare shoulder. He ran his tongue lightly over the spot. The salty taste of the seawater still clung to her warm skin.

"Shower or pick up Sylvie?" Chris asked, grinning.

"Whatever. . . ." Mike shrugged agreeably and again lowered his lips to her shoulder.

"Later, Michael." Chris pressed her open palm against her chest as he eased his arms around her. "Here." She handed him the picnic basket and pointed him toward the kitchen. "You throw out the garbage, put the good stuff in the refrigerator, take a shower, have a cold beer, maybe take a nap—and I'll be back in a while. After Sylvie is settled tonight we'll compare suntans." Fuller stood staring after her as Chris ducked up the hallway and returned seconds later with cutoff jeans and a loose T-shirt tugged over her bathing suit. "See ya." She kissed his cheek and stepped past him.

Fuller carried the woven basket to the kitchen counter and dutifully unloaded its contents. They had taken the toll road to Savannah Beach, sprawled in the sun, and picnicked under the trees. They had walked along the ocean's edge, laughing and talking, occasionally racing out into the water and plunging into the swell of a wave. He had slid his arms around her, pressing her wet cool skin against his, and he had wanted to make love with her.

Later. He smiled to himself as he remembered her words. *We'll compare suntans.* Beer in hand, he strolled toward the bathroom. As the pulsing flow of water beat upon his chest, Fuller closed his eyes, thinking of the golden-haired creature who filled

his senses. Abruptly he leaned forward, twisting the
shower control to cold. *Later*, he chastised himself
as the chilly water shocked his system into submis-
sion. *Later*.

The steady soft-rock rhythm of the music swept
over Chris as soon as she pushed open the door of
the roller rink. Bright lights circled the room,
illuminating the conglomeration of youngsters
skating on the one-way oval painted on the blue
floor and sending dizzying reflections into the
mirrored panels of the ceiling and walls. Chris
settled onto the carpeted benchlike steps that separated the sunken skating area from the upper level,
which was lined with pinball machines, electronic
games, and a refreshment area. Her intent gaze
followed the pale blond ponytail that swayed gently
amid the continuous arc of skaters.

Lauri Taggert skated next to Sylvie—not holding
hands, but reaching out occasionally to touch
Sylvie's arm as they laughed and chatted. On
Sylvie's right side the other girl skated, sharing the
jokes and antics of her new friends. Finally Sylvie
noticed their spectator and skillfully cut through
the other skaters toward Chris.

"How are you?" Chris stared cautiously into the
younger one's green eyes. "Are you OK?"

Sylvie flashed a bright smile. "I can handle
it—really," she insisted. In the next few seconds
Lauri and the second girl completed a full circle of
the rink and glided to the carpeted area to follow
their friend.

"Hi, Miss Martin." Lauri perched beside Chris,
easing into the welcoming curve of her arm.

"This is my aunt, Chris Martin," Sylvie told her

new friend eagerly. "Chris, this is Jenny. Jenny Barth."

"Nice to meet you, Miss Martin," the youngster replied politely.

"Here, join us." Sylvie motioned for Jenny to sit next to Chris. Then she announced, "I've got to go to the bathroom," and promptly departed. "You guys wait right there," she called back. "Don't tell Chris what we've been eating!"

"Oh, boy," Chris muttered. "I guess that means two milk shakes each—and four chocolate bars." She nudged Lauri for a response.

Grinning conspiratorially, Lauri patted Chris's knee. "Two chocolate bars," she blurted out.

"And some popcorn." Jenny Barth crouched closer so her knees pressed against Chris's leg.

"You've been stuffing yourself too?" Chris draped her right arm across Jenny's shoulders. "You sure fit in with these two culprits." She forced her voice to remain light as she looked into the wide brown eyes. "I don't suppose I could offer you some orange juice or something healthy. Just a parting gesture," she teased.

"Oh, it's time to go?" Lauri groaned.

"We agreed that your folks would drop you two off and I'd take you home. Your mom gets home from work at four today. I'm supposed to get you there about the same time. We've got twenty minutes," Chris explained.

"So let's have a Coke," Lauri said. "We've got time."

"Come on, girls." Chris stood and offered them each a hand. "My treat," she added to reassure Jenny.

"Hey, I told you not to leave," Sylvie pouted as

the trio climbed up two steps to the refreshment area. "I wanted to show Chris our new turns." She stood, hands on hips, waiting for a response from the girls.

"Can we have just another minute?" Lauri begged. "Just to show you?" Chris smiled and nodded. Abruptly Lauri and Sylvie dashed out onto the floor into the vacant center of the rink, where the flashier skaters occasionally did stunts and twists. Jenny Barth still clung to her arm as Chris watched the two girls.

"They're very good," Jenny whispered self-consciously.

"I should hope so," Chris kidded her. "When they're not taking lessons or practicing, they're on the telephone talking about skating. You should hear them giving directions over the phone." A slight smile brightened Jenny's face. Out in the center of the floor Sylvie circled backward, then in one-two-three order turned forward, backward, and forward again without missing a beat of the blaring music. Sylvie waited on tiptoe while Lauri Taggert did the same routine, reversing direction rhythmically and ending up facing forward.

"Very *nice*," Chris said as the two beaming girls glided back beside her. "Very impressive," she insisted sincerely. "So now how about a cool drink?" Without protest they crossed the carpeted area to a wall booth and squeezed in side by side. "I don't suppose you could handle a few French fries?" Chris asked. "With puddles of catsup?"

"Please, please," they yelped together.

"OK. I'd hate to take you home hungry and thirsty," Chris conceded, then strode off to the counter to place their order. When she returned with a tray laden with fries, catsup, drinks, and

napkins, the conversation had switched to swimming.

"Could Jenny come to watch us practice on Monday?" Sylvie begged as she stripped the plastic lid from her orange juice. "If her folks drop her off after school, could we take her home? Please. . . ?"

Chris was already nodding. "If Lauri makes the same arrangements, I'll take all three of you to dinner after practice. How about it?" Three heads bobbed agreeably while each girl clutched her drink in one hand and stuffed fries into her mouth with the other. "We should all be good friends by then," Chris said, grinning, "after a couple of rides with the four of us in a two-seater MG."

They giggled happily. Across the table from Chris, Jenny Barth's eyes were wide and moist. Chris held her gaze, trying to tell her wordlessly that everything would soon be all right.

Later, when they were alone in the MG, Sylvie reached out and clasped Chris's hand. They proceeded home without talking, for between them no human words were needed.

"Lay off the sugar," Chris said, interrupting the silence as the car swung onto River Street. "You're overworking your system, Sylvie."

The pale-haired young one let her hand drop back against the seat. "The other children eat that stuff," she noted. "So I bought what Lauri bought."

"You are not . . . the same. You aren't used to so much sugar and chocolate. Besides, the food today isn't like it was when you were young. Now everything has preservatives and colorings and chemicals that we need to avoid," Chris continued evenly. "You are under enough of a strain. Please—purify your body."

"I'm sorry," Sylvie sighed. "I got carried away."

Chris cast an apprehensive look at the profile of her young ward. Already the substances had begun to drain the color from Sylvie's cheeks, and grayish blue half-moons were forming beneath her eyes, making the childlike face seem drawn and weary.

"Early to bed tonight." She squeezed Sylvie's hand. "I'll make some soup and you can skip dinner." Sylvie didn't need to respond. The hand Chris clasped was clammy and limp. The juice would help. The fries would counter some of the effect. But the herb broth would restore the young one. Ralph Taggert's final warning—the third dream—had been scheduled for tonight. *Tomorrow*, Chris decided. *We'll wait till tomorrow, when Sylvie is better.*

"Fancy meeting you here," Traci Callazo greeted Chris and Mike as they wandered hand in hand through the art displays scattered along the waterfront plaza between River Street and the Savannah River.

"Oh, hi. See anything you like?" Chris smiled at her friend.

"Just a big guy with mitts like ham hocks. But he's wandered off somewhere, prowling around after more of his weird finds.' " Traci shrugged, then shaded her eyes and peered out into the crowd. "I absolutely refuse to hunt for him," she finally asserted. "He does this every time—at the supermarket, the movies, flea markets, stores. He just gets absorbed and wanders off."

"You want to sit in the shade and let me browse around?" Mike offered with a smile. "I've got a few inches on you," he kidded the petite brunette. "I

may spot Burt above the crowd. You're forced to hunt at belt-buckle level."

"Very funny," Traci groaned. "If my feet weren't so sore, I'd kick you in the toe. However, since you offered, I'd appreciate your expert help. You'd think that one of Savannah's finest detectives could find a two-hundred-and-ninety pound, gray-eyed prowler in a ten-block art show. Besides, he's wearing a sombrero." She grinned.

"You're kidding," Chris said, laughing.

"I wish I was," Traci muttered. "But he doesn't like too much sun, so he wore his damn sombrero. One of his better finds that he picked up at a garage sale."

"I'll give it my best shot." Mike waved and took a few steps. "By the way, lady," he said, turning back with a grin, "do you know what color the sombrero is?"

"Go!" Chris told him, laughing. "I'll sit here with Traci and wait for the great sleuth to return with the Frito Bandito. Go." She waved him off.

A minute later Mike spotted Burt, head down, darting through the plaza.

"I'm not lost—I'm sneaking around," Rambo said, tucking his sombrero under his arm so Fuller could step closer. "Traci saw a nifty music box in a shop up ahead a few days ago and I want to surprise her with it. Come on, I'll show you." The two men walked along River Street close to the row of shops that opened onto the street to receive the strolling Sunday afternoon shoppers—the overflow from the open-air art show.

"What the hell's that?" Mike pointed at a grayish papier-mâché hand perched upright in one window.

"Magic shit." Rambo glanced over the masks and magician paraphernalia that filled the small shop window.

"I mean the hand. Chris has one like that, but hers is gold or something."

"You're kidding." Burt stared intently at the grotesque hand. "It's just a rip-off. Ain't the real thing. It's called a Hand of Glory. See the twisted ends on the fingers?" He glanced at Fuller. "Well, it's like a magic spell. If someone goes to sleep in the house and you light the finger, the person won't wake up until you put out the flame. Supposedly robbers used them so they could work inside a house without any of the occupants waking up."

"What if someone was still awake when the robber lit the finger?" Fuller asked.

"That particular finger wouldn't light. It would flicker, then go out. So the guy had to wait till the damn thing stayed lit," Burt explained as he studied the hand. His round gray eyes turned again to Fuller's face. "You say Chris has one?"

"She has a candelabrum thing sorta like it. Hers is pretty, though." Fuller shrugged.

"She probably doesn't know anything about this voodoo shit. She must've bought it because it looks good on an end table or something. Women are like that," Rambo finished, dismissing the issue. He plunged again into the crowd moving along the sidewalk. "Come on, I've got to get this box thing for Traci," he called over his shoulder as he hurried toward the nautical shop three buildings away.

A few minutes later Rambo stuffed the gift-wrapped music box with the scrimshaw inset into the cavernous opening of the sombrero. "Smart, eh?" He chortled. "I told Traci I had to keep my delicate brain out of the sun so I could get away

with wearing this thing. But it fits in just fine—
look." He showed Mike how snugly the package
rested in the crown of the hat. "And old eagle eye
won't spot it." His big face glowed with satisfaction. "Say, you wanna see something your girl
likes?" He headed down an aisle toward the shell
displays.

"Miss?" Rambo called over the slender saleswo-
man with the frizzy red hair. "What happened to
the nautilus shell? The one on the little brass stand?
It was right here." He pointed to the glass counter
top.

"I guess someone bought it," the woman replied.
"Just a moment and I'll see if we have anything
similar," she added sweetly, walking off to consult
the gray-haired woman behind the counter.

"Chris has a pelican too." Fuller pointed over
two counters to a row of ceramic pelicans in shades
of brown—some about to swallow fish, others
basking in the sunshine on pilings. "Any voodoo in
a pelican?" he half joked.

Burt rubbed his chin in thought. "Pelicans are
the quintessential symbol of motherhood. A mother pelican will bite open her own breast and let her
blood flow so her young can feed and survive."
Suddenly he chuckled. "They're such floppy,
dopey-looking characters. You'd never expect them
to be so conscientious."

Before Mike could reply, the red-haired woman
returned with a shell and stand similar to the one
Rambo had been seeking, though this shell was
larger. "That's it," Burt said enthusiastically.
"That's just like the one Chris wears." He took the
shell and held it under Fuller's nose. "What do you
think?"

"I think I like it." Mike took the shell and turned

it over in his hand. When he saw the ten-dollar price tag, he decided he really liked it. "I hope your hat is big enough for this too," Mike said, eyeing the outlandish sombrero Rambo clutched under his arm. A few minutes later the big fellow graciously spread open the rim so the saleslady could deposit the gift-wrapped shell beside Traci's music box.

"We're such nice chaps," Rambo commented in a terrible mock-British accent as they crossed River Street toward the place where Mike had left Traci and Chris. "A woman would be a fool to pass up either of us."

"Boy, if you don't look like the cat that just demolished the canary." Traci crossed her arms and stared up at the large man with the Mexican hat. "Congratulations, Inspector Clouseau," she said to Mike with a grin.

"Say, would you two like some lemonade?" Rambo asked. "Maybe you and Mike could join Traci and me. There must be a place around here where we could get something cold and refreshing."

"No, thanks." Chris rose and took Mike's arm. "We were just getting started when we bumped into Traci. We still have to look at the paintings. Thanks for the offer, but I really want to walk around and admire the artwork."

Rambo shrugged uncomfortably and glanced meaningfully at Mike. "I suppose I'll see you around," he stalled, his eyebrows rising toward his hat.

Mike smiled. "I'll drop by the swimming pool before I go to work tomorrow afternoon. I'll see you there." He winked.

Rambo nodded in relief, glad Mike had caught his meaning and would collect Chris's gift the next day. "Yeah, sure. See you both tomorrow."

"Bye for now," Traci added as she slid her small hand into Burt's larger one.

Arm in arm, Chris and Mike walked among the displays in the bright afternoon sun. "You think Sylvie will go to sleep early tonight?" Michael whispered.

"Your sunburn acting up again?" Chris countered with a smile.

"No. . . ." Mike stopped and looked into her eyes. "I just want to make love with you," he said hoarsely.

"Well, since you put it like that—" Chris stood on tiptoe and breathed against his ear, "I'm sure something agreeable can be arranged."

"I think I've died and gone to heaven." Mike grinned at her. "I love you, Christina," he said, using the name he usually called her only in their lovemaking.

"I love you too, Michael," she answered solemnly.

"So—" he began.

"So let's look at the paintings," she said, cutting him off and steering him toward a watercolor display. "We have the whole day," she reminded him. "And the whole night, Michael."

"Since you put it like that. . . ." He rested his hand on the curve of her waist. Slowly they strolled the length of the plaza, then turned back toward Chris's apartment. The shimmering Savannah River sparkled in the sunlight as tour boats chugged up and down amid occasional freighters and private motorboats. Across the walkway a brown pelican squatted next to a sea gull on the low gray stone wall. With a flap of wings and a swoop, the larger bird plunged into the river and emerged with a silvery fish pinned in its beak.

"You know what Rambo told me about pelicans?" Mike confided as they headed home. The sea-sweet breeze fluttered the rigging of the ships and the skirt of the tall blond as the twosome strolled along the walkway toward the statue of the Waving Girl.

Sedna was a gentle Eskimo girl, a pretty child who lived with her father, Angusta, a widower. Their cabin sat beside the sea from which her father had received bountiful catches, enough to make him a wealthy man. When Sedna reached a marriageable age, many young men sought her; however, Angusta refused to give her a dowry, and the suitors were discouraged.

One day there arrived from a distant land a suitor who was not deterred by Angusta's refusal. Cloaked in the rich furs of a hunter, the handsome suitor did not land his kayak on the shore. Instead he remained a short distance away, gently rising and falling with the waves, as he called to Sedna.

By night he sang an enticing song, imploring her to come down to the sea. "I will take you to the land of birds, where no one hungers, no one thirsts. You shall sleep in my tent, warmed by skins of bears. You will always have oil for your lamp and meat for your cooking pot."

Timid and confused, Sedna stayed inside the cabin. Her father forbade her to answer the stranger.

"Come with me . . . " he implored her. Sedna felt it was her duty to refuse. But the stranger persisted, promising necklaces of ivory, foot coverings of finest skins. Gradually he wore away her resistance, until one day she walked slowly down to the shore.

Captivated by the marvelous tales the stranger told, Sedna stepped into his boat. As soon as she did, the stranger stole her away.

He took her to the land of birds. There she came to know the truth. Her lover was not a man; he was a Kokksaut, a bird spirit who had fallen in love with her and longed for her affection in return. Phantomlike, he could assume a human form, but in his true nature he manifested the shape of a gull or some other seabird. Sedna was horrified that she had been deceived.

"I will always care for you," the bird spirit promised. "I will keep you safe and well fed and warm." But his promises did not relieve her despair. She spent her days weeping and longing to be returned to her people.

"No one can love you as I do," the bird spirit insisted. "In your stubbornness you fail to recall how unkind man can be." Sedna would not listen to the Kokksaut.

One day while the bird spirit was away Angusta rowed his boat to the distant shore where his daughter had been taken. He seized Sedna in his arms and carried her off to his waiting boat.

When Sedna realized that her father's concern was not for her happiness, that he only wanted her to care for the household and bring him luck with his catch, she began to cry out in anger. The bird spirit, returning from his flight, heard her cries upon the sea wind and guessed what had occurred.

Again he assumed the phantom form of a man, pursuing Angusta and his captive daughter. When Angusta saw that the Kokksaut's canoe would overtake them, he forced Sedna to conceal herself beneath some skins.

The phantom-lover drew alongside and demanded to see Sedna, but Angusta refused him. In spite of the bird spirit's pleas Angusta rowed on.

Suddenly the sky above Angusta's head was filled with the furious beating of wings. The Kokksaut had transformed himself back into a gigantic black bird. Uttering the strange cry of the loon, he hovered above them, then disappeared, filling the sky with darkness. The sky thundered as a terrible storm, the Dark Storm of the Arctic, swept across the seas. Terrified, Angusta seized his daughter, willing to sacrifice her in order to appease the angry waves that threatened to engulf the small boat.

With one thrust he cast her overboard, letting the dark water claim her. Sedna struggled against the waves. Desperately she grasped the side of the boat. Unwilling to join his daughter in the swirling water, Angusta lifted his ivory ax and chopped at the small hands. Three times she managed to regain her hold on the craft. Each time Angusta chopped frantically, repeatedly mutilating her bleeding hands. Then at last she sank beneath the surface, the sea grew suddenly calm, and Angusta made his way to shore.

From the wounds of Sedna, from the drops of blood that mingled with the seawater, were born the creatures of the deep—seals, walruses, and whales. These creatures bore her to the island of the bird spirit, where she willingly married him. She became the protectress of the sea animals while the Kokksaut was guardian of the seabirds.

In the night, after Angusta had taken refuge,

there came an unusually high tide that pulled him out into the depths of the sea. There he reigns over a morose domain called Adliden, the watery place in which souls must dwell after death in order to expiate the sins committed while they lived. The duration of their stay is determined by the gravity of their sins. Angusta must stay there throughout eternity.

CHAPTER 8

❖❖❖❖❖❖

"What's the matter with Sylvie?" Traci Callazo leaned toward Chris and spoke quietly.

"She's just getting over a bout with a stomach bug," Chris replied without taking her eyes off the young swimmers in the near lanes. "I'm letting her sit out today, just to be safe." She held her thumb lightly on the button of her large chrome stopwatch.

Traci nodded. "She looks pale, all right. I was a little worried. I've got six out with some virus or other. It sure thins the ranks."

Chris jotted down the times of the three swimmers who had finished, then walked to the end of the pool and called out three more names. "Dixon, Yates, Taggert—ready." She waited till they stood on the starting blocks, then barked, "Ready . . . set . . . go!"

Three young bodies sprang forward, stretching out over the water; then they hit the surface and raced toward the far end.

"Stay in your lanes, girls!" Chris reminded the ones waiting their turn. "Check yourself on the lines while you dig under." Thirteen heads nodded dutifully.

Far across the parking lot Chris could see Mike Fuller's blue sedan easing out into the traffic on Victory Drive. A few seconds later Burt Rambo appeared at the side gate leading into the pool area. The two men had been leaning against Mike's car when Chris had arrived at three forty. Mike had strolled over to talk with her for a few minutes while Rambo waited patiently. When Chris headed into the locker room to get the girls moving into the showers, Mike had returned to Rambo's car. She had glanced back once from the doorway and found both men with their arms folded over their chests, leaning against the car and staring at her in silence.

"Are you guys up to something sneaky?" Chris had kidded them. Neither had budged. With a shrug Chris had gone about her duties, leaving the men to their schemes. Something about Rambo and Mike together made her uneasy.

Chris watched the big man step up into the bleachers and sprawl out on a row a few feet from Sylvie and Jenny Barth. She could see that he was smiling and talking to the girls, but she couldn't hear what was being said. Then, abruptly, Rambo's round gray eyes shifted to her. He flashed a self-satisfied grin. Traci had teasingly called Burt Rambo weird, but as Chris turned her gaze to the kids in the pool, the peculiar uneasiness returned. Rambo was disconcerting. He watched and joked, he occasionally played the buffoon—but beneath it all was an uncanny mind. He noted, sifted through, and juxtaposed bits of data in bizarre and brilliant combinations. Rambo was more than weird, Chris concluded. He was dangerous.

"You three finish your food and let's get going. You all have homework to do," Chris pro-

tested as Lauri Taggert held a drinking straw full of
Coke over Sylvie's french fries. "Enough horsing
around."

Jenny Barth obediently began stuffing her child-
sized sandwich into her mouth. Her wide brown
eyes were fixed on Chris's blond braids. Jenny had
silently admired them from the moment she'd seen
Chris today at the practice session at the pool. Chris
smiled at the shy girl. "You know, Jenny, we may be
able to French-braid your hair. Sylvie is good at
it—and you'd look very elegant." Jenny chewed
the large mouthful of food more rapidly. "Maybe,"
Chris continued, "you can stay over with us one
night and we'll try it."

"Oh, could I? I'd love it! Do you think my hair is
long enough?" Jenny said in a burst, eagerness
overcoming her reticence. "I just love your hair."

"I think your hair would work just fine," Chris
answered. "Now, let's get this table cleaned up and
I'll chauffeur you home. You can introduce Sylvie
and me to your folks and we will set up a night for
you to stay over. Maybe Lauri could make it the
same night and we'll have a slumber party." Now
she had their attention. The three youngsters rapidly finished every last trace of food, then promptly
wadded up napkins and wrappers.

"I'll drop you off first, Lauri," Chris announced
as Sylvie and Jenny Barth wedged themselves in the
small space behind the seats of Chris's sports car.
The arching streetlights were already glowing, although the sky still held a rosy purple glow. With
their still damp hair blowing in the wind, the three
young girls draped themselves over the little MG,
attempting to appear nonchalant as the car eased
through the light traffic toward their destinations.

"Mama, this is Sylvie and this is Miss Martin,"
Jenny announced to her mother as the two blond

females stood beside her on the doorstep.

"Well, what a coincidence," Chris said, beaming at the small woman. "You're the lady who saved me from falling into the cereal boxes."

"I thought there was something familiar about your voice." Caroline Barth shook Chris's hand. "When you called to invite Jenny to the swimming practice and dinner, I just felt like I knew you from somewhere. Her daddy would be furious if he thought I let her go with a stranger—even a teacher."

"We really enjoyed Jenny's company," Chris asserted. "In fact, Sylvie and I would like her to spend the night soon—whenever it's convenient."

"It's nice of you to ask." Caroline Barth nodded uncertainly, then motioned for Jenny to go inside. "Let's just wait a bit. I don't want to press her. I'm sure you read in the papers about it." She avoided Chris's eyes. "Her sister . . . Marsha Barth."

"The young girl who was killed last month," Chris said sympathetically. "It must be sad for all of you."

Caroline Barth sighed, then looked up at the darkening sky. "I've been doing better now that I'm going out to do the shopping and such. Just getting out of the house was a help. That outing at the shopping center, when we first met, that did me a world of good." She smiled fleetingly. "I'm not sure Jenny is doing as well. She was quite close to Marsha," she confided.

"We're very sorry." Sylvie spoke from beside Chris.

"Oh, I didn't think, won't you come in?" the sad-eyed woman asked, jerking herself upright. "Jack told me not to mope around. I get carried away sometimes," she apologized. "He should be

home any minute now." Her apprehensive gaze shifted out toward the street.

"No, we can't stay," Chris said. "We have school-work to do. I just wanted to tell you how much we enjoy your daughter's company."

"Well, maybe we can return the favor. Sylvie could have dinner with us this week. Is there an afternoon you are free?" She forced herself to be cheerful.

"I don't have swimming Thursday," Sylvie replied. "Chris can drop me off here after school, couldn't you?" She turned eager eyes to her aunt.

"Sure." The tall blond smiled agreeably.

"That would be great." Caroline Barth seemed genuinely pleased at the prospect. "We could use a little fun in this house."

"See you Thursday, Mrs. Barth," Sylvie called. She waved as she followed Chris's movements and stepped toward the car at the curb. "Good night."

Halfway to the street Chris said under her breath, "I think we may be in for a bit of trouble." She continued on to the curb, opened the driver's-side door, and let Sylvie slide through to the passenger seat.

"I can handle it, Chris. Really," Sylvie protested.

"That's not the trouble I mean." Chris eased in beside her and thrust the key into the ignition. "Don't turn around—but Michael's car just turned the corner." Chris guided her sports car out into the traffic without glancing back. Mike's blue Ford pulled to the curb in front of the Barth residence.

"Maybe he didn't see us," Sylvie said hopefully.

"Two blonds in a silver convertible—" Chris sighed. "I don't think we're that lucky, my friend."

"Well, what if he did see us?" Sylvie asked, frowning.

"Then I'll have some explaining to do," Chris replied grimly.

"It won't be the first time," the younger one consoled her.

"No, but I care about this human. That complicates things considerably," Chris sighed.

"It will be all right." Sylvie patted Chris's hand on the wheel. "Really, it will be all right."

At nine thirty the quiet knock on the door drew Chris's attention from the stack of homework papers she was grading. Quietly she crossed the room. "Michael?" she called, guessing.

"Yeah, it's me."

"I thought you were working tonight." She pulled open the door and smiled at him.

"I am," he said flatly. "I came by to see you about some business." He shifted uneasily in the doorway.

"Come in," Chris whispered. "Let's talk in the kitchen. I'll get you some tea."

Mike followed her in silence. He leaned against the counter watching her deposit the full kettle on the burner, then lift cups and saucers from the cabinet.

"So tell me about it," he said finally.

"About what?" Chris concentrated on measuring the tea leaves into the metal oval tea steeper.

"About being at Marsha Barth's house earlier tonight."

"Oh." Chris shrugged. "Sylvie met Jenny Barth Saturday afternoon at the roller rink and I invited her to watch the practice and eat dinner with us."

"And you didn't mention it to me." Fuller watched her closely.

"No," Chris answered. "Was there some reason I

should have brought it up?" She turned her steady green gaze to meet his.

"It just seems curious." Mike's jawline tensed as he pressed the issue. "You're with me when the Barth girl is killed; you get real chummy with the witness, Angela Jackson; you get upset over the Lolita newspaper articles; and now suddenly you're big buddies with the dead girl's sister."

"Not big buddies," Chris replied coolly. "Just friends."

"Well, whatever you call it," Mike countered impatiently, "it just seems a bit more than coincidental."

"I'm not sure what you're driving at." Chris turned to retrieve the steaming kettle from the burner. Deliberately she poured the hot water into the teapot.

"I want to know what you're up to," Mike demanded. "I have the distinct impression that you are poking your nose into my business—police business."

Chris motioned for him to sit at the table. Efficiently she placed the teapot and cups between them.

"Well, what do you have to say?" Mike grumbled.

"Nothing," Chris said flatly. "What can I say? I met the girl . . . Sylvie and I like her. We're friends." She raised her eyes to his. "Sylvie and I are allowed to choose our own friends, aren't we?"

"I'd rather you chose someone not connected with one of my cases," he shot back. "I'll take care of my business myself."

"You are taking care of the case," Chris acknowledged. "I'm a friend of the survivors."

"You aren't trying to dig up something about the poor kid's sex life, are you?"

"You mean the poor kid who is dead—or the one who is still living?" Chris responded icily.

Mike expelled a long breath. "I was afraid you were up to something," he groaned. "You've gotta stay out of this, Chris. It's my business, not yours."

"I think things are becoming overly tense between us." Chris lowered her voice. "I don't function well with a supervisor. I don't intend to seek permission or approval for whatever I choose to do. I'm not interfering in *your* business, Michael. You are interfering in *mine*. Perhaps it would be easier if we stopped seeing each other."

Fuller opened his mouth in protest. Chris reached across the table to rest her cool hand over his.

"But . . . Chris . . ." he breathed.

"I love you, Michael," she said sadly. "I have so much that I must do. Loving you only complicates things. I just don't think we can work this out." For several long seconds Mike looked down at her slender fingers on his hand.

"Chris, I simply don't like you butting into my work. I don't butt into yours. I understand that you'd like to do something to help these people, but you're interfering in police business. I can't let you do that. Please don't drag a professional dispute into our personal lives—they're separate issues." He caught her hand between his larger, rougher ones.

"Michael, I'm not that compartmentalized," she declared softly. "Everything all runs together for me. I don't want to upset you, but I can't comply with your hands-off instructions. Jenny Barth needs a friend. She has Sylvie now—and I'm part of the package deal." She paused. Mike looked up from their hands. "Michael, she's got some big problems in her life. Sylvie and I can make a difference. You

can get along without us. I don't think Jenny can. I'd rather break off our relationship now than see you so unhappy."

"I don't want to get along without you," Mike argued. "You make me feel good . . . alive . . . and peaceful." He reached out and wiped away the single tear that trickled down Chris's cheek. "Please—don't do this to us," he said huskily. "Don't do this." He stared at her graceful tanned arms, now lying limp on the table. The uncharacteristic droop of her wide shoulders made his own eyes fill with tears.

"Look, next week I go back on the day shift and school ends for you. Things will seem a lot less hectic then. It's been rough on both of us lately. I know the Lolita stuff in the papers has you upset. With Sylvie feeling sick and school grinding to a halt for the year, maybe you're a bit depressed. We'll work out our problems—but don't cut yourself off from me." He stroked her pale gold hair. "Don't leave me alone. I don't want a life without you, Chris."

She raised her head and regarded him thoughtfully. Her green eyes were still distant and inscrutable. "I think we both need to take a little while to think things over," she said finally. "Just a few days. I'm going to the beach this weekend. I'll call when I get back."

The teapot sat untouched between them in the soft circle of light. They were on opposite sides of the table, only their fingers touching. Finally Mike patted her hand. "Can I see you Sunday night?" he asked quietly. Chris nodded wearily.

Without another word Fuller eased out of his chair. He glanced down at the lowered head with golden hair spilling over the shoulders. Quietly he headed toward the front door, pausing momentari-

ly to glance into the dim living room. The basket of seashells sat on one end of the mantel. The alabaster pelican still perched on the driftwood on the other end. The gold candelabrum was nowhere in the room.

A slight movement over his right shoulder caught his eye. Chris now stood in the kitchen alcove watching him as he surveyed her sanctuary.

"Just looking." Fuller shrugged. "I like the room." His voice trailed off uncertainly.

"So do I," Chris said softly.

"Well, I'd better get back to work. You take it easy." He tried to sound cheerful. "Get some rest. I'll see you late Sunday."

Chris nodded as he pulled the door shut behind him. Solemnly she walked toward the bedroom where Sylvie lay sleeping. For several minutes she stood at Sylvie's bedside, staring at the slight form beneath the covers.

She reached down and brushed a stray strand of pale gold hair from the young one's cheek. "Perhaps you are not ready after all," Chris sighed sadly. "You are brave—but you are just a child." She pulled the soft covers up to the young one's chin, resting her hand on Sylvie's shoulder.

Sylvie had sent the last dream to Ralph Taggert on Sunday night. While Fuller had lain asleep and oblivious in Chris's bed, the young one and her mentor had lighted the single taper and made the circle of shells. Pallid but resolute, Sylvie had performed the last ritual—the third serpent dream. She had completed her part, hopeful that the ancient warning would save Lauri Taggert from further violation.

Now, as Chris crouched beside her ward, large tears slowly trailed down her cheeks. Tomorrow she would have to teach Sylvie the saddest lesson. She

would teach the young one that eventually the man's fear would dissipate—and when that occurred, he was likely to turn to his child again. Sylvie would have to be ready for the powerful depression that would follow. As a guardian she would feel for the first time the anguish of the sisterhood—and in that moment of anguish she would have to act alone.

"Did you see the paper?" Traci Callazo called out to Chris.

"No, why?" Chris stood waist deep in the rec center pool, disconnecting the float rope that divided the pool between four- and six-foot depths. "Something good or something bad?" She shaded her eyes with a hand and peered up at Traci.

"The Lolita case." Traci held out the evening paper. "The grand jury indicted the guy."

"So?" Chris waited apprehensively.

"For manslaughter," Traci said grimly, "not for murder. 'If he is convicted,'" she read from the paper, "'manslaughter carries a maximum of twenty-one years, but with mitigating circumstances the term can be suspended or reduced by good behavior.'"

"I doubt that Bertram Willis will find any sixteen-year-old girls to knife in prison, so his behavior should be very good indeed," Chris muttered angrily as she looped the rope over her arm. "So we can all relax, knowing that justice will triumph." She stalked through the water, pulling the rope out of the pool and slamming it down beside the locker room door.

"I'm sorry." Traci patted her shoulder. "I know it was Mike's case. I'll bet he's disappointed. I just thought you'd better know before you saw him. Is he coming to the meet tonight?"

"He's still on the evening shift. I doubt if I'll see him tonight." Chris concentrated on folding a stack of extra towels.

"Well, tell him I'm sorry whenever you do see him," Traci added. "I sure wish I knew what made the jury settle for the lesser charge. I wonder if the newspaper stuff had any impact."

"If Marsha Barth had still been a high school student, living at home and attending club meetings—if she'd been killed in a shop downtown or on the school grounds—it would have been different," Chris said evenly. "But put a sixteen-year-old runaway in the back hall of a bar, and suddenly you have another picture. It's not the crime but the victim who is judged. She—not Willis—was on trial." Her hands trembled in anger.

"You want to swim a few laps and cool off?" Traci suggested. "The kids will be here in about fifteen minutes. You need to calm down before they show up."

"Good idea," Chris conceded.

"Well, I'll get the stuff inside," Traci volunteered. "You burn off some calories." Traci hoisted the buoy rope and ducked into the locker room.

Chris strode to the end of the longer span of the L-shaped pool, hesitated a moment, then bent low, her muscles tense. With a sudden explosion of energy she sprang out well over the water in a racing dive, then pierced the surface of the light blue pool. That single dive thrust her forward through the entire length of the span. With exquisite precision she executed a flip turn, lightly rippling the pool surface, then returned to where she had begun without drawing a single breath. Again the perfect flip, this time bringing her even with the surface as her long, slender arms sliced through the water and

a swirling wake spread out behind. Midway through her fourth lap the water directly ahead of her erupted as something hit the surface.

"You said we were never to do that here." The wide eyes of Sylvie Martin were leveled at her. "You said we had to do it just like them," she reprimanded Chris. "You were going far too fast . . . and you weren't breathing like they do."

Chris was nodding. "You're right . . . you're right."

"Mr. Rambo is on his way in here. I didn't think he should see you like that," she said, grinning, "so I decided to drop in." Her pale green eyes narrowed suspiciously. "What's the matter? Why are you upset? It isn't like you to make mistakes."

"Just a little tense," Chris answered vaguely. "Let's do a couple of laps together—and this time I'll go slowly." She smiled. Side by side the two blonds glided the length of the pool, stroking evenly so that neither one inched ahead or fell behind. They halted by the end ladder after three laps, then crawled out of the pool to sprawl on the ledge so the sun could warm them.

Burt Rambo had crossed the pool area to retrieve a long low table. As official timekeeper and record keeper for the informal meet, Burt was making himself comfortable.

"I had to bring my own pencils too." Rambo directed the comment to the two sunbathing blonds. Sylvie looked up and laughed at the big man with the table balanced above his head. Rambo simply winked and kept walking. He finally deposited the table near the starting blocks, then strode off into the locker room in pursuit of something else.

"He's funny," Sylvie said, giggling, as she lowered her head back onto her arms.

"He's also smart," Chris noted. "So thanks for the warning. He already seems to think I'm a little strange. I don't want to give him more spectacular evidence." She reached out and rested a hand on Sylvie's cheek. "I don't think we will be here much longer," she confided. "It's almost time to move on."

"So we keep a low profile." Sylvie guessed what would come next.

"Right. And we honor our commitments."

"Right." Sylvie smiled. "Will you go with me on the next mission?"

"I'm not sure." Chris shrugged. "I haven't decided where my next mission will be." They settled back down side by side in the sun. Moments later the giggles and excited chatter of early arrivals echoed in the locker room. Metal doors slammed and showers sprayed as the young girls changed from school clothes to swimsuits.

"So much for tranquillity." Chris slapped Sylvie's fanny. "Time to get going, my friend."

Arm in arm they headed into the locker room to greet the young swimmers. Outside Burt Rambo lined up three chairs by the officials' table, dumped a pocketful of pencils on the clipboard, and sat clutching the stopwatch and scanning the list of events while he fiddled with the button on the clock. There would be more spectators tonight. This swimming session would end when school ended, so most of the parents would make an effort to watch this meet.

Rambo smiled at the first few girls who emerged from the locker room. Wide-eyed and somber, they scanned the bleachers for familiar faces, then grinned when they spotted their particular fans. He watched the serene Sylvie and her sandy-haired

friend Lauri Taggert zigzag through the cluster of youngsters and then station themselves slightly apart from the others.

She could take 'em, Rambo thought of the young blond swimmer. *She could take 'em all if she wanted to.* But Sylvie always finished second—effortlessly, without shortness of breath, without spectacle.

Even from his side of the pool Rambo could see the glimmer of the golden shell the child wore. *Generation upon generation,* he mused. *Timeless change. Immortality.* He pursed his lips in thought. Nautilus . . . pelican . . . children. Touching, circling, and touching again, one upon the other the images floated to the surface, then settled to submerge and mingle in the flow of thought. Rambo smiled and shrugged, directing his full attention to the dark-haired coach approaching with a clipboard. Then a final specter surfaced: the gray papier-mâché Hand of Glory in the window of the magic shop. "Chris has one . . ." Fuller had said. "Hers is pretty, though."

Rambo's pale gray eyes shifted once more to Sylvie.

"You ready to score?" Traci's cheerful voice interrupted his contemplation.

"Is that a proposition?" Rambo smiled up at the petite coach.

"Weird, Burt. You are really weird." Traci shook her head and shoved neatly columned pages in front of him.

"I'm also ready to keep score." He sat upright, dutifully clasping his pencil in one hand and the stopwatch in the other. "By the way," he added casually, "at precisely nine twenty-three this evening, in the laundry room of the Riverside apartment complex, I intend to propose to you. I'd

appreciate your cooperation in making the procedure as smooth and efficient as possible." He kept his eyes riveted on the pages before him on the table. "I mean a real proposal—diamond ring and everything. Nine twenty-three."

Traci stood motionless, staring at him, for several seconds. "Fine," she said finally. "I'll be there."

"Bring your tennis shoes." Rambo looked up shyly. "One if it's no, two if it's yes."

Traci smiled at him; then her chin began to quiver.

"Nine twenty-three," Rambo said, dismissing her. "Remember the code."

Traci straightened and sniffed, then turned back toward the lineup. "OK, you guys," she called with a slight catch in her voice. "Let's get this show on the road."

Sylvie sat up in bed and peered toward the window. The pink shutters were closed and the shade was drawn, but the bright morning sun shot narrow streams of light across the floor. On the far side of the bed, Lauri Taggert lay asleep, half-covered by the flowered sheet. Sylvie eased out of bed and padded toward the adjoining bathroom, tugging shut the door.

"Christina will be so angry," Sylvie groaned as she stared at her reflection in the mirror, remembering what had led up to this.

Lauri's folks had come to the swim meet with brother Robbie in tow. Afterward Marion Taggert had sought out Chris and Sylvie. "Whatever you two have done to make Lauri more self-confident, I really want to thank you," the brown-haired woman had said. "I don't know if it's the swimming or just being around you, but I've noticed quite a

change in my daughter. She's simply a lot happier."

Sylvie had spoken before with the thin-faced woman and had responded automatically, with childlike politeness. But as she stood in the steamy locker room with the odor of chlorine swirling about and the echoing laughter of the young girls filling her ears, Sylvie had studied the woman carefully. Marion Taggert's hands fluttered as she spoke. Her dark eyes, so much like Lauri's, shifted anxiously from Sylvie to Chris, then off toward the showers where Lauri had disappeared.

"You really don't know how much I appreciate your efforts with Lauri," Marion Taggert had repeated. "Ever since I went back to work she's been a little withdrawn. But you know how the economy is, and Ralph and I always dreamed of fixing up an old house." The explanations and apologies tumbled out. "We got in a little over our heads," she continued, smiling nervously, "so I went to work. Robbie doesn't seem to mind at all. We have a nice neighbor who sits with him. He has a nursery school . . ." She hesitated. "But Lauri hasn't adjusted too well—at least until lately." Her dark eyes returned to Chris. "I do intend to sign her up for the next swimming session, and I hope now that school's ending, Sylvie will come over any time she can."

Chris had nodded and smiled sympathetically throughout Marion Taggert's narrative. Sylvie had moved closer to the woman, so that occasionally Mrs. Taggert's hand would come to rest on her shoulder.

Chris had finally gotten a few words in. "We enjoy Lauri. She and Sylvie have brought out a lot in each other," she had said with an affectionate glance in Sylvie's direction.

"Perhaps—" Mrs. Taggert had started, paused, then gone on. "Perhaps if you two aren't committed somewhere else, we could all go out together for dinner. We were going to celebrate anyway," she asserted. "I just received a little promotion. Tomorrow I'm going to Atlanta with the buyer from our shop. She's training me to take over the junior department."

"Well, congratulations," Chris had said, grinning. "That's really wonderful."

"Would you be our guests for dinner? I'd love to have some time to visit with you two. Perhaps Sylvie could even stay the night," she had ended hopefully.

"I'd love to"—Chris had shrugged—"but I have some work to do here and I'd planned to turn in early." She had glimpsed the disappointment in Marion Taggert's face. "However, if Sylvie feels up to it," Chris had conceded, "she can go along. If you've got an extra pair of pajamas, she can stay the night. Tomorrow we're going to visit relatives at the beach. Sylvie can recuperate there."

Alone in the bathroom, Sylvie stared at the dark circles under her eyes. "Boy, do I need recuperating," she muttered. "Too much dinner, too many Cokes, and too many doughnuts," she chanted, reciting her vices.

"Purify your body," Chris had warned her.

"Am I in trouble," Sylvie sighed.

Hesitantly she crossed the bedroom and retrieved her clothes. She tiptoed back into the bathroom, stripped off the borrowed pajamas and sponged her naked body with warm water. Then she dressed slowly, dreading the appraisal that would come when Chris arrived. As she crouched to tie her tennis shoes, Sylvie heard footsteps.

Cautiously she cracked the bathroom door and peeked into the dim bedroom.

"Lauri, honey," Ralph Taggert called softly at the bedroom door. "Daddy loves you, baby." He crossed the room and settled onto the bed beside the sleeping child. "Lauri, baby doll," he cooed, slowly stroking her hair to wake her.

Lauri stretched and rolled onto one side, then jerked her head back to stare up at him. He was unshaven and red-eyed. Apparently his celebration had lasted long after everyone else had retired.

Lauri opened her mouth to speak, but Taggert pressed his hand over it. "Shhh. Robbie is downstairs watching TV. Your mom has already left for Atlanta. I locked your door," he whispered. "It's all right, baby." Lauri's wide eyes shifted to the vacant space beside her, then across the room to the chair where Sylvie's clothes had been. Slowly Taggert moved his hand from Lauri's lips to her shoulder.

"No, Daddy," she said firmly. "I mean it. No."

Taggert, bleary and hung over, began massaging her shoulder. Abruptly Lauri rolled away and climbed out the opposite side of the bed.

"I'm going to the bathroom," she stated without looking back. "Just go away—please."

Lauri pulled open the bathroom door just as Sylvie raised a finger over her lips to commit them both to silence. The door slammed shut behind the child and Sylvie turned the lock.

"I can handle this," Sylvie whispered, embracing Lauri. "You will wait here," she told her friend, "and you will not remember." She pressed her open palms against Lauri's temples and stared into her eyes. Then she placed the still child on the closed commode.

"Baby doll." Taggert's whine came through the

bathroom door. "Lauri, baby. Daddy needs you, honey. Come on out, baby," he coaxed. He stood there, his forehead pressed against the wooden door as he spoke. "You know I'd never do anything to hurt you, baby."

Finally the door lock clicked. Taggert straightened and stepped back expectantly. Slowly the door swung toward him. Ralph Taggert stared into cold green eyes.

"Oh—Sylvie. I forgot you were here . . ." he floundered. "I just wanted—"

The green eyes transfixed him. Below them the firm, straight mouth parted over clenched white teeth. Taggert momentarily seemed bewildered, as if some memory had floated to his consciousness. In a shudder of comprehension his left hand dropped to his crotch, but he was intact.

Sylvie stepped out, closing the bathroom door behind her. She chanted softly, pacing around him in a wide arc, compelling him to turn and face her. Methodically she breathed the ancient melody while Taggert's hands fell listlessly to his sides. She grasped the bottom of her T-shirt, tugged it over her head, and dropped it onto the floor. She reached back and unhooked the small beige brassiere that covered her slight breasts. Then she crossed her arms, pressing her right wrist upon her naked chest. Still humming, she began to breathe, inhaling and exhaling in regular, rhythmic beats.

Taggert stared, unable to move or look away. The green eyes became luminous—distant and implacable. The room seemed to expand and contract with the rhythm of the wordless music. Taggert watched the rise and fall of her chest as she breathed deeply. He could not take his eyes away. Then it happened. He saw the flesh of her bosom

begin to fade like a pale mist until the ribs, then the lung beneath, were visible, along with the oval heart, pounding out the rhythm of her song.

Then the air began to shift around him, sliding away toward the rows of gleaming teeth. A slow, steady hissing grew louder as Taggert's own heart thudded faster. Gasping for breath, he wheezed noisily. Then the hissing faltered, resumed, and faltered again.

Desperately Taggert bellowed. The creature fell silent. Taggert broke for the door, twisting the lock open and then slamming into the doorjamb as he fled. The chant began again, sweeping from the bedroom into the hallway, pursuing the screaming man. At the head of the stairway Taggert glanced back. The creature was on the upper landing, staring at him, grinning. With a final shriek Taggert lurched down the stairs, half falling, half rolling. Huddled on the lowest step, he crouched with knees pulled to his chest, his hands between his thighs clutching his genitals. Sobbing loudly, he rocked back and forth, hollow-eyed and rigid.

"You'd better come over right away." Sylvie's voice came shakily over the telephone. "Something went wrong."

"Are you all right?" Chris demanded. "What's the matter, Sylvie?"

"Mr. Taggert came into Lauri's room," Sylvie whispered. "I tried to do it," she sobbed, "but I couldn't do it right."

Chris gasped. "Did he hurt you? Is Lauri all right?"

"We're OK. He can't hurt anyone now. He's just sitting downstairs and rocking. Chris, he's crazy—*really* crazy. He's lost his mind."

"I'll call the police when I get there," Chris said, taking over. "You get the kids away from him. Keep them away. I'll be right over. It will be OK, Sylvie," she reassured her ward. "It will be all right."

"I tried your apartment last night." Fuller stood in the hallway outside Chris's classroom, deliberately keeping his voice hushed.

"Sylvie and I stayed at the beach with Elena. I just drove in this morning for school." Her voice conveyed a weariness that contrasted with her pinkish gold tan. "I guess you heard about Lauri's father."

"No, something wrong?" Fuller arched his brows.

"Do the signals ten-fifteen and one-oh-three-M mean anything to you?" she asked.

"Prisoner—mental case—some kind of disturbance. The guy flipped out?"

"With three children in the house. I called the police and they came to take him to the hospital."

"That's grim," Fuller said softly. "Everyone else all right?"

"Sylvie isn't too good. The whole episode really upset her. Lauri doesn't remember much of it. Robbie was in the back of the house watching cartoons. He didn't know what was going on until just before the police arrived." Chris stepped to the classroom door and glanced in at the twenty-eight students bent over their mimeographed examination sheets. She watched them for a few seconds, then returned to Mike's side of the hall. "Mrs. Taggert came back from Atlanta and took over. She did really well. Anyway," Chris sighed, "Sylvie and I had to get away. I'm sorry about last night."

"No problem," Fuller assured her. "As long as

you're OK. I just wanted to check on you." He fell silent and shifted feet awkwardly, waiting for her to speak.

"I've got two more swimming sessions," she said finally, "just today and Wednesday. Then school's out and the swimming class ends. Could you wait until Thursday, Michael? We can talk then. Right now I'm stretched a bit thin. I've got to finish up here and get back to Sylvie and . . ."

Fuller was nodding agreeably. "Sure, I understand. You've got your hands full. Just let me know if there's anything you need, anything I can do. Call the station if you need me." He stepped closer and grasped her shoulders, holding her until she raised her eyes to meet his. "You don't have to do everything yourself, you know," he said earnestly. "You could lean on me once in a while—just to remind yourself that you're human. Wonder Woman is for the comic books, Chris."

The sound of multiple footsteps in the adjoining hallway made him release her. "If you need me—" he reminded her. A trio of students, each carrying a stack of test papers to deliver to a teacher, turned into the hallway and stared with interest at the blond teacher and her tall, curly-haired companion.

"Good morning, Miss Martin," the youngsters chimed as they passed, trying not to grin at the twosome.

"Good morning," Chris replied, then waited while the three continued down the hallway. Once more her eyes shifted to her classroom, where her students were still diligently at work.

"I'll let you get to your class," Fuller said. "I've got to get back to the station. I'm on days again," he added pointedly.

"Oh, by the way." Chris turned abruptly to face

him. "I'm sorry about the manslaughter indictment on Willis. You were hoping for something more severe, weren't you?"

Fuller shrugged. "I'm a cop, not a lawyer. I just do the investigating. The DA's staff decides about the rest. But it'll do; we settle for whatever we can get." The weak smile Fuller mustered drooped unconvincingly.

"Sure." Chris tried to sound understanding. "See you later," she whispered.

Fuller stood alone in the vacant hallway for several seconds after Chris disappeared into her room. Finally he turned toward the end doorway leading to the parking lot.

"Taggert," he muttered, remembering the pretty sandy-haired girl who had become Sylvie's friend.

"How's blondie?" George Parsons greeted him at the car.

"You're not gonna believe this one," Fuller told him, ducking the question. "Chris had to call in a nut case this weekend—the old man of one of her kids."

"Nice friend you've got. She hangs out with cops and loonies. She ain't into whips and chains or anything kinky, is she?"

Fuller frowned and slid in next to Parsons. "Nothing kinky," he protested lamely.

"Too bad," Parsons muttered as he shoved the gearshift into drive. "I once knew a girl—"

"I don't want to hear about it," Fuller groaned, a slight smile playing at the corners of his mouth. "Just head for the station, smartass."

In France the tale is told of *mère* Lucine, or Melusine, the spirit of the fountain at Lusignan. Melusine was the only daughter of the fairy Pressine and the river spirit Fleuve. While Pressine was off in a meadow stringing together chains of wild flowers, Melusine dallied by the side of the river. Fleuve approached his daughter and tried to entice her into the water. Melusine waded into the cool river up to her waist. Fleuve tried to lure her in farther.

"Come beneath the rippling surface," he invited her. "Come with me."

Melusine began to back away toward the river's edge, but Fleuve swirled the water around and tried to sweep her under the currents. Melusine grasped a branch from an overhanging tree and pulled herself to safety. In fright she fled into a mountain cave. Fleuve followed her there, but once he was inside, he could not see her. With her magic powers Melusine slipped by him. Outside she spoke to the mountain, seeking its aid. With a massive rumble the cavernous mouth of the cave closed tight, sealing Fleuve within.

When Pressine returned, she demanded to know where her husband had gone. Melusine told her the story but refused to release Fleuve from his prison. In anger Pressine decreed that on one night each week Melusine would be transformed into a serpent from the waist down. She would be spared from this transformation if she could find a husband who would never seek to view her in her changed state.

At length Melusine met a young man who agreed to marry her and obey that prohibition: he would never look upon her on that night each week. Her husband, Raymond of Poitiers, became rich and powerful due to her wise counsel. With her magic she built the castle of Lusignan and many other fortresses for the Lusignan family. Raymond's happiness was complete, except for his increasing curiosity over the secret ritual his wife forbade him to witness.

One night when Melusine had withdrawn into her private quarters to pass the night alone, Raymond could no longer resist. While she bathed in scented waters, Raymond stole into her chamber. Concealed by a curtain, he peered into her bath and saw the deformity of her lower body. With a chilling shriek, Melusine flew into the air, still in serpent form, and fled from him forever.

From that time on she has been known as the protectress of the house of Lusignan, an invisible creature who haunts the fountain and heralds the death of any Lusignan with a mournful cry. Her name is often invoked in childbirth when an expectant mother cries out in pain. Melusine's reply is heard in the first breath of the newborn.

CHAPTER 9

❖❖❖❖❖❖❖

I have learned
To look on nature, not as in the hour
Of thoughtless youth; but hearing often-times
The still, sad music of humanity . . .
—WORDSWORTH

Four mature females sat cross-legged in a circle of
shells while the sea wind swept into the room. Each
wore the symbols of her power: the ring of pearl, the
serpent bracelet, the golden shell. Each had placed
her summons—a single feather from a seabird—
upon the naked figure in their midst.

"I misjudged the situation," Christina confessed
before they commenced the ritual. "She was not
ready for such an ordeal." Her melancholy voice
caused all eyes to shift to their youngest member.

"*We* misjudged the situation," Elena, the eldest,
corrected her. "We all assumed she was ready to act
alone. In our eagerness we miscalculated. She simply lacked the judgment to resist human tempta-
tions. Her system is not that resilient." Elena spoke
without censure, only with sorrow. "Sylvie will stay
with me here until she is well. Then she will begin
again as a contact—only an intermediary—until
she is more mature. There is no fault here," Elena
continued, turning to Christina, "that is not shared.
We must all learn from this."

"I still feel responsible," Chris said.

"We all feel responsible. You did not advance her

189

to the sisterhood alone," Elena reminded her proté-
gée. "We all agreed. We were overly eager. Each of
us becomes so overwhelmed by our own contacts in
the human realm. Their time moves by so quickly.
Like minnows in a stream, bright flashes of silver,
they pass by us. We can only save a very few from
the predators. Sometimes, in our distress, we get
caught up in the current. Then we make mistakes."
She reached out and touched Christina.

"There are more children than we can reach,"
Elena said evenly. "It is the acuteness of their pain,
the urgency of their needs, that tugs at us. Sylvie
insisted she was ready. She pushed herself because
the friend she loved was in danger. No one could
have known that Sylvie was too vulnerable to
withstand emotional pressures. No one could have
known that her powers of concentration were not
sufficiently strong."

The others nodded in understanding. Each one's
first encounter had been harrowing indeed.

"We must keep our human attributes in check,"
Elena cautioned them. "Our human fathers gave us
the capacity for anger, frustration, jealousy—even
the desire for revenge. But they also gave us the
wonder of human longing and a sense of kindness
and humor. However, it is with our mothers' traits
that we must rule our choices. Our actions must not
be dictated by transient emotion. This time the
boundaries were indistinct and we acted unwisely.
As a result we will have to continue without Sylvie's
help for quite some time. She must retreat from
human influence. She must draw from our strength.
She must rest and contemplate."

"I think Christina needs to rest also," Katie said.
Her narrowed eyes inspected the pallid face of the
one next to her in the circle.

"You are weary?" Elena's inquiry drew a silent nod. "How soon can you complete your commitments in this place?"

"I have Jenny Barth," Chris replied. "Once she is safe I will be ready to move on."

"What steps have you taken to protect the child?" Elena asked.

"I have eased the grief of the mother," Chris answered quietly. "I have given her some comfort for the loss of her child, and perhaps increased her strength so she can transform her sorrow into a closer bond with the daughter who needs her now." Christina's tone became more chilling. "I have sent the second dream to the father. For the moment that has deterred him from further advances. He has not manipulated the child into any genital contact, but the preliminaries had begun." The solemn recitation needed no further clarification. The tale had been reiterated with few modifications throughout their time.

"What work remains at your school? What other responsibilities continue in your human role?"

Chris shrugged. "My classes ended today. So did this session of swimming. I simply have to clear out my schoolroom and file some records. I will be finished with everything by Friday."

"And Sylvie's friend," Elena said. "What about the Taggert child, Lauri?"

"I have helped her understand. She will not blame herself for the crimes of her father, nor for the condition in which he remains. Humans are quite tolerant of aberrations of the mind," she noted with a rueful smile. "Particularly once the offender is no longer in a position to do them harm."

"The Taggert man is no threat to anyone," Katie

interjected. "He is being held in our hospital for observation for ten days. I have seen him and I have seen the preliminary reports. The man has become catatonic. He is to be transferred to a permanent institution."

"So that leaves your Jenny Barth," Elena concluded.

"And Michael . . ." Alicia said.

Elena nodded. "Yes—Michael Fuller. What will you do about Michael?" Her noncommittal gaze settled on Chris.

"I can leave him," Chris replied quietly.

"Knowing that before you do, you must take from him all memory of your existence. Will that be so easy to do?" Elena asked, pressing the issue. "He loves you, Christina."

"I know." Chris lowered her eyes to the floor.

"And you love him?"

"I do."

"So leaving him is but one of the choices open to you," Elena observed. "Have you eliminated the other possibilities?"

Two glistening rivulets inched their way down her cheeks. Slowly Chris shook her head.

"You are still undecided," Elena said.

"You could bear his child," Alicia suggested. "You could create a daughter who could one day replace you."

"She knows what can be done," Elena said, hushing the younger one. "She also understands the consequences. Let her consider them in peace. The choice is hers, not ours."

"But if she loves him?" Alicia persisted. Elena raised her eyebrows in disapproval.

"If she loves him, the choice is difficult indeed," Katie asserted. "It is a commitment to one part of

our nature that requires a sacrifice of the other. You have not reached that moment, Alicia. Do not force it upon others prematurely."

"As we did in Sylvie's case," Elena said, resuming command of the discussion. "Caution, my sisters. Caution. We must all proceed with discretion. For now, we must combine our efforts in ministering to Sylvie."

The four pale-haired females fell silent, clasping each other hand to hand, closing the circle within the circle. Eyes closed, lips parted, they breathed in unison, summoning the sea wind to restore the young one. Each creature inhaled as the wind grew more intense, then each expelled her breath in an even, unseen stream that mingled with the breath of the others and swirled softly about the young one who lay in their midst.

Much later one of them would carry the child to bed and stay with her through the night, cradling her gently, singing to her softly, so the night dreams would not come.

The gray fog hung above the sea grass, which rustled in the night breeze. The woman hesitated at the far end of the wooden pier. Then she plunged silently beneath the inky surface of the Atlantic. Sleek ridges continued to roll toward the shore, collapsing into white rows of frothy sea foam illuminated by the moonlight filtering through the fog.

A second figure, white-haired and robed in ivory, crossed the boardwalk and strode along the coarse sand. She stood at the water's edge waiting, while somewhere beyond the pier the first one swam unseen and alone. After a few moments the white-robed female stepped into the gentle waves, extend-

ing her right hand out over the water. She clasped a feather, which she moved in a circle above the water. Then she whispered an ancient word of summons and let the feather drift from her grasp onto the surface of a receding wave. She lowered her hand and waited once more.

Far out beyond the pier the blond-haired woman emerged above the swell of an incoming wave and began swimming steadily in to the shore.

"Something is wrong?" Chris asked as she waded toward the older woman.

"Your Michael called," Elena replied grimly. "Jenny Barth's father is dead. He shot himself this afternoon—in Marsha's bedroom." There was no triumph in the creature's voice, only a hint of weariness.

Motionless, Chris stood ankle deep in the sea foam. Water trickled down her bare arms. In the moonlight and mist she seemed like an ancient sculpture, shaped from marble. She closed her eyes, knowing what Elena would now tell her.

"Christina," Elena said softly, "your sojourn here can now end. There is no need to send a dream tonight. It is finished."

Chris opened her eyes to see Elena's slender hand extended toward her. "Come," Elena whispered. Chris reached out and clasped the hand, letting the one who had been her mentor lead her from the water. Elena wrapped a large towel over Chris's shoulders, holding it in place as they walked toward the house. Side by side they moved soundlessly along the boardwalk. Only the whisper of the sea grass and the rhythmic rush of the waves broke the silence of the night.

The Norsemen knew the Valkyries, ferocious goddesses, helmeted in gold and bearing spears tipped in flame. The Valkyries were the dispensers of destiny. Warriors courted their favor, since these creatures could grant victory or defeat in any conflict. They soared above the heads of warriors in battle, protecting those they chose and taking to Valhalla—the great hall of the immortals—the heroes who must perish.

The Valkyries were also gracious and exquisite beings who, in swan plumage, could float through the air or glide upon isolated lakes and pools.

The Valkyrie Kara stopped by a cool lake to refresh herself. Casting aside her swan plumage, she dived into the clear blue water. As she swam beneath the surface, the warrior Helgi passed that way and found the abandoned plumage. Immediately he recognized the garment of a Valkyrie and knew that he could keep the swan maiden captive and make her obey his commands. A Valkyrie was compelled to obey any man who possessed her feathery cloak.

195

However, when Kara emerged from the depths of the lake, Helgi was so enchanted by her beauty that he returned her plumage. He would not force obedience from so lovely a creature.

Touched by Helgi's tender sentiment, Kara was overwhelmed with love for the warrior. She could not bear to be parted from him. They vowed eternal faithfulness.

Kara accompanied Helgi into every battle and on every hunt. Soaring above him, she would sing so sweetly that his enemy would lay down his arms and fail to resist. The beasts on the hunt would forget to flee, so glad were they to stand and be charmed by Kara's songs.

One day, in the fiercest throes of battle, Kara flew too near the affray in an attempt to protect her beloved Helgi. He raised his broad sword to strike his adversary, but his blade pierced Kara's breast. Her final cry was sorrowful and beautiful; her swan song moved the warrior to tears.

Helgi took the dead creature to a still lake and let her slip slowly beneath the water. As he stood mourning at the water's edge, Helgi cast his sword into the lake, yielding his title of warrior. He watched the widening circles spreading from the spot wherein the sword had plunged and saw a pale hand rise above the center, holding aloft his battle sword. Once again his beloved Kara surfaced, bearing the prized weapon to her hero, restoring him to his rightful rank.

"Go bravely into battle," Kara whispered. "I am waiting to take you with me to the feasting place of Odin. Valhalla awaits you." With that she disappeared into the lake.

Helgi returned to battle with the ferocity of

velve men. Then at last, amid the clamor, he heard
.ara call his name. With a final cry of triumph
Ielgi bade farewell to his comrades to take his seat
mong the company of Valhalla, drinking mead
nd beer at Odin's feast. Once more he would be
·ith Kara.

CHAPTER 10

❖❖❖❖❖❖❖

"Miss Martin?" The clean-shaven young patrolma[n] stood in the classroom doorway, his peaked cap i[n] his hands.

"That's right." Chris stared at him apprehe[n] sively.

"A Katie Baker asked that someone contact yo[u] She was injured in a traffic accident—nothing t[o] serious," the young officer added hastily. "Just [a] couple of cuts. She's in the emergency ward [at] General." He smiled suddenly. "They'll really ta[ke] good care of her. She said she works there."

Chris grabbed her purse from behind a cardboar[d] box she was packing. "I'll go see her. I've got to s[ee] her," she insisted.

"You want me to drive you down there, ma'am?" the patrolman offered. "Don't want you racing o[ff] all upset—might end up with another collision."

Immediately Chris stopped. "I'll calm down," she said. "I can get there by myself." Assuming [a] more relaxed demeanor, Chris headed out the do[or] with the patrolman at her side. "I'll drive carefu[l] ly," she assured him after a deep breath. "I ju[st] want to be with her."

"Sure, that's real nice of you," the young ma[n]

id, keeping in step with her. "I'll drive along
head of you, though," he added, "just to see that
ou get there all right."

Once they reached the school parking lot the
fficer veered right to his blue and gray patrol car.
hris crossed to her little MG and pulled out
ehind him. One block from Savannah General,
hris stopped at the traffic light as the patrolman
anced into his rearview mirror. He smiled and
aved, then pulled into the left-turn lane. "You'll
e fine from here on," he called.

"Yeah, thanks." Chris waved in return, then
ulled ahead toward the hospital parking lot.

At the desk inside the double doorway of the
mergency room, Chris waited until the white-clad
urse returned to her post.

"Oh, you're Katie's cousin." The graying woman
miled. "Well, don't worry a bit. We just patched up
few cuts and boosted the blood supply. She's right
n here." The nurse led her to room A.

"How are you?" Chris looked closely at the blond
voman propped on the table. The only repair work
mmediately visible was a large white bandage over
Katie's left temple.

Katie flashed a welcoming smile. "A bit rough
round the edges," she replied. "Some guy in a
•ickup hit my car—and I hit the window. Just four
titches." She shrugged, looking up toward the
•andage. "However," she said, wrinkling her nose
nd pointing to her left leg, "I also caught my leg on
he handle of the emergency brake. Really sliced it
•pen."

Chris walked around the table to stare at the
welve-inch bandaged area.

"Twenty-one stitches—and a few pints of
•lood," Katie informed her.

The nurse waved and ducked out the door towar
her buzzing telephone.

"Blood?" Chris whispered. "You had a transfu
sion? Of *their* blood?"

Katie's brave smile wavered. "It would hav
looked odd if a nurse like myself had refused. Bu
keep cool, my dear." She cast a cautious eye at th
door. "They could detect no difference. Besides,
was just enough to keep me tap-dancing," she trie
to joke.

"Does Elena know?" Chris asked softly.

"You and I will have to tell her," Katie answered
"No sense in upsetting her now. What's done
done."

"Katie, what will this do to you?" Chris steppe
forward and clasped her hand. "The human bloo
I mean."

Katie pursed her lips in thought for a second
"Well, from the way I feel now, I'd say I'm out o
commission for a while. I'll come to the beach t
recuperate. They'll get someone to fill in for m
here," she said calmly. "But someone will have t
carry out my other commitments until my syster
returns to normal."

Chris opened her mouth to protest, then glance
once more at Katie's bandages. It was too late fc
words of caution. "So . . . OK," she conceded
"Can you go home yet?"

"It is normal procedure for them to stick me in
room for a few hours," Katie said. "Just as
precaution. I don't want to make a fuss. I don
want any more attention than I already have. Yo
just go on with your normal business. Call here thi
afternoon after you finish packing your school stuf
If I haven't any other ill effects, you can come an
get me."

"You're sure you don't want me to stay?" Chri

eyed her warily. "I don't want to leave you alone just now."

Katie smiled. "I'll hardly be alone. This place has a staff of over two hundred." Her smile faded as she added, "Just get back to school and close out your files. I'll be fine. I promise." Chris squeezed her hand. "Tonight, Chris, when we're with Elena, she'll tell us what needs to be done. I will transfer my commitments to one of you. For now, don't worry."

Chris obediently backed out, letting the heavy wooden door swing closed quietly.

"She's a tough cookie," the desk nurse said suddenly. "The doctors in the intensive care unit really love her. She never loses her cool. You can bet we're taking extra good care of her," the warm voice reassured her. "You give her a few hours to rest, then we'll have her ready to be moved. The X rays didn't show anything unusual, so there's no need to worry."

"X rays?" Chris breathed softly as she stepped toward the elevator. X rays. *What will X rays do to Katie's system*? Chris brooded as the elevator stopped at the ground floor. She walked slowly along the corridor past the cafeteria. In all the long years of human time Chris had lived, she could not recall any of their sisterhood being exposed to X rays. The infusion of human blood was serious enough. But X rays . . .

"You look like you could use a cup of coffee," the familiar voice said, stopping her.

"Michael!" Chris turned as Fuller loped out of the cafeteria toward her.

"What are you doing here? Something wrong?" he asked, examining her face. "Or are you just losing your tan?"

"Katie was hurt—a traffic accident."

"Bad?"

Chris started to speak, then pressed her lips together, struggling to retain her composure.

"Not bad," Mike guessed. "Not *too* bad?" He waited until she nodded. "You've really been having a hell of a time." He slid his arm around her shoulders. "Come on. Have a cup of coffee with me."

"I'd rather just walk outside," Chris answered.

"So we walk," Michael agreed. Still holding her, he swung around toward the exit. Chris slid her arm around his waist and eased closer to his large frame. With slow, even steps they strolled through the doorway, then along the flower-lined walkway that bordered the otherwise bleak premises of Savannah General.

"You want me to take you anywhere? Home? Lunch?"

"No, I've got some loose ends at school. I'll go back by myself."

"Will you be home tonight? I'll stop by," he offered hopefully.

"I don't think so, Michael. I've got to check on Katie later. I'm going to take her to the beach. Elena doesn't know yet."

"Speaking of not knowing, neither do I," he said, shifting subjects abruptly. "I know you've got a lot on your mind, but, Chris, you gotta talk to me about you and me. One way or the other. Something's gotta give."

"I need a little time, Michael," Chris protested quietly. "Just for things to calm down a bit."

"Things never do," Mike groaned. "They never will. One thing crowds in right over the last—good or bad, happy or not. If you want me, you have to grab on and drag me with you through it all. God knows I want to hold on to you."

"Then give me a few more days," Chris replied.

They walked some more, no longer touching. At the stone bench beside the high brick wall they stopped and sat down.

"How's Sylvie?" Mike asked, surrendering. "I miss the kid."

"She's still a little shaky, but she's coming along."

"I looked up the Taggert reports. Pretty weird bird," Mike observed as he watched the light clouds above the hospital building. "The patrolman who answered the call thinks Taggert was into some kind of voodoo stuff. There's always been a trace of it around Savannah. Anyway, on the ride to the hospital, Taggert kept muttering about snakes and glowing eyes and melting flesh and bare bones— and he kept clutching at his crotch and moaning. Real basket case. No wonder Sylvie was petrified."

"She was pretty upset," Chris admitted.

"It's been a grim week: first Taggert, then the Barth fellow blowing his brains out. The papers are makin' it out to be some kind of protest by Barth over the indictment. Like he felt manslaughter wasn't enough."

"We would all like to feel that some sort of justice has been achieved," Chris observed flatly.

"So you think he wanted justice?" Mike asked dubiously.

"I didn't say that." Chris smiled slightly. "I'm a teacher, not a psychiatrist. I settle for whatever I can get."

Mike grinned. "I'm easy. Settle for me."

"Give me a few days." Chris found herself grinning back at him.

"I'd give you anything." Mike reached out and tucked a strand of pale hair behind her ear. "Anything." He cupped his hand behind her head and

eased her toward him, twisting his body to bring her close. Chris didn't resist. "I shouldn't be doing this," Mike breathed as his lips brushed hers. "I'll spend the rest of the day trying to remember every single detail—how you look and smell and taste." He kissed her again. "It would be a hell of a lot easier if I simply dropped dead with you filling my senses—like going out on a high."

"I never pictured you as an escapist." She moved back and stared at him. "What happened to good old durable Sergeant Fuller?" she asked, trying to joke.

"He woke up alone one day too many. You wanna get married?" he blurted out. "Make babies and house payments?"

"Are we both in the same conversation?" Chris countered. "Michael, we were talking about me taking a few days to reestablish my equilibrium."

Fuller shrugged. "So marry me in a few days. I'd even settle for living in sin." He grinned. "I told you, I'm easy."

"And I'm leaving," Chris said as she stood and stepped from the pathway onto the grass, heading for the parking lot.

"Call me," Michael shouted after her. "I'm in the book."

"Under Easy," Chris muttered as she jammed the key into the car door lock.

Fuller stood on the walkway, his hand shading his eyes from the glare of the June sunshine, his lips parted in a slight smile.

"Easy, my foot," Chris grumbled, pulling out into the traffic. As she maneuvered the small car, she tried to shake his words from her mind. "I'd give you anything . . . Going out on a high . . ."

"Oh, Michael," she whispered softly, her eyes full and sad. "Michael."

Chris had cleared out everything but the contents of one small bookcase in her diligent effort to leave the classroom just as she had found it.

Burt Rambo peered in through the open doorway. "You seen Traci?" he asked as his curious gaze surveyed the room.

Chris shoved two more books into the packing box. "She was heading for the library a few minutes ago." She smiled. "By the way, congratulations on the engagement."

Rambo stepped into the bare room and grinned. "Thanks." He stood staring at her. "You need a hand with some of that stuff? I'll carry it to your car."

"Sure." Chris grabbed some language tapes and poked them in beside the books. "You take this one, I'll be right behind you with the plants." She picked up a bushy fern and a small philodendron.

"It sure looks bleak in here." Rambo hoisted the box of books onto his wide shoulder and gazed around the room. Chris had removed all the bright posters and maps from the drab beige walls. With the plants gone the room had resumed its institutional anonymity.

"Schools are always bleak when the kids are gone," Chris remarked as the large man braced the door with one arm for her to pass. "They're quiet and cold and grotesque."

"Sounds like my apartment," Rambo joked.

"Traci said you two were looking for an old house." Chris walked beside him through the empty hallway, their footsteps echoing gloomily.

"If we get a place with a few extra rooms, I can move some of my machinery home and work there. I'm going to take care of the kids while Traci teaches school," he asserted.

"And raise a bunch of computer wizards with a penchant for physical fitness." Chris smiled.

"Just two kids. One of each. Or whatever combination we happen to hit upon," he said agreeably.

"Sounds like you've got it worked out nicely." Chris deposited the philodendron on the front floorboard of her convertible and pulled the passenger seat forward so Rambo could wedge the box of books behind it.

"The planning is the easy part. I can plan the slickest systems you've ever seen. Getting them to run—that's tricky. Somehow the pieces never quite fall together the way I thought they would."

Chris nodded as she plopped the fern on the passenger seat. "I know what you mean. Something about the best laid schemes—"

"—of mice and men," Rambo chirped. "John Steinbeck," he added with satisfaction.

"I was thinking more of Robert Burns." Chris arched her brows with exaggerated smugness.

"Is Burt pulling his trivia routine on you?" Traci Callazo bounded toward them. "He worked on undergraduate degrees in everything from astronomy to Zen Buddhism. Unfortunately, both of us missed out on home economics."

"Then I'll give you a cookbook," Chris declared. "Just when and where are you two planning this event?"

"I haven't figured that one out yet," Rambo sighed. "I had trouble enough buying off the five folks who wanted to use the Laundromat the night I proposed. It took eighteen quarters to set it up," he

joked. "Then one of the tenants phoned the land-lord because we were necking when she wanted to wash her undies."

"It will be sometime this summer," Traci said. "And it will be within the general vicinity."

"You're invited," Rambo added. "Bring your cop friend along."

"Just let me know when you work out the specif-ics," Chris told them. "I'll be there."

"Let me know too," Traci said, nudging her fiancé. "In the meantime I have sixteen smelly gym suits and innumerable tennis shoes to get out of the locker room. I thought you were going to help me." She yanked Rambo's hand off the back of Chris's car.

"Did you say tennis shoes?" Rambo hugged her. "Oh, you sweet-talkin' thing." He lifted the petite brunette off the pavement.

"See you later," Traci called over Burt's back as he carried her off over his shoulder, fireman-style, toward the gym.

Chris stood smiling at the departing twosome. "Tennis shoes." She chuckled over their shared joke. Traci had bounced into school on Monday flashing her diamond and babbling excitedly about answering Burt's proposal by tying her tennis shoe to one of his. "He's weird, but he sure is sentimen-tal," she said, giggling. Chris slid into her MG and rapidly raised the top and rolled up the windows.

"Is Miss Katie Baker ready to be released?" Chris stood in the school office. She traced the telephone cord with her fingertips, waiting for the informa-tion.

"Are you a relative?"

The cautious reply prompted an anxious frown.

"I'm Chris Martin, Katie's cousin," she managed to say.

A second voice took over. "Miss Martin, could you come down to the hospital for a few minutes? This is Dr. Orbach. There have been a couple of complications. Some paperwork needs to be taken care of."

"Is Katie all right?" Chris demanded. "What's happened?"

Orbach cleared his throat. "She's had a slight reaction," he answered vaguely. "We're going to keep her overnight while we run some tests. I'd appreciate your coming down to take care of a few details."

"I'll be right there," Chris whispered.

They had moved Katie to another room. Outstretched on the bed, her slight form barely moved. Only the steady zigzag pattern of the light on the monitor suggested that something remained consistent. Katie's pulse beat with precise regularity.

The moment Chris stepped into the room, Katie's eyes snapped open. "I can't stay here," Katie said flatly. "You've got to get me out of this place," she insisted. "If they put me on any kind of drug, I won't be able to concentrate and keep all the instruments normal."

"Dr. Orbach wants to keep you overnight." Chris tried to keep her voice steady as she stared at Katie's near-white countenance.

"They are killing me," Katie gasped. "I have managed to conceal anything that would give us away, but if you don't get me out of here, I'll die for sure. You've got to get me home—to the sea. We've got to make the circle," she begged, her eyes wide and desperate. "They cannot make me stay, Chris.

Just sign a release and get me out of this place."

Chris rested her hand on Katie's arm. The skin was cool and damp.

"I think it was the X rays," Katie whispered. "Something is going wrong inside me. I cannot stop it alone. Maybe if we all tried. Maybe if we were all together."

"All right." Chris patted her reassuringly. "I'll get it arranged. Stay calm." Hastily she left the room and hurried down the hallway to the floor supervisor's desk.

"I'm taking Katie home," she announced. "Right now." She raised her voice. "I need an ambulance. How do I get one?"

The red-haired floor nurse pressed several buttons on a console and began placing numbered forms on the desk in front of Chris. While she spoke into the telephone, the nurse pointed from one space to the next, indicating where a signature was required. Chris filled in the blanks, then took the forms into Katie's room. Within minutes a tall, gaunt physician, Dr. Orbach, arrived.

"She's a nurse—she should know better," he told Chris, frowning anxiously.

"She wants to go home," Chris said evenly. "So she's going home."

Finally resigned, Dr. Orbach followed the procession down to the main floor so he could brief the ambulance attendants. "We're concerned about a shock reaction setting in," he warned the two men. "Just keep her warm," he concluded in distress.

"You want to ride with her?" the mustachioed attendant asked Chris.

"I have my car. I'll be ahead of you. We're going to Hilton Head. You follow me." She took another look at Katie, then hurried off toward her car. As

she wheeled into the heavy traffic Chris sobbed, "Hold on, Katie. Hold on." She turned onto Central Avenue and accelerated, catching sight of the hulking orange and white ambulance in her rearview mirror. "Just hold on. . . ."

In the fading daylight three golden-haired women bore a fourth one aloft as they made their way along the wooden boardwalk. A fifth one, smaller than the other four, followed behind. Swiftly they crossed the beach and walked, fully clothed, into the amber-crested waves. Shrouded in gold by the sinking sun, they waded into the glistening water, which eased the burden they carried. Amid the slanting ridges of collapsing waves, the females removed their garments, letting the wet clothing sink down into the salty water.

Repeatedly they submerged the one they bore. Each time, the older woman accompanied the stricken one beneath the surface, clasping the listless form to her bosom. Each time the twosome submerged she pressed her lips to those of the injured one, sending her own breath into the other as they lingered beneath the surface. Each time they reappeared above the waves the bearer sighed a low, melodic, melancholy strain, as if sending skyward some remnant of her companion's affliction. The youngest one served as sentinel, her pale green eyes constantly scanning the shores lest anyone observe this ritual.

Gradually the sun settled below the horizon. Their shrouds of gold became once more simply damp hair clinging to bared arms and bodies. Now the injured one could float suspended by the sea. They left her there and proceeded in to shore. If she wished to join them on the land, she would have to

do so under her own power. Or if she so chose, she could drift away into the arm of the sea until she was restored.

So they waited. At last she stirred. Buoyed up by the incoming waves, she skimmed over the water toward her sisters. When the waves were no longer sufficient to support her weight, she struggled to her feet and laboriously moved landward.

Supporting her between them, the other females walked mutely back toward the darkened house. They placed her on her bed, draping across her body a cloak woven from the down of seabirds—pelican, heron, and gull.

The sentinel arrived last. Disrobing like the others, she helped them encircle the bed with a line of shells. Standing within its bounds, they stretched their arms, linking fingers, so the circle-within-the-circle encompassed the figure on the bed. Swaying from side to side, they chanted, summoning their powers to aid the weakened one. They continued into the night as the damp air whispered in the throat of the conch.

"We can leave her now," Elena said finally. "Katherine will survive—but I do not think she will ever serve again."

The other three had sensed the loss of something they could not define.

"It is fortunate that she already has given us a child who will one day be able to serve in her stead." Elena stood looking down at Katie. "She will never bear another. It would be too dangerous." Gently she touched the pale cheek and turned to leave.

"May I stay with her?" Chris asked quietly from within the circle. "May I keep watch over her?"

"I want you to rest, Christina," Elena cautioned

her. "You will need your strength in the days to come. You must be her surrogate."

"I could lie beside her," Chris pleaded. "I will sleep. But if she should need something, I will be here. I do not want her to be alone."

Elena nodded in concession. "Summon us if you need us," she said. In the harsh light from the hallway deep lines of age streaked her gentle face. With a solemn glance she signaled for the others, Sylvie and Alicia, to follow her.

"Sleep peacefully, Christina." From the wise Elena the comment was more than a good-night wish. It was an instruction that had to be heeded.

"I will," Chris agreed. "You rest too." She moved beneath the cover, protectively placing her hand upon the softly rising and falling chest of her companion. Assured at last that Katie was safe, Chris closed her eyes. Outside the wind picked up. Dark clouds hung low, obscuring the pale moon. Obsidian waves rolled in and pounded against the beach, relentlessly grinding pebble against pebble, sand against sand.

Chris parked in the narrow roadway beyond the tall electrically wired fence surrounding the Steinlach Pharmaceutical Company truck depot. The blue-green numbers on the dashboard clock read nine fifty. She was early.

Inside the massive warehouse Andy Russell rocked back in his swivel chair, propped his feet on the console, and stared at the six security monitors. A slow spiral of smoke drifted upward from the cigarette drooping from the corner of his mouth. Russell picked a piece of lint off his dark gray pants leg, rolled it into a tight ball, and flicked it across

the room. Then he turned back listlessly to the monitors. Finally he grabbed a paperback book off the counter and thumbed through it until he reached the page where he'd left off the night before. He sprawled out with the book propped on his stomach, just below the level of the monitors.

Chris watched the headlights of the approaching car. They crossed the center line and pulled up against the curb facing Chris's car; then they were switched off. Chris stepped out and walked to the driver's window. The young girl at the wheel looked up at her.

"Come with me, Kelly," Chris said softly. The girl emerged and stood beside her. Without hesitation the girl offered her hand to the surrogate. They walked together through the shadows beside the security fence, then turned along the waterfront side of the building toward the entrance.

Three glaring floodlights caged in metal filled the area with harsh white light. The girl held Chris's hand more tightly.

"The camera is there." Kelly pointed to a Plexiglas-covered grid directly above the doorway.

"Then you go on alone." Chris released the girl's hand and gazed into her eyes.

"What the hell are you doin' here?" The faint voice came through the intercom speaker beside the door.

Kelly pushed the intercom button to reply. "I need to see you, Daddy."

"Now?" Andy Russell barked angrily. "Can't it wait?"

"It's important, Daddy," Kelly answered evenly. "And it's private."

"Jesus Christ," Russell muttered. "Lemme get

the goddamn override system in gear. This had better be good. Just a damn minute." He clicked off.

Kelly stood motionless as the steady mechanical whir of the shifting camera broke the silence. Then a dull click sounded. The girl reached forward, easily pulling open the dual doors, and stood between them, preventing them from closing. The tall blond stepped close to her and they entered the inner foyer as the doors resealed tightly.

"What the hell is she doing here?" Russell bellowed at the sight of the intruder. A second camera rotated above their heads. "I'm gonna call the cops," he threatened.

"You'd better let us in, Mr. Russell. Your daughter has confided in me. I know about the videotape. I have come to see you. I am not interested in the contents of your warehouse." Chris felt her voice waver as she spoke.

Russell swiveled the camera toward the stranger, then jammed the zoom button till the screen of unit two held a close-up of her face. "What is it you want, then?" he demanded. "Money?" The eyes stared back at him. The woman began to hum.

Slowly Andy Russell reached for the button that released the inner security door. The transparent Plexiglas barrier swung open to admit the creature.

Alone, the blond female passed along the main corridor toward the central elevator. Andy Russell stood immobile as the creature's image moved from one video unit to the next.

Finally she confronted him in the glass-walled booth. "I want the videotape," she said.

Russell's eyes shifted involuntarily toward the locked file drawer. "You will get it," she directed.

Wordlessly Russell complied. He held up the tape for her to see.

"And I want you," she said evenly, "to put it in the machine." Again Russell did as he was told.

The woman stationed herself in front of the sixth unit. Abruptly the screen flashed in shades of gray. The show had begun.

The pale-haired female stared at the images of the man and the young girl. She watched their lips moving. She could guess what was being said.

Elena had instructed her to view the tape. Katie had called Kelly Russell and, charming the girl with her song, had compelled her to come to this late-night meeting. But in order for Chris, the surrogate, to act effectively in Katie's place, she must share the rage—so in horrified silence she watched the grotesque performance while her heart thundered in protest.

Then she whirled to face Russell for the last time. Her vivid green eyes fastened upon him.

Red lips parted as she inhaled. In one smooth motion she unfastened the tie that held her pale shirt wrapped about her. Slamming her wrist above her bared chest, she arched her back, pulling herself erect as she drew the breath out of the ashen-faced human. The small room resounded with the surge of air that swept books and papers into a whirlwind, then ceased suddenly. The airborne residue slowly fluttered into bizarre patterns on the floor where the dead man lay.

Chris closed her shirtfront, picked up the video cassette, and stepped out of the office. She walked the length of the empty hallway, her eyes on the girl standing at the Plexiglas doors. "You will not remember," she said, embracing the young one, as her kind embraced any child who had witnessed a

part of the final ritual. "You were coming home
from the movies." Chris worked to erase the gap in
human time. "You are still in your car, going
home." She walked the girl to her vehicle. "Nowhere else, just home." She closed the girl's car
door. "Home."

Alone in her own sanctuary Chris paced the
living room, clasping her arms across her chest in
an effort to calm her misgivings. Something wasn't
right. She shook her head, going over the details she
had extracted from Katie. It hadn't felt right when
she parted with the Russell child. Maybe Katie had
not told her enough. "It wasn't enough," she said
into the silence. Perhaps when Katie was better
they could go over it all again.

Anxiously Chris glanced at the kitchen clock.
Then she sighed and picked up the telephone. "I
don't want to be alone," she announced to no one.
She dialed Mike Fuller's number.

"I know this is rather short notice," she said
softly, "but could you come over?"

"Sure," Mike answered immediately. "Where are
you?"

"Here in town, at the apartment. I came in to
take care of some business for Katie and I'm just
too tired to drive back to the beach."

"I'll be right over." Mike stifled a yawn. "Is
everything all right?" he asked. "You sound funny."

"I was just lonely. I wanted to see you." She
paused briefly. "Were you already in bed?"

"I still am." He chuckled. "Now I'm standing on
the floor."

"I didn't mean to interrupt your sleep," she
apologized. "Go back to bed. I'll see you tomorrow."

"It is tomorrow," Mike countered. "And I couldn't sleep now if I tried. I'll be there in fifteen minutes."

"I hate to sound ungentlemanly—but you look less than radiant," Fuller whispered into her hair when Chris met him at the elevator and stepped into his arms. "Are you *sure* you are all right?" He eased her away and looked closely at her.

Chris nodded.

"Sylvie's OK? And Katie?" Again she nodded. "So it's you and me." He smiled warily. "You wanna go inside and continue our discussion in private?" He guided her into the darkened apartment. "Good news or bad, I don't want to hear it in a hallway."

"I miss you," Chris said simply once the door was closed behind them.

"I miss you too." Mike pulled her close.

"I'm so tired, Michael." Her soft voice was warm against his cheek as she leaned against him. Silently he held her, stroking her long pale hair.

"Let's both go back to bed. Not for whoopee," he added, countering the look in her eyes. "We'll just snuggle down under the covers, no skin-to-skin stuff, and hold each other." He led her down the hall then, into her bedroom.

"Set the alarm for six," he suggested.

"Is that when you get up for work?"

"Nope." He grinned. "I thought maybe we could find something to do with an extra hour."

Chris padded across the room and adjusted her alarm clock. Then she slid into bed next to him.

"I love you," he whispered as he settled back onto the pillow with her head resting on his shoulder. "Anytime . . . tired or not."

Chris closed her eyes and listened to the steady beating of his heart. Just for the moment she had someone for herself. The slow motion of the water bed subsided as she lay pressed next to him, warmed by the heat of his body.

"I love you too, Michael," she answered.

"So go to sleep. I'll stick around."

Within minutes his warmth and the murmur of the sea wind had lulled her into unconsciousness.

A gentleman planter from Tennessee, with a money belt full of New Orleans gold from the sale of his cotton, turned his mount toward an inn below the Natchez bluff. Above, the Trace began, a high, winding passage that led back to Nashville and the stagecoach depot where a traveler could find more comfortable means of continuing on. However, the Trace was the frequent haunt of unscrupulous ambushers who would readily slit a throat for amusement and for the chance to search one's pockets and saddlebags.

At the inn the planter hired himself an escort, a gray-eyed gunman who rode the Trace for hire. With his money belt secure beneath his coat, the planter took a final stroll along the river, watching as the dull brown waters of the Mississippi bore barges full of timber and cotton southward. There he passed a pale-haired woman who elicited his smile with her own. Arm in arm they returned to the inn, speaking softly as they sat together. He bought her one drink, then another, as the lone piano man began to play. Then the woman sat with half-closed eyes and blood red lips and sang an

unfamiliar tune. When she finished her serenade the planter took her hand and led her to his room. There they passed the night together behind the wide oak door.

In the morning neither the innkeeper nor the hired gunman could rouse the planter by knocking. Finally the innkeeper brought the key and turned it in the lock. Both men thrust strong shoulders against the door to dislodge the bar that held it closed from within.

The planter lay lifeless upon the bed, his gold, like his last breath, long gone. His pale outstretched form bore no marks at all to explain his sudden death. The room showed no signs of disruption. When the marshal tried to track down the pale-haired singer who had been seen with the man, no one knew her name, nor where she had come from, nor where she might have gone. No one could explain how she had departed unnoticed or what had become of the heavy belt full of gold, much less how anyone could escape from a windowless room with a door barred from within.

So the story spread along the Trace of the river witch with the pale hair who sang to the planter on his final night and beguiled away his life and his gold. In taverns from New Orleans to Nashville the tale was told in song and verse. Many a cautious man who wished a different fate heeded the warning and passed his last night in Natchez all alone.

CHAPTER 11

❖❖❖❖❖❖

"I saw Burt Rambo at city hall yesterday," Mike yelled from the bathroom. "He was getting a marriage license." He poked his flushed face into the bedroom, where Chris was dressing. "Give you any ideas?" He grinned.

"I thought I'd give them a cookbook," Chris answered, ducking the issue. "I guess I'd better start shopping around."

"That's not what I meant." Mike stalked out and grabbed his shirt. "I was thinking of something nice and normal and mundane—like you marrying me."

"Some folks can lead normal and mundane lives and some just can't." Chris tucked her shirt into her jeans.

"That's what my ex-wife said," Mike mused, stopping to stare at her, "just before she saw the lawyer. I'm beginning to think there's something wrong with me."

"It's not you, my love. It's me." She stepped forward to brush his hair back from his forehead after he'd pulled on his T-shirt.

"You said last night that you love me," he protested.

"I do."

"So . . . ?"

"So—I still love you." She uncrossed her arms and hugged him.

"You wanna go steady, then?" Mike refused to release her.

"Sure," Chris answered. "I can get that close to normal."

"Good, because I've got something for you. It's been knocking around in my car for weeks. You make me a cup of coffee and I'll bring it right up." He pulled on his dress shirt, slid the tie under the collar, and headed toward the door.

By the time Chris had filled the little coffee maker and lifted two mugs from the cupboard, Mike had returned with a gift-wrapped box, slightly bedraggled at the corners.

"For you." He grinned, presenting it with a great flourish. "Rambo said it was kinda symbolic." Mike watched eagerly as Chris unwrapped the square package.

"Oh, Michael," Chris breathed, smiling as she pulled back the tissue paper and lifted out the curving shell. "It's beautiful." She poked into the box and retrieved the brass stand.

"He said it's the symbol of immortality—one thing building upon another." Mike spoke over her shoulder as Chris set the spiral-shaped shell on its brass support. "Maybe it will bring us luck."

"You'll need some luck to get to work on time," Chris reminded him. "Your coffee is ready so you'd better finish getting dressed."

"You'll be here when I get off work?" Fuller asked. "Or are you going somewhere?"

"Both," Chris replied. "I've got to check in on some friends and I'll be back here when you get off work."

"How do I tactfully ask if I can come over and spend the night?" Mike's neck reddened as he spoke.

"You just did." Chris smiled and handed him his jacket. "Bring clothes for one night only. I'm going back to the beach tomorrow afternoon. If you like, you can come out and spend the weekend."

"I'd like that. You plan to announce our new status to Elena and the others?" Mike asked as he scooped up watch and wallet from the dresser. "I've never gone steady before," he said, grimacing as he accepted his car keys from Chris.

"Don't tell anybody. They'll never notice." Chris smiled, then ducked into the kitchen to return with a mug of steaming coffee. "We'll work out the details as we go along."

"See you tonight." Mike kissed her nose. "We'll mull over our irreconcilable differences."

Long after Fuller had gone Chris stood before the curving shell on the mantel. "We must replace ourselves," she sighed as her fingers traced the outward spiral. "There must be a next generation. We must continue."

As Mike Fuller edged through the cluster of men, all in shirt-sleeves, milling about in the main corridor of the Steinlach Pharmaceutical warehouse, he spotted Burt Rambo. "What are you doing here?" he asked.

"Just checking some stuff." Rambo extended a hand and shook Fuller's. "No one knows what the heck went on here last night. My company set up all their electronic systems, so I came in to browse

around and see if anything's been tampered with."
He winked at Mike. "Now you know I have a real
job."

"Come on, Mike," George Parsons bellowed,
urging his partner toward the elevator. "I gotta see
this."

"You guys look around, just don't move anything," the senior member of the homicide squad
greeted them. "We got a real prize this time. Medical examiner says the guy suffocated—like somebody stuck a vacuum cleaner over his face and
sucked the air outta him."

"Upright or canister model?" George Parsons
asked innocently.

"Knock it off, Parsons. It wasn't a vacuum cleaner. It was . . . something else. No marks on the
body. Just a very unpleasant expression and collapsed lungs."

"The stiff had his eyes wide open like he saw
something real *bad*," Detective Lindsey said as he
stepped up to the group. "Like *bad*." He slid into
the black-jive routine he sometimes assumed to
irritate Parsons.

Fuller moved past Lindsey and stepped into the
glass-walled security booth. The chalk outline on
the floor marked the position of the now-removed
body. The rest of the floor space, cluttered with
papers and pages from books, had been dutifully
photographed and examined by the lab team.

"So what did they bump him off for?" Parsons
asked from the doorway. "What kind of drugs do
they have here, anyway?"

Lindsey eased past Parsons and surveyed the
room again. "They got every kind of narcotic ever
made, but nothing's turned up missing so far. There

are three guys from the drug squad and two
Steinlach inventory experts poking through the
warehouse. So far, nothing wrong."

Fuller and Parsons looked down on the long
parallel rows of boxes extending the length of the
warehouse.

"But here's the pisser. . . ." Lindsey heaved a
sigh. "The day-watch security men arrived to find
every gate and door locked, every camera and
alarm working except that one." Lindsey turned to
look at the six TV monitors. Five carried clear
views of parts of the Steinlach facility. The sixth
was turned off. "So how'd whoever did it get in?"

The homicide sergeant filled the doorway. "No
tellin'. No signs of forced entry, nothing weird
about the remote systems. Looks as if the fool just
let 'em in and they wasted him."

"With a vacuum cleaner," Parsons hooted.
"Maybe it was the janitor!"

"Right on, brother." Lindsey did his Stepin
Fetchit routine, shuffling and pulling along an im-
aginary vacuum cleaner. "Yazzir, Ah's a-comin'.
Yazzir."

"Up yours, whitey." Parsons smiled pleasantly,
barely moving his lips as he spoke.

"It wasn't no vacuum cleaner, asshole," the
sergeant barked, cutting them off.

"Hey, maybe he had a hot date and she turned
out to be one hell of a kisser." Burt Rambo peered
over Fuller's shoulder.

"I could use some of that a little lower," Lindsey
said, guffawing.

"You could use about six inches a little lower."
Parsons slid behind the broad form of Burt Rambo
and strode off, chuckling.

"You two knock it off." The sergeant thrust a finger under Lindsey's nose. "Just lay off each other and solve the fuckin' case."

"Nice sensitive guys," Rambo sighed with feigned innocence as Lindsey and the sergeant wandered off toward the elevator.

"Sure is weird." Fuller looked once more into the cluttered room. "You say no one tampered with the security system."

"Everything was found five by five—in civilian talk that means turned on and running smoothly. Only the doors were opened at ten oh two and then again at ten eleven."

Fuller narrowed his eyes. "What?" he said softly.

Rambo smiled. "One of my minor systems we installed here. A simple program in the security computer that records every time any checkpoint is opened—to prevent inside-job burglaries."

Mike shook his head in amazement. "Would you be so kind as to mention this fact to Kline and Lindsey? I'm sure they would like to know the exact time of the crime they are investigating."

"Already did." Rambo grinned broadly. Then he scanned the security booth with narrowed eyes.

Mike walked around the small cubicle, carefully avoiding the scattered papers on the floor. "He must have known them. Whoever did it."

"He sure didn't do it himself. You should go down and take a look at him." Rambo hesitated. "Something scared the shit outta him."

Fuller paused before the console of monitors. "Why is that monitor turned off?" he asked, jerking his head toward the mute set.

"It had been disconnected from the system. The videotape recorder was hooked up to it. Here they use the recorder to check on certain employees or

suspicious areas, but apparently last night it was set to replay a videotape," Rambo answered evenly. "Only trouble is," he added, "there aren't any tapes in the office. No one's even found any downstairs."

Fuller sniffed in disbelief. "So he was murdered for some videotapes."

Rambo shrugged. "Maybe the tapes were an afterthought."

"Maybe somebody he knew didn't like what he had on the tapes." Fuller's look brightened. "Maybe he was into something weird. Maybe he was using the tapes to extort money or something."

"Sure," Rambo muttered. "Maybe he had the great kisser on tape and she came after them."

"She?" Mike raised his eyebrows. "With a mop and a vacuum cleaner, no doubt." He chuckled.

"Alas, we're back to the rational. This is where I came in. I'll just wander off downstairs and run a few items through the funny box and see how the inventory is going. Give me a call if you find hot lips or the tapes." He raised a beefy hand in salute and strolled off, whistling lackadaisically.

"Back to the rational." Fuller nodded, staring once more into the cluttered room.

"So how's the week been?" Chris asked, descending the front steps of her aunt's beach villa to greet Fuller.

"Not bad." He stepped out of the car and reached out to embrace her. "You are sure looking great," he said, beaming down at her. "Either the sun has done wonders for you or I'm a lot worse off without you than I realized."

"What's that?" Chris pointed to the bulging manila folder on the front seat of his car. "You brought your homework?"

"My mail. Stuff from my box at the office. Nothing that can't wait."

"How about a quick swim before dinner?"

"I thought you didn't go in for quickies," Mike teased.

"Afterward, late tonight." Chris lowered her voice. "You and me on the beach—reconciling our differences." She nudged him. "*Very slowly.*"

"I need the swim," Mike groaned. "A little sublimation till after nightfall."

"I'll help you carry your stuff. By the way, what's going on in that pharmaceutical warehouse case?" she asked casually. "Who's handling it, anyway? The newspaper didn't say."

"It's Sergeant Kline's case. Lindsey is partnering with Kline. Nothing much has come out of it so far except the fact that the guy had some kind of videotapes that were taken. They're checking with all his friends to see if anyone ever saw them or knows what was on them." Fuller seemed unconcerned. "No one's figured out just what killed him yet," he said, handing Chris the folder to carry, "other than the fact that his lungs were collapsed. The medical examiner is working on the possibility that it was a violent allergic reaction. But that would explain only the collapsed lungs, not the rest of the weird stuff." He hoisted his suitcase in one hand and draped his free arm over Chris's shoulders. "I won't bother to tell you what Burt Rambo suggested," he said, chuckling, as they started up the front steps.

"I won't bother to ask," Chris replied, trying to match his easygoing attitude. There was never a need to press this man. Eventually he would tell her whatever perverse observations Rambo had made and she would listen closely.

"Since we're going steady, does that mean we

share the same room?" Mike asked eagerly as they reached the upper landing.

"Maybe the same bed; but sharing the same room, no. I'll put your stuff in the guest room. When it's time for bed I'll join you there."

"Fair enough." Methodically Fuller unpacked the suitcase, stuffing socks and underwear in the drawers and hanging shirts and slacks.

Chris propped the folder on the dresser. "I'm going to get my swimsuit—and a cold beer for you. Meet me downstairs in the kitchen when you're finished changing. I stuck a couple of lounge chairs down on the beach. We can sit and watch the ocean without getting sand in our crevices."

"Stop talking like that or I'll lose control and ravish you right here on the bed." Fuller grabbed her and kissed her neck.

"Save it for tonight," Chris said with a giggle as she pushed him away.

"Where's Elena and the others?" Mike lowered his voice guiltily.

"They're out in the boat—at least, Sylvie and Katie and Elena are. Alicia is in Charleston. She won't be coming down this weekend."

"You want to talk some more about crevices?" Mike grinned as he peeled off his tie and shirt.

"Downstairs. Cold beer. See you soon." Chris ducked out the door.

Late in the night three pale-haired females passed a paper from one to the other, each scanning its contents. Chris watched the progress of the sheet she had removed from Michael's bulging folder of mail.

She had only intended to glance at the assortment, to peruse and ponder over the simple communications that touched Michael's life. But this

envelope had made her hesitate. The hand-printed address, with its neat, slightly back-slanted letters, had caught her attention. She had sat alone staring at the familiar penmanship—the same back-sloping writing neatly columned on the time charts at the swimming meets. The message was from Burt Rambo. Burt—the one who joked and smiled and watched with calm gray eyes.

Now Chris folded the note and laid it on the table before her.

"You have to stop this man," Elena said from across the table.

Between them lay the discarded computer print-out sheet with the curious notations from Burt Rambo to Fuller. On the top of the page Rambo had printed the words SIREN/LAMIA, and just below, "An interesting fact for you, Mike. In many languages the word for *breath* is identical to the word for *soul*." Then Rambo had jotted a column of names under the heading "Possibilities for your hit-*woman* list":

Lamia
Sirens
Apsaras
Valkyries
Vampires

Below was a list of sources: an encyclopedia of the supernatural, an anthology of African folklore, a medieval myth collection, and citations of several poems by Keats and Coleridge.

"You thought I was kidding about old hot lips," Rambo had printed. "Two points for the counter-culture!" At the bottom he had inscribed his name inside a doodle that resembled a sombrero.

"Your Michael has not seen this yet." Elena tapped the paper with a slender finger. "He would probably dismiss it as a mere intellectual game," she said thoughtfully, "an amusing but frivolous jest between friends."

"Probably," Chris agreed. "However, he enjoys the tales Burt tells him. He remembers them."

"Even so," Sylvie asserted from beside Chris, "even if he read this, Michael would not draw any connections with us."

"Michael is too reasonable and objective—and overworked—to pursue such bizarre angles on any crime," Chris added. "Besides, it isn't even his case."

"This Burt Rambo does not reason like your Michael. He makes leaps in logic that put ancient tales in juxtaposition with the world in which we function now," Elena observed calmly. "He is in contact with the officers who are investigating. Mr. Rambo is a problem," she insisted as she scanned the list again. "He needs to be silenced." She aimed the comment at Chris. "Just as a precaution."

Chris held Elena's level, intent gaze.

"I will take care of it," Chris replied solemnly.

"And this note—it will not need to be delivered." Elena folded it neatly.

"No, it won't be delivered," Chris echoed.

"Now you go back to your Michael." Elena patted her hand. "Cherish your time with him, my dear. Etch the moments in your memory, for the moments will pass."

The three females held hands briefly, then Chris rose to go. "Weird Burt," she murmured as she made her way back to the wide bed where Michael lay asleep.

Downstairs Elena pressed Sylvie's hand sympa-

thetically. "Our sister has great wisdom," she declared. "She will do what has to be done."

"But I like Mr. Rambo," Sylvie responded softly. "And I love Michael." Her pale green eyes brimmed with tears.

"There are children somewhere waiting for our touch. They are confused and tormented and terrorized. They are defenseless."

Sylvie nodded in understanding. "And we must protect them," she said, reciting their commitment, their ancient mission.

"Extinguish the candle," Elena directed the younger one. "Even now our sister needs this human love." Obediently Sylvie blew out the single flame that burned. Elena took the hand-shaped holder and pressed it to her chest. With her arm around Sylvie she proceeded with the young one upstairs toward their separate rooms.

"Chris. . . ." Michael stirred and rolled over in the darkness, reaching for the silent form. He snuggled closer to her, cradling her in the curve of his body. With his arm draped across her, he sighed. Chris brushed away the salty tears that had dampened her cheeks.

"Michael. . . ." She inched closer and pressed her warm lips against his throat. Without a word he closed his arms about her, then slid his hands over her velvet skin.

"Oh, Michael," Chris breathed as his body tensed and the steady pulsing of his blood accelerated. Fuller chuckled low in his throat as her long, graceful arms stretched out, then folded around his neck.

"Anytime," he murmured into the pale golden hair still faintly scented by the salty ocean breeze.

* * *

The bright morning sun sent streams of pure white through the regular diamonds in the latticework that rimmed the eastern windows of the villa. Mike Fuller replaced the telephone receiver and grabbed his mug of coffee. "You'll never guess what Lindsey dug up," he said, strolling out onto the rear porch. Chris sat sipping orange juice, staring out at the still, gray-green Atlantic.

"I thought you came here to relax," she countered without lifting her gaze from the water.

"I did, but I have to keep in touch with the office." He picked up the scattered pages of the Sunday paper, then settled down next to her at the wrought-iron table. "Anyway, he found out that Russell, the pharmaceutical warehouse guy—well, he made nudie photos of his own daughter. He was going through some of Russell's stuff and there they were."

"That's awful," Chris said evenly. She kept her eyes locked on the shimmering surface of the ocean. She felt the aura of uneasiness concerning Russell growing in intensity.

"Yeah. The creep took Polaroids." Fuller breathed a long sigh. "Some of them are damn rough—not just stand-and-show-it stuff, but the real thing. He was some shit to use his own kid for stuff like that."

"To say the very least," Chris agreed solemnly. She now saw that Katie, in her sickness and confusion, had not told her everything about the Russell girl and her past traumas.

"And guess what Lindsey is figuring now?" Fuller pressed on.

"I wouldn't know," Chris replied with a slight catch in her voice.

"Well, he thinks this picture stuff has been going

on a long time. Some of the pictures are two or three years old."

Chris was still facing the water, so Mike didn't see her close her eyes tightly. This was the missing information that had troubled her: the deep secret shame of Kelly Russell that Chris had not been able to know and remove.

"Just over a year ago Russell bought a videotape setup, camera and everything, for do-it-yourself movies. Maybe the still pictures didn't do it for him anymore. Maybe——"

"I don't want to hear about it," Chris said sharply. "It isn't your case. It has nothing to do with you. And I'd rather just not let it crowd into our lives." Fuller looked at her intently. Even from the side he could tell that her lower lashes were glistening with tears.

"I'm sorry." He reached out and rested his hand on her arm. "I sure didn't mean to get you all upset. I just got carried away and let my mouth run. I guess by now I shoulda seen it all," he said, pausing while Chris turned to face him, "but along comes some damn pervert and I just get caught up. Somehow, when I talk about it, it helps take the kick out . . . toughens me up for the next round."

Chris placed her hand on top of his. "I don't think I like you getting tougher," she said quietly.

"Occupational hazard." He tried to smile.

"So I'm beginning to understand." She patted his hand, then turned in her chair, once again facing the Atlantic. Fuller glanced at her uncertainly, then turned his attention to the paper. Chris sat without speaking for almost thirty minutes while Mike read. Finally the irregular rustle of the pages ceased and she realized that he was no longer reading. He was just sitting and looking at her.

"You want to go out in the boat?" She grinned at him.

"I'm not much of a sailor," he hedged. Chris continued to grin. "Well, I'm not *anything* of a sailor. I've never been on a sailboat in my life."

Chris chuckled. "What about your legendary career in the navy?"

"The U.S. Navy taught me Chinese, stuck me on an island, then came and got me when my hitch was up. In a big boat—with a motor," he said pointedly.

"This one has a motor," Chris replied. "Besides, I'll take care of you. Promise."

"You've run that thing single-handed before?" he asked, jerking his thumb toward the sleek sailboat moored by the pier.

"That or something like it . . . millions of times," she assured him. "Trust me."

"Millions. . . ." He shook his head in amusement. "Then I guess we go sailing. Just remember, my life is in your hands."

"I'll remember." Chris took his hand and tugged him to his feet. Arm in arm they crossed the rough sand toward the waiting boat.

Urvasi was an Apsaras, one of the beauteous water nymphs that haunted the rivers of India and often frolicked in the forests and the mountain streams. One day King Pururavas was hunting in the Himalayas alone when he heard a sweet voice calling out for help. Although unaccompanied, he hurried to assist the one in peril.

Urvasi and a second Apsaras had been playing amid the flowers that grew along the bank of a stream. They had been set upon by demons of the forest, who were dragging them off into the dark woods. The brave Pururavas challenged the demons and drove them away, rescuing the Apsarases. When Pururavas gazed upon the beauty of Urvasi, he became so enamored that he begged her to marry him. Urvasi consented on one condition— that she never see her husband undressed.

Only in the darkness of night did they lie with each other. Pururavas diligently adhered to the condition of his marriage. However, the Gandharvas, air spirits who were the customary consorts of the Apsarases, resented that a human had taken one of the nymphs for his own. The

mischievous Gandharvas crept into the room
where Pururavas slept beside his wife. They stole
one of a pair of young lambs that Urvasi kept
beside her bed at night.

"Who dares steal from my chamber while my
fearless husband is beside me? Do they forget that
he is a hero?" she exclaimed.

On the next night the Gandharvas returned and
carried off the remaining lamb. Again Urvasi cried
out, "Who dares steal from my chamber while my
fearless husband is beside me? Do they forget that
he is a hero?"

In order to prove that he was still courageous
enough to pursue the thieves regardless of what
they might be, Pururavas leaped out of the bed
without dressing. Immediately the Gandharvas
filled the night air with flashes of lightning that
illuminated the room. Urvasi saw her husband
unclothed. The triumphant Gandharvas fled into
the night. When Pururavas returned to his bed and
sought his beloved wife, she had disappeared.

In desperation Pururavas returned to the moun-
tains, seeking the place where he had first seen
Urvasi. In the clear stream he found three swans
swimming. Suspecting that the Apsarases had
transformed themselves into swans, which was one
form they often assumed, Pururavas knelt by the
water's edge. His tears fell into the stream. At last
one swan came near to him. It was indeed Urvasi,
and she took sympathy on him.

"I am with child," she told her husband. "You
must leave me until the end of the year, then you
may come again and see your child."

Grieved by the harsh condition, Pururavas returned to his kingdom until the appointed time.

Urvasi prevailed upon the Gandharvas to let her

husband spend one night with her and her newborn child. She reminded them that he had not broken the condition of their marriage of his own accord. He had also stayed away for the prescribed time. The Gandharvas relented, admitting that this mortal was indeed honorable.

When Pururavas returned on the last day of the year, he was allowed to spend the night with Urvasi in a splendid palace of gold. As the first light of dawn appeared, Pururavas caressed his beloved. "I do not wish to leave you," he wept.

"You have always been an honorable man," Urvasi replied. "You have asked nothing, you simply obeyed. Now the Gandharvas must show that their honor equals yours. It is a custom to grant one's guest a boon if he should ask it. In the morning you must ask the Gandharvas to grant you one wish."

"What can I request that will allow us to be together always?" Pururavas asked.

"You can ask to become one of them," Urvasi replied wisely.

In the morning he told the Gandharvas of his wish. They knew that Urvasi had helped him determine what he should request, so they decided to test the wisdom of Pururavas alone.

"Take this dish containing the sacred fire to your home," they directed him. "Make sacrifices with this fire and you will become one of us."

Pururavas took the fire and returned to his kingdom. For a moment he left the fire unguarded, and when he returned it had disappeared. In the place where he had left the dish grew the tree *Sami*. Where he had placed the fire stood the tree *Asvattha*.

Pururavas cut two sticks, one from each tree, and rubbed one against the other. Soon he had created a spark of flame that burned brightly. Now the Gandharvas were convinced that he was indeed wise enough and honorable enough to be one of them. Having cast his offerings into the fire, Pururavas was transformed into a Gandharva. Forever after he dwelt with his beloved.

Thenceforth, whenever a wise and honorable man died, the part of his soul that moved on from life to life was called *gandharva*, and his passing was one of great joy.

CHAPTER 12

❖❖❖❖❖❖❖

But when Night is on the hills, and the great Voices
    Roll in from Sea,
By starlight and by candlelight and by dreamlight
    She comes to me.

—H. Trench

Burt Rambo leaned back in his swivel chair. His glance moved steadily from one column of figures to the next as the steady moan of the computer produced square-shaped green numbers across the gray display screen. Low fluorescent lights cast a whitish haze in the section of the large room where Rambo worked alone.

The pale-haired female stood watching him for several minutes while he studied the mathematical message, typed something on the keyboard, then waited as the machine spoke back to him in a number language she could not comprehend. When she moved closer, Rambo shifted his attention from the display to the female who stepped from the darkness into his lighted arena.

"Welcome to the inner sanctum," he greeted her. "I never expect visitors, but I'm always glad when I get one." His jovial smile faltered when he saw her somber expression. "There's nothing wrong with Traci. . . ?" he asked, rising.

Chris rested her hand on his chest. Immediately he stood still. "I came to talk to you." She leveled her green eyes at him. "There is nothing wrong with

Traci." Her voice had a rhythmic quality. "Sit down and relax, please. You and I have some business that must be settled."

Rambo's large frame settled back into the chair. Chris knelt before him so that her eyes, still riveted to his, were level with them. She reached toward him, placing her palms on his temples. Rambo neither spoke nor resisted; he simply stared back and did precisely as she instructed.

"You must rest," she said softly. Then she hummed until his eyelids fluttered and finally closed. She remained motionless before him, strangely relieved that the gray eyes no longer looked back at her. They had often made her uneasy. But now they would follow her command.

As the large man sat very still Chris stood and surveyed his domain. Machines with sets of circular tapes, rows of keyboards waiting for instructions, books and papers, notes and cards spread across his desk . . . the bewildering array fascinated her as she circled the room twice, each time pausing to stare down at the man who was the beloved of her friend.

At last she cradled his head against her as she chanted softly. Then she pressed her palms against his temples and began to speak in human words.

"You have no interest in the manner in which Andrew Russell died. You have no time for speculation . . . neither for amusement nor for satisfying your curiosity. Your concern in the case is only with the computers and your programs." Her statements followed one another with methodical precision. "Let the time to come occupy your thoughts, not the time that is past."

Rambo swayed slightly beneath her touch, his eyes closed, his breathing easy and deep.

"You must forget your tales of sirens and lamias, of snatchers of souls and beguilers of men. Send them deep beneath your consciousness. They shall not surface again in your mind." Rambo's breathing became more rapid and shallow for a moment; then he heaved a sigh and resumed the earlier steady pace, as if he had complied with her wishes and now waited for her next command.

"You sent no message to Michael Fuller. You have no reason to discuss the death of Andrew Russell with him. Your interest is only with the computer systems. You are simply sitting in your office, engrossed in your work, reading numbers on the screen," Chris concluded. "You have seen no one. You have not been disturbed."

Then she stepped back, releasing the man. Still humming softly, she turned away into the darkness.

Rambo remained still, his eyes closed, until the door slid shut behind her and he was once more alone with his machines. He breathed deeply, opened his eyes, blinked at the screen, then glanced uncertainly about the room. He rolled his head from side to side, rubbing the back of his neck to ease the tension in his muscles. He yawned and stretched his long arms. Then he refocused his attention on the rows of green figures that had not moved since he had lifted his fingers from the keyboard.

"I didn't know you'd be back on the job today." Fuller stepped back out of the path of an attendant with a hospital cart as he greeted Katie Baker. "How's the leg?" He looked down at the slight ridge beneath her thick white stockings.

"The leg is doing fine. And as for coming back early," she said, rolling her eyes good-naturedly,

"folks keep showing up here insisting on being treated. I figured I'd better show up too. What are you doing down here?"

"People keep cutting the crap out of each other, so I've gotta come and talk to the survivors. A couple of fools went at it on the docks this morning. The winner is in the emergency room getting his face stitched back together."

"Dumb. . . ." Katie shook her head reproachfully.

"And what's going on in your department?"

"A nine-year-old with gonorrhea." Katie bit off the words. "Her sixteen-year-old stepbrother is down at juvenile."

Fuller frowned. "He gave it to her?"

"He certainly did."

"Sounds like a nice family. Where the hell were the parents?"

"There were several fathers—different ones for different kids," Katie explained. "One mother—she's upstairs in the waiting room."

"And what's she got to say about it?" He stepped back momentarily as several young girls in candy-striped uniforms passed by.

"For one thing, 'They ain't real sister and brother.'" She duplicated the jargon of the projects. "For another, 'They gotta learn sumwhere. If it ain't fambly it'll be sumbuddy else.'"

Fuller shook his head wearily. "And I think *my* job is depressing." He reached out and patted her shoulder sympathetically. "How about a cup of coffee?"

Katie raised her hands in protest. "Not allowed. I'm on strict orders. No caffeine. I'll take a glass of juice and watch you ruin your constitution, though."

"I don't mean to cramp your style." Lindsey ambled up the hall toward them. He was speaking to Fuller, but his heavy-lidded eyes were on Katie. They dropped to the name tag above her pocket. "Mind if I interrupt long enough to ask Nurse Baker a couple of questions?"

"Cop," Fuller said tersely, jerking his thumb toward the detective. "Lindsey."

Katie smiled politely.

"Do you happen to know a kid named Kelly Russell?" Lindsey held a black-and-white photo in front of her. "Blondish, sixteen. She worked here as some kind of volunteer."

Katie looked at the picture apprehensively. "I've spoken with her a few times," she answered cautiously. "She's a candy striper in OB."

"Sorry to have to tell you this, ma'am, but the girl is dead. She was found this morning. Overdose of pills."

"Russell's daughter? The one he used in his pictures?" Fuller blurted out in astonishment. Katie turned almost gray.

"Afraid so," Lindsey said dully. "I'm just lookin' for any information about her. Seein' if she had any other problems—somethin' we didn't know about." He took a slow breath. "It was me that got her to talk about those photographs," he volunteered. "I don't know if that was enough to do it—or if she had other troubles besides." The firm line of his mouth shifted to a weak smile that faded as abruptly as it had formed.

"It's not your fault," Fuller assured his grim-faced colleague.

Lindsey shrugged. "That won't make it any easier to get to sleep at night. If you've got a few minutes, ma'am," he said, turning back to Katie,

"I'd like to ask you some questions about her."

Katie shook her head. "I really didn't know her that well." Her fingers moved to the slender chain about her neck. Fuller's eyes followed the motion, lingering on the familiar shape—the spiral shell—that rested on her chest. "I'm sorry I can't be of any help. I'm sorry," she whispered, retreating hastily down the hallway.

"I'm sorry too," Lindsey muttered dejectedly.

"Quit blaming yourself," Fuller said as they stood watching the blond nurse walk away. "The girl must have had a lot of things on her mind. You were just doing your job."

Katie Baker disappeared into the intersecting hallway.

"Yeah, well . . ." Lindsey tried to smile. "I'd just like to know for sure," he concluded weakly.

Mike left Lindsey at the elevator. Just before the doors closed in front of Lindsey's face, Mike said softly, "Blame her old man. He had a hell of a head start on all of us."

The doors slid shut and Fuller was alone in the hallway.

Fuller sat watching the eleven o'clock news, staring dully at the commentator as he sipped a cold beer. He emptied the can and dropped it beside his chair, then lurched forward to answer a knock at the door.

Chris stood on the step. "I had a change in plans, so I thought I'd come to see you here for a change."

"Come on in." Mike yanked the door open all the way and stepped aside to let her enter. "I thought you were up in Charleston visiting Alicia. What happened to your trip?"

"I came back early. More loose ends," she said

noncommittally. She deposited her large shoulder bag on the floor beside the door.

"Good. I was getting gloomy without you." Fuller picked up two empty beer cans and pitched them into the garbage bag near the kitchen door. "I saw Katie yesterday."

"So I heard." Chris walked around the large living room slowly, pausing occasionally to contemplate the pictures on the walls and the books on the shelves. This was her first visit to his apartment.

"Did she tell you about the Russell girl—the suicide?"

"She told me." Chris sighed, continuing her tour.

"Well?"

"Well, what?"

"Nothing. How do you like my apartment?" He crossed his arms and leaned against the wall, watching her.

"It's nice," Chris said softly. She leaned forward to inspect a black-and-white photo of fifteen uniformed officers. "Is this you?" She rested a finger on a young policeman sporting a narrow mustache.

"That's me." He grinned. "Second in my class at the academy."

"I'm impressed," she replied without lifting her eyes from the youthful face.

"You want a drink or anything?"

"No, I just want to be with you." She turned to face him, her expression solemn, emotionless.

"So come here." He opened his arms. Chris walked to him and slid her arms about his waist. Softly and tenderly he kissed her. "I missed you. I'm glad you're back."

"I need to discuss something with you," Chris said, leaning back and looking up at him.

"Business or pleasure?" Fuller inquired uncer-

tainly. Something in her voice made him uneasy.

"A bit of both."

"You want to sit down? I don't know what's coming, but I'd rather be sitting when I hear it." He took her hand and tugged her toward the sofa. He sat with his arms braced on his knees and looked at her. "So talk to me."

"Michael, I want to have your child," Chris said calmly.

"Jesus!" Fuller stared at her. "I'm glad I sat down."

"I need your permission."

"That's not all you need," he said, grinning.

"I'm serious, Michael. I cannot conceive without your agreement."

"Does this mean we're moving up from going steady? You *are* talking marriage, right?"

"I'm talking conception," Chris replied. "I cannot marry you, Michael. But I love you—and I can conceive your child . . . if you let me."

"And then what?" Fuller asked bewilderedly. "We keep on as we are? I just don't get this."

"And then I go away."

"For how long?"

"Until after our child is born," she answered.

"Will I see you again?" His voice had faded to a whisper.

"No, Michael."

"Will I see the baby?"

"No."

"Then I refuse," he said firmly.

"I'm going away anyway, Michael. I cannot stay here any longer." She looked up with wet eyes. "I have to go away."

"And you just dropped by to say so long."

"I came by to ask your help in creating a child. A

child who can make a difference, just as you wanted to. I cannot take you with me, but I can take a part of you." As she spoke, the tears overflowed and slowly trickled down her cheeks. "There are not enough of us, Michael," she said sadly. "And our children must be conceived in love."

"I don't know what the hell you're talking about," Fuller groaned. "I'm sitting here, dying inside because I love you and you're leaving me. You're sitting there crying—and still insisting you're going away. On top of it all you want to conceive a child because we love each other. What's going on?"

"It is my commitment, my duty," Chris said, sniffing. "It is my function while I live—to do what must be done. I must replace myself."

"Don't I matter?"

"Yes. Without you I would not know human love."

Mike turned on the sofa to stare at her closely. "Human love? What the hell other kind of love is there?"

"My kind," Chris answered quietly. "Something you can help to continue—by creating a child from both of us."

"Jesus Christ," Fuller muttered. "I think I'm losing my mind." He bent forward, thrusting his hands into his hair.

"I am not like you, Michael. There is no reason to tell you how we differ—but we do. Your human lifetime is but a fraction of the time I will spend on the earth, unless some illness or accident takes my life before I complete my span. I must replace myself while I am strong and whole. I have not chosen to do so before because I had not found you. I had not shared a love."

Michael stared at her in disbelief. "Now I think it's you who's lost her mind. You think you're some kind of . . . alien?"

"Something like that." Chris reached out and slid her hand into his. "I don't expect you to understand. I just want you to trust me once more. Say you will help me. Love me once more." Her fingers tightened. "I'm asking you to put your life into my body so a new generation can arise from our love."

Fuller raised his head slowly. His eyes sought the golden spiral that hung between her breasts. "You could have done this anytime—conceived without my knowing anything. Why now? Why this way? How do you know it will work this time?"

"Because this will be the last time . . . and because we *will* it."

"What if I refuse?"

"Then I shall make you forget me."

"Impossible." Fuller shook his head. "You're the only part of my life worth remembering."

Chris did not respond. She sat quietly, watching him, waiting for his answer. Fuller looked at her solemnly. His gaze shifted from the green eyes to the pale hair that fell across her shoulders, then to the golden nautilus shell. His fingers closed over hers as he slowly turned her arm. He studied the unfamiliar serpent bracelet that encircled her wrist and coiled at its end about the same spiral-shaped shell he'd seen before—suspended below the slender throats of Sylvie . . . Elena . . . Alicia . . . Katie . . . and Chris.

"You really believe all this, don't you?" he asked, staring into her eyes.

"I believe it."

"A hell of a way to say good-bye," he said hoarsely.

"You will agree?" Chris whispered.

Fuller nodded. "I always wanted to go out on a high," he said, his voice cracking.

Chris reached up to wipe away his tears. "Then I will show you what must be done."

Standing naked in the dim bedroom, Chris lifted the purple-throated conch from the shoulder bag. They pulled Fuller's bed away from the wall, into the center of the bedroom. Michael sat crosslegged on the bed, watching Chris without speaking. His naked body glistened with a film of scented oil.

Chris made a circle of seashells on the carpet around the bed. She opened the windows, standing for a moment silhouetted by the pale moon as she listened for the night breeze. Then she anointed her body with a sweet-scented balm and stepped inside the circle.

She sat facing Fuller, softly whispering the words he would have to repeat. "With my heart . . ." she began, resting her right hand on her chest. Fuller mirrored her movements with his own. "With my spirit . . ."—she lifted her fingers to her lips— "with my embrace . . ."—she opened her arms —"I create a new life."

Now Fuller cleared his throat and raised his chin as he held his gaze locked with hers. His voice, clear and sad, filled the small room. "With my heart . . . with my spirit . . . with my embrace . . . I create a new life."

As he spoke the words the wind outside stirred the leaves; then it wound its way into the room, sliding into the depths of the conch shell and emerging as a subdued moan.

Gently Chris entered his outstretched arms, guiding him back upon the bed. She lay beside him,

humming softly, caressing his reclining form. Then she moved above him, easing herself against him. Fuller grasped her waist, holding her while she rocked slowly, her pale hair streaming in the encircling breeze.

She crossed one arm over her bosom, pressing the serpent bracelet to her breast. "With my heart—*ki-ag*," she breathed. "With my spirit—*sussuru* . . . with my embrace—*gu-da-la* . . . I create a new life."

Her movements became more rapid as Fuller's fingers dug into her sides. The building spasm began its irreversible course. The pale-haired creature arched her back and cried out.

In the semidarkness Fuller saw the torso above him become transparent. Then soft, shining green eyes enveloped him. Pale streams of gold cascaded down across his face. Blood red lips parted to receive his final sigh.

"I love you, Michael," she breathed. The wind within the room subsided. The purple-throated conch was silent once again.

All movement beneath her had ceased. It was done. In an instant one life had slipped away and deep within her another was beginning. Her tears overflowed, trailing down her pale cheeks as, still gasping from her passion, she swayed to and fro, lamenting.

The creature moved about the room, methodically removing every trace of her presence. The body beneath the clean sheets had been bathed and placed slightly to one side, an arm draped across the pillow, as if Fuller had snuggled into bed and peacefully drifted off.

She paused one final time and touched her fingers

to the lifeless lips. "She will be a special child, my love," Chris whispered. "Perhaps she will change the world."

She withdrew into the outer room. Stopping by the framed picture of the young officers, she touched once more the mustachioed face she knew. Quietly she lifted the picture from the wall and slid it into the large shoulder bag. Then she stepped out the door and strode toward her car.

The warm summer breeze tinged with the scent of the sea rippled through her golden hair. Far away the gray gulls huddled against the sand and melancholy pelicans spread their feathers over seagrass nets. Farther still, the slick black swells of the sea rolled toward the shore, spreading ivory ruffles over ancient sands.